"YOU TOLD M̲   ,"

"Yes, I did," Julia replied. "But I expected—"

"What?" Garth's eyes, so seductive and warm, flared with the amusement which was so very innate to him. "You expected platitudes from me, perhaps? Or poetry?" He shook his head. "Wrong, Julia. I know you."

"I s-said you may s-top now," Julia stuttered, and placed her one free hand upon his chest.

"I will not let you turn me away." Garth's voice was fierce.

Julia jumped. His gaze was a mix of teasing and earnestness. "But . . ."

"I must have your hand!"

"You have got it," Julia squeaked. Yet she tugged it away, nervous and frightened for some reason.

"No, sweet liar." Garth smiled. "You have not given anything. You hold it all back. Give me your hand, your heart, your love."

His lips were mere inches away. Julia closed her eyes. "Er, ah . . . Garth?"

"Yes?"

She frowned. "I . . . forgot what I was going to say."

"Just say *my love*," Garth murmured. His lips covered hers.

Never had she been kissed in such a manner, and she responded with a sudden and natural fervency, her growing desire the teacher. "Hmmm," she breathed in pleasure. Tingling, heat, and Garth were the most perfect, irresistible blend.

"Now is when you say you will marry him, dearest," Aunt Clare chirped.

THE MISSING GROOMS

Cindy Holbrook

ZEBRA BOOKS
Kensington Publishing Corp.

http://www.zebrabooks.com

ZEBRA BOOKS are published by

Kensington Publishing Corp.
850 Third Avenue
New York, NY 10022

All Kensington titles, imprints and distributed lines are available at special quantity discounts for bulk purchases for sales promotion, premiums, fund raising, educational or institutional use.

Special book excerpts or customized printings can also be created to fit specific needs. For details, write or phone the office of the Kensington Special Sales Manager: Kensington Publishing Corp., 850 Third Avenue, New York, NY, 10022. Attn. Special Sales Department. Phone: 1-800-221-2647.

Zebra and the Z logo Reg. U.S. Pat. & TM Off.

First Printing: January, 2001
10 9 8 7 6 5 4 3 2 1

Printed in the United States of America

One

"Lucinda!" a heavy baritone voice roared.

"Lucy," Garth whispered to the redhead in his arms. "Someone is calling you."

"Hmm?" Lucy murmured, her eyes closed and lips pursed. "Oh, kiss me again."

"Lucinda!" Rather, the voice bellowed once more.

Lucy's eyes popped open. Passion drugged, they showed dawning fear. "Oh, my God! It is Jason!"

"Jason who?" Garth asked, his brows rising.

"My husband!" Lucy scrambled away from Garth. "Of a certain, he's in high dudgeon. He is so jealous!"

"You have a husband now? Why did you not tell me?"

"I . . . forgot! I was just that pleased to see you again." She tugged at her gaping neckline. "Quick. You must hide."

"I will not." Garth sprang for his discarded shirt and jacket. "It never pays."

"You are right." Lucy ran toward the balcony doors and swung them wide. "You must escape down the trellis."

"Don't be daft." Garth paused to frown at her. "I will break my neck."

"No, you will not, for it is very strong," Lucy vowed

sincerely. "I assure you, other men have done it without injury."

"Ah, in that case"—Garth's eyes lit with humor, and he bowed even as he struggled into his shirt—"I can do no less."

A pounding shook the bedroom door.

"Hurry!" Lucy whispered.

"Excellent advice, my dear." Grinning, Garth blew her a kiss and bolted toward the open doors and out onto the balcony. A stone wall, waist high, enclosed it. The trellis in question was easy to spy and built on sturdy lines. Lucy no doubt had drafted the design herself. He swung his leg over the wall, seeking to catch his foot upon the latticework.

"Good-bye," Lucy called. "It is famous to have you back in town."

The panels of the bedroom door cracked as its wood heaved. "Lucinda!"

"I doubt Jason agrees," Garth laughed. He began his unplanned, hasty descent down the trellis. "Faith, I am getting too old for these capers."

A loud crash from above resounded.

"Jason, is that you, sweetheart?" Lucy's voice asked. "You are home early. How was your day?"

"Where is the bounder?" a male voice roared.

"Who, darling? There is no one here but me. I am alone. I have been alone all—"

"There was a man in here."

"A man? Jason, how could you think such of me?" Lucy's voice turned weepy. "Never would I!"

"Then what, madame, is this?" Jason's voice demanded. Garth cursed. What item of evidence had he left behind?

"Th-that? Why, that is mine." Lucy's laugh was rather strangled. "It—it is the newest fashion, darling. Er, Lady Jersey started it."

"Ah! The balcony doors are open. The impudent dog has gone down the blasted trellis!"

"No, Jason, I vow he has not. I-I was just taking the air."

Garth chuckled at this. An act that proved fatal. The "out-and-outer" misjudged his footing and crashed the last length into the shrubbery, a very prickly and brittle shrubbery at that.

"I love you, Jason!" Lucy shrieked. "I love you!"

"He *is* down there! Bedamn, I have had enough. I'll kill the scoundrel."

"Jason, no! My God, you can't shoot him!"

"Leave me be, woman. Else I will shoot you!"

Garth fought free of the bush. He looked up. Jason appeared. Apparently Lucy had decided to "leave him be." Jason lumbered over the balcony wall and onto the trellis. Garth found he could not fault the woman, fickle though she was. The man was huge.

Garth could only hope that the trellis might break under Jason's mighty weight. Not tarrying, however, to observe the Goliath's fate, he took off at an uneven lope, slowed by a pained ankle. "Hmm, yes, I am decidedly too old for this."

He successfully traversed the townhome's private garden. Coming to the thicket dividing it from that of the next residence, Garth bolted through it and into the adjacent yard. He headed toward the protective shadows of the next building. Slowing only marginally, he jerked his jacket on over his unbuttoned shirt. The sound of ripping material greeted his ears. He cursed. Then cursed more loudly as he rammed into a pole. A screech sounded. He stumbled backward.

The pole, in truth, was not a pole. It was a ladder, a shaking and teetering ladder to which a woman was desperately clinging farther above. "Oh, no! Drat!"

A cloud of petticoats descended upon Garth.

"Blast!" He worked to regain his balance and maneuver into position to catch the live bundle. He succeeded. The impact, however, sent them both rolling to the ground. Garth was the first to achieve an upright stance. He reached down his hand. "A thousand pardons, ma'am. Are you all right?"

"Of course not," the lady snapped, grasping his hand. She was swathed in a voluminous cape, her head entirely concealed beneath a deep-brimmed calash.

Garth thought he heard a strong expletive come from her as he drew her up, but was certain he must be mistaken as he took in the delicate hand grasping his.

"Forgive me, I fear I was not watching where I was g—" He halted as the woman looked up and he saw beneath her bonnet's brim. A soft light from the windows above revealed the most classically beautiful face, framed by honeyed gold hair. Wide, golden brown eyes fringed with dark lashes studied him. Only the blatant fullness of the woman's lips (for she was certainly no *jeune fille*) and the resolute strength of her chin could be considered by critics to detract from her perfection. Though in Garth's opinion those features were far more distracting than detracting.

Astonishment washed over him. "Julia?"

"Oh, my God. Garth!" Her eyes widened in consternation.

He frowned severely. "What the devil are you doing here?"

"What am *I* doing here?" Her finely shaped brows snapped down. "Rather, what are *you* doing here?"

"You first." Garth laughed. "Never say *you* are engaged in a lover's tryst? You, of all people, set on a path of vice. For shame, I am shocked."

"You are never shocked. You are too preoccupied in *doing* the shocking. And no, I am not engaged in a lovers' tryst." Julia jerked her hand from his. Her gaze raked over him, taking in his open shirt and awry jacket. "That, is *your* department."

"Then it is an elopement?"

"No, indeed, it is not!"

"Come, it is all too obvious. An open window. A ladder." Garth feigned sympathy. "But, alas, where is the redoubtable fiancé? I fear you have been jilted. Stood up at the . . . ladder, alas."

"I told you, I am not eloping." Julia's body stiffened, and her fists clenched. Garth suppressed his laugh. Plainly, she would like to clout him. "I have no lovers' tryst."

"You there!" a man shouted.

Garth peered toward the darkened hedge line. He could hear Jason making excellent time in his advance. He shook his head ruefully. Danger lay in either direction. Garth opted for the danger that did not wield a firearm. "You do now."

Moving quickly, Garth seized Julia and dragged her into his arms. He planted his lips firmly upon hers. He breathed in her objection and clinched her close as she struggled. He knew better than to weaken in his resolve. It would be letting go of the tiger's tail to be sure. Desperately, he held his position, and his kiss.

Julia grew still. Her lips trembled, softened and warmed all at once. Garth lost all sense of reality in an instant. Thoughts of whom he kissed or where he was were quelled as he reveled in the taste of this new kiss that captured him. There was a teasing hint of passion, and something else. Something far more illusive. Garth deepened the kiss, seeking the answer.

It was his undoing. An all-to-rare fire of emotion flamed through him. Shocked, he pulled back. He held Julia's fulsome body close against him now, in need of support.

Julia, her eyes wide, her lips ravaged from his kisses, stared at him in bewilderment. Righteous anger put paid to that enchanting look. "Why, you—"

"Not now." Garth was actually relieved to have Jason bearing down upon them with a pistol. It gave him an excuse to ignore what had just happened. He lowered his head and nuzzled Julia's ear. "We have company."

"Stop that!" Julia twisted her head away from him. It was in the direction of the approaching Jason as he thrashed forward from the hedge and plowed across a planting of impatiens. "Oh, Lord, Garth, what have you done now?"

Jason pounded up to them, panting. In his right hand, he waved a gleaming Manton, the reflection of lights bouncing off its fierce-looking, long barrel. "Did you see a man run by here?"

"A man? Why, no." Garth looked down at Julia, who glowered up at him. He smiled with encouragement. "I did not see a man run past. Did you, dearest?"

"I did not." Julia's words were crisp. "Though I believe I did see a dog pass by. A mangy, slinking cur at that."

"This man would be missing a cravat." Jason hoisted up said article in his left hand.

"Indeed?" Garth asked. Of course, that was what he had missed when scrabbling for his expeditious departure. "How improper of him."

Jason's eyes narrowed. He pointed the pistol at Garth and cocked it. "Just like you are missing one, sirrah."

"Please, no." Julia stepped directly in front of Garth. She clasped her hands together. "Please, sir, do not shoot. You shall awaken the household." She paused. It was clear that what she was about to say choked her painfully. "We . . . we are eloping, you see."

"Yes, by Jove, that is what we are doing." Garth

looked at Julia with respect. Faith, but she *was* a quick thinker. "Only we, uh, became carried away."

"Did you, now?" Jason's voice was surely, though his pistol did waver.

"Please, it is true." Julia rushed forward. With a graceful movement, she knelt. Her cape fell away. The white of a nightgown, simple and virginal, was displayed. She looked down demurely. "If you shoot him, I-I will be dishonored. W-we must marry, you see."

Jason stared. He then looked at Garth, indecision rife upon his face. "There cannot be two scoundrels both missing their cravats in one night."

"Sir, I fear the world is populated with scoundrels, with or without cravats," Julia said, her voice sad. "This scoundrel, unfortunately, is mine. He has—has been with me this entire eve."

"You ought to be ashamed of yourself," Jason admonished.

"I-I am, frightfully." A tearful sob escaped Julia. "B-but I did not realize he was a bounder until it was too late, *far too late*. My parents warned me, but there you have it. I have thrown my hat over the windmill with this loose fish, and I must wed him posthaste."

"Forsooth, lass." Jason lowered his pistol. "You poor thing."

"So you see . . ."

"Betina!" A voice shrieked from above. A woman, a nightcap of point lace askew to one side upon her head, leaned from the window, waving her hands frantically. "Come back! Come back!"

"Pardon me, but this blackguard and I must flee!" Julia sprang up, lifted her skirts, and ran.

"Hope you find that other scoundrel." Garth nodded, and pelted after her.

He caught up with her at the front street. A hack

with coachman waited there. The door was open, and Julia was already settled within the vehicle.

"Hurry!" Julia waved a beckoning hand.

Garth dove into the coach. "Spring them, man!"

"Not yet, Meeker! Hold for my order," Julia shouted. She lowered her voice. "Hide, for pity sake!"

"What?" Garth asked, bemused. The front door to the residence burst open. People spewed forth from its portal. "Go, man! What are you waiting for?"

"Not yet!" Julia shoved at Garth. "Get on the floor!"

"Very well," Garth conceded. In truth, the force Julia was applying left him with very little choice. He crouched on the hack's floor. Julia flung part of her cape over him. Garth manfully maintained his silence, though he twitched the cape up a tad to watch what transpired.

Julia continued sitting with the door wide open. Why, the vixen was luring them to her. When the crowd was but one meager foot from the coach, Julia called out in a strange, high-pitched voice. "Go. Oh, please go, coachman!"

She leaned over and pulled the coach door shut directly in their faces.

Meeker jerked the carriage into action so fast that Garth toppled into Julia. He wrapped his arms about her legs for anchoring.

"Stop that," Julia's voice commanded.

"Pardon." The coach took a hairpin turn, which caused Garth to hold on even tighter.

"I said, stop that!"

"I will," Garth gritted. "Whenever Meeker stops driving neck-or-nothing."

"He will in a moment."

"Then I will refrain the moment thereafter." True to Julia's prediction, the coach slowed. Out of sheer deviltry, Garth slid his hand up to the curve of Julia's waist. 'A pity. I was beginning to enjoy this."

"Will you cease your mauling!" The enveloping cape was flung from him.

Garth grinned up at Julia with a severe lack of repentance. "Alas, I am uncovered."

"It is clear France did not change you one wit," Julia said, her tone sour. "You remain the disgraceful womanizer you have always been."

"*Voyons*, it is sad to own, but yes. You must blame it on the French women. They simply refuse to let a man reform. I tried; I truly did. I would tread a path of rectitude, but then I would chance upon another Brelendiére. The seductress would put paid to all my fine resolutions, and there I would go again. Yes, those beautiful, lusty French ladies would not permit reform. They take it as their national duty, I believe." Garth cocked a brow. "Though I see that you have changed. The most respectable Saint Julia running about in her night rail? It is a wonder and a calamity all at once." A sudden, odd twinge passed through Garth. "Confess. You were eloping. Who's the poor chap? Would you like me to take him to task for missing his own elopement?"

"I told you, I was not eloping." Julia snorted. "As if I would make such a frightful mistake as that."

"Ha, that's my girl." Garth shifted to a more comfortable position, one arm resting upon Julia's lap. "You have not changed past all recognition, then."

Julia smiled. A mischievous twinkle entered her eyes. "Indeed, not. Our view upon marriage is the singular subject we both agree upon, I believe."

Garth froze. Time faded away. He was not looking at the woman Julia had become during the four years of his absence but rather the girl Julia had been fifteen years ago. The girl who had been his adopted sister, his co-conspirator in pranks and mayhem, his best friend. Time shifted, and the woman Julia sat before him once more, awaiting his answer. He forced a smile. "Marriage is to be avoided at all cost."

Julia nodded graciously. "Exactly."

"Then what *are* you doing?" Garth asked, intrigued. "If this is not an elopement and it is not a tryst, what in blazes is it?"

"I have no doubt you will laugh. I am helping a friend of mine. It is she who is eloping. I am merely acting as the decoy for her family to chase. If I am not mistaken, Betina is well on her way with her beloved Thomas to Gretna Green. Since she has my coach and cattle, I expect them to make good time."

"Isn't that a little hypocritical?" Garth asked dryly.

"What?"

"You refuse to step into a parson's mousetrap yourself, yet you will gladly push a friend into it. Sacrificing her to the marriage god in appeasement, are you?"

"I am doing no such thing!" Julia said, her tone wroth. She shrugged her shoulders. "That is where your opinions and mine depart. I do not dislike marriage comprehensively. I accept it as a necessary institution, and even an advantageous one, for that matter, for many women. Fortunately, I am not forced to be one of those women. I need not give up my independence for a suitable existence. I do not need to curry to a man's whims and megrims merely to possess the comforts of home and society."

"A man's whims and megrims? Faith, you do think highly of us fellows, don't you?"

"What of you? Do not try and gammon me with a profession of your respect for us ladies."

"But I do respect you ladies. Of a certainty, I love women. All of them."

"Forgive me, but it is not love that you feel for

women," Julia said, a hearty dose of cynicism within her voice. "Desire, perhaps. Lust, most definitely. But not love."

Anger flared up in Garth at her cut. Still, he offered her a rakish smile. "You know me too well."

"Indeed I do." Julia lifted her chin in regal disdain. "Just exactly who was the behemoth with the Manton? We left before I was properly introduced."

Garth clenched his teeth. "He is the husband of . . . a friend."

"A friend?" Julia shook her head. "You will never stop."

"No, I have," Garth said, irritated. "I have not dallied with a married woman since my salad days. I value my life more than that. I didn't know the lady had acquired a husband while I was abroad."

"Indeed?"

"She said she simply forgot to inform me." Garth grimaced. "She saved that particular bon mot for when hulking Jason was pounding at the boudoir door."

"My!" Julia's lips twitched. "How positively *unsporting* of her."

"I was forced to the indignity of an escape down the trellis, no less. I balked at the thought at first. She assured me, however, that many had exited safely by that route before."

"Oh, no!" Julia's laughter filled the carriage. Garth warmed. It felt as if it had been ages since he had heard her laugh. Julia had the kind of laugh that could set an entire room aglow. "Whoever said the path, or shall I say the trellis, of unrighteousness is easy?"

Garth studied her with the slightest wonderment. "I do not know you since you have grown up. I have heard about you in France . . ."

"I must be honored."

Garth frowned. "They call you the Citadel."

"How positively unoriginal." Julia actually yawned.

"I believe 'capricious and unattainable' were terms also used." Garth cocked one brow high. "Have you never suffered from—ah, to use your words—desire and lust?"

Something illusive flickered through Julia's eyes. She laughed. "Most certainly not. That is why I am the Citadel, I believe. A stronghold against such mundane passions." Garth gazed at her, his disappointment showing. There had been no honesty within her answer. Julia looked away. "I am intending to exchange coaches shortly. Betina's father and party should be able to follow this one for what remains of the night. They will find themselves in the wilds of Devonshire by morn if all goes well. Once we have made the switch, where may I take you?"

"Why, home with you."

Julia rolled her eyes. "Please, I am the last one you should attempt to ply your charms upon."

"I wasn't." Garth frowned. "Did your father not tell you I was expected?"

"What do you mean?"

"I have returned to London at your father's request. He wrote that the matter was urgent. He assured me I may stay with him."

"What matter?" Julia exclaimed.

Garth shrugged. "I do not know. He did not say. He merely said it was important. After everything your father has done for me, I certainly would not deny his request."

"Tsk, tsk, the famous Citadel sneaking in the back entrance like an errant servant." Garth shook his head mournfully. "What would the *tôn* say to this? I wonder. I can not believe they would consider this *comme il faut!*"

"Do be quiet!" Julia admonished as she led him around to the kitchen entrance of the Wrexton townhome at Cavendish Square.

She purposely ignored Garth as he leaned against the doorframe and watched her. The years had not changed him one wit. He was still one of the handsomest men in England. No doubt he had now claimed that title in France as well. It was not simply his superior height of two and six or the perfect balance of strong muscle to his lithe frame. Nor was it the deep russet color of his hair, which made a woman think of fine Bordeaux in amber glass. All of that was indeed alluring, but it was Garth's eyes that drew and conquered a woman. They could be described simply as hazel gray. Yet when Garth looked at a woman, the glint of amusement and pleasure in them would change their color to so many different shades as to make her head spin.

Julia smiled grimly. Since she had known Garth all his life, and also knew his here-and-there nature, her head did not spin. Not unless, that is, he made her angry, which he did more times than not. Faith, he was not even back in London one night and he was in trouble and had drawn her into it as well. No, the man had not changed one wit.

"May I ask why such stealth?" Garth whispered.

Julia sighed. "It does not matter that I am eight and twenty and have been on the town for more years than I care to recall. Father still believes a young lady should be home by midnight. I have found it simpler to have Ruppleton inform him that I have arrived home and gone to bed, and then I use this entrance. I would not be forced to these measures if Father would not persist in remaining in the library every night until the wee hours. The library is directly off the entry hall, and he unfortunately has the best of hearing."

"How very inconsiderate of him, forcing you to stoop to such chicaneries."

"Yes, isn't it?" Julia drew out her personal key.

"And what of the other servants? Do none of them ever spill their budget to your father."

"Heaven forefend." Julia smiled wryly. "The servants who survive in this house are the kind who can accept minor and major eccentricities and keep mum about them all. I have never known how Ruppleton finds such, but thank heaven he does."

"His first question, no doubt, is whether they are odd themselves and wish to feel at home."

"Charming notion. Here I thought he merely offered them obscenely large wages." Julia reached to put the key in the keyhole, but the door swung open as if by magic. Julia jumped. She then saw her father standing there. *Make that black magic,* she thought as she mustered a smile. "Hello, Father."

"Hello, Julia," Bendford Wrexton said. His distinguished face was stern. Well, in truth, it was actually thunderous.

"Look who I have found?" Julia tried for a light tone. She brushed past her fulminating father. "Why did you not tell me you had invited Garth to London?"

"Ah, Garth, my boy, greetings." Lord Wrexton trailed Julia into the kitchen. "I intended to tell you this very night, but *you* could not be found. Ruppleton was finally forced to confess."

"Poor Ruppleton." Julia moved quickly through the kitchen and succeeded in reaching the green baize door on its far wall. If she could brazen it out, she might be able to escape to her rooms.

"It is fortunate for Ruppleton that he is the only butler I know who can tolerate this impossible family, else I would have sacked him promptly. And that would have been upon your head as well, miss. We are in the library, Julia."

"I see." Julia's hope fled. She knew her father's tone. She dare not press him any farther.

"How have you been, Garth?" Lord Wrexton asked then as the three moved through the darkened house.

"In the best of form, sir." Garth's tone was despicably cheerful. "And you?"

"I have been better. It is a blow to a man to discover the flagrant deception of his only child."

"Indeed, sir?" Amusement was rife within Garth's voice. The man never took anything seriously. "Did you truly just discover this about Julia?"

"No." Lord Wrexton sighed heavily. "I have known for years that she has been playing me this way."

"Father!" Julia skittered to a halt in utter shock. "How . . . ? When . . . ?"

"You have confounded her, sir," Garth said. "She is positively beautiful with her mouth agape like that, is she not? Indeed, it quite brings to mind an exotic fish I viewed in a pond at Versailles."

"It has brightened *my* night." Lord Wrexton grinned in return.

"You both are . . . odious!" Julia stamped her foot.

"The library, my girl." Lord Wrexton frowned darkly at her once more.

"Yes, sir," Julia said, realizing her error. Garth's chuckle galled her all the more. Yet she refused to be the bear of his baiting. She stepped into the library, head held high. She froze.

"Julia, dearest!" Her aunt Clare rose from a large wing-backed chair. She was a petite but plump woman. Her hair was the lightest silver blond. With her age in consideration, one might have thought it white, but in truth, not one strand was due to her years. Nor were her large blue eyes lined particularly or her lips marked by time. Her gown of bright, rose-hued crepe pasemé, trimmed with far too much blond lace twirled into rosettes arranged with clusters of plum-colored satin peas, was neither in the fashion of her day or the fashion of the present, but in Aunt Clare's fashion alone. She bobbed her head, the spangles on her turban of pleated gauze twinkling in the candlelight. "We have been waiting for you."

"So I have been informed." Julia's heart sank. The "we" of Aunt Clare's statement happened to be twelve cats. Much to Lord Wrexton's displeasure, Aunt Clare always included her felines as part of the family.

That, however, was not what caused Julia's foreboding. It was that Aunt Clare had called all of her cats to the meeting. Generally, only the presence of Percy, her favorite, was considered necessary for daily issues. Aunt Clare only required all of her pets' attendance below when there were important affairs to consider.

As a rule, at Lord Wrexton's demand, the clan was confined to the third story, where Aunt Clare's rooms resided. That her father had permitted all the "family" into the library—and for the length of an entire evening—might very well portend the end of the world.

"And Garth, dear boy!" Aunt Clare had been approaching Julia with outstretched arms. She promptly veered to Garth, enveloping him instead. Julia took no offense. Aunt Clare was the dearest of women, but her mind was easily diverted. "I have been so eager to see you again."

"You knew he was coming?" This time Julia *was* offended. "You never told me!"

"I am sorry, dear." Aunt Clare's expression turned sad. "I have tried to persuade your father differently, but he has refused to listen."

"Persuade him differently about what?" Julia asked cautiously.

"Clare, for God's sake," Bendford said. "Let me do the talking."

"Oh, dear, yes." Aunt Clare blinked in confusion. "We have not reached that discussion yet, have we?" Deserting Garth, she came back to Julia with unnerving focus. "Come, Julia, let us all sit down." Julia permitted Aunt Clare to lead her over to a chair. "You may sit next to Percy. Percy is such a comfort at times like these."

"What 'times like these'?" Julia obediently sat and permitted Aunt Clare to undo her cloak and take it from her.

"What in blazes!" Bendford exploded.

"Oh, dear," Aunt Clare murmured.

"What?" Julia was distracted at the moment by Percy, who had jumped into her lap and was offering her what sounded like a sympathetic yowl. "What is the matter?"

"I fear you did not look in the looking glass before you went out, Julia." Aunt Clare's voice was kind. "You forgot to change from your nightgown. Indeed, it is the easiest thing to overlook, I own, but Marie should have noticed. It is the most important reason for employing a dresser. Bertha spies it very quickly for me, I assure you."

"What the devil were you doing, Julia?" Bendford Wrexton asked. "And do not think to palm me off with some faradiddle or I will take a whip to you as I should have a hundred times when you were a child."

"Father, it is not what you might think." Julia flushed. Even she must admit the evidence was damning. "Truly. It was perfectly innocent. I was merely assisting my friend Betina to elope."

What? You call that innocent?" Lord Wrexton looked at her as if she had turned traitor to the Crown, and that for a guinea. He staggered over to a chair and fell into it. A screech arose from beneath. In a moment,

Esther, a gray-and-white tabby, scrabbled out from between his legs. "You unnatural child."

"Father?" Julia frowned. "There was nothing unnatural about it. Nothing immoral or depraved, I assure you."

"Witness the cotton of the nightgown," Garth interjected, his voice amused. "Good, sturdy, no lace. Nothing going there, sir."

"It was quite simple. I went to the Carlyles to visit Betina, who was playing sick. Her parents have been watching her for days and all but keeping her prisoner. I stopped to visit her. I said I was attending a masquerade and came dressed in domino and mask. I exchanged clothes with Betina and sent her with my maid in my coach. I then remained to set up the 'other escape' to lead her parents astray. Betina and Baron Sherwood should be well on their way to Gretna now."

"Do you dare to tell me that—that platter-faced Betina is escaping in *our* coach to be married?" Lord Wrexton sprung from his chair with a roar. "Have you no feminine feelings whatsoever? How could you help another woman become married when *you* are not married yourself? You, a diamond of the first water, are left upon the shelf, and that pale little Betina is now married, thanks to *you*. And those Carlyles will see their grandchildren before they die. While *I* will not. Not unless something drastic is done." Lord Wrexton puffed out his chest. "Since my child will not look out for herself, I shall do so."

"Bendford, please." Aunt Clare's voice was gentle and pleading. "Could you not reconsider?"

"No," Bendford said.

"Reconsider what?" Julia asked in frustration.

"This last escapade of hers only proves I am right," Lord Wrexton growled. "Something must be done."

"What must be done?" Julia tried again.

"Indeed. What, sir?" Garth inquired. "As you noted, it is much too late to beat any sense into her. I fear it would be a waste of a good whip and naught else."

"Oh, do be quiet. Of all people, you are the last person who should cast stones at me." Julia looked to her father. "Do you know what Garth was doing tonight when he . . . stumbled across me? He was running away from—"

"You need not continue." Garth cast her a dark look. "Aunt Clare, I am sure, is not interested."

"Children, children," Aunt Clare soothed. "Do not bicker. You really—"

"Well, it was he who started—" Julia began. Percy meowed, and soon Peaches and Cream and Strawberry added their voices.

"It was not," Garth objected. Shakespeare added to the chorus of yowls. Radcliffe joined in as well.

"Everyone be quiet!" Lord Wrexton commanded.

Julia and Garth continued to bicker. The cats yowled with a higher pitch. Aunt Clare's clucking and tsking made no impact.

"Deuce take it!" Lord Wrexton's chin jutted out rather in defiance of the pandemonium. "I demand you marry within six month's time, Julia. Else I will cut you out of my will and from any other funds prior to my demise."

The room silenced within a second. Human and feline alike sat mumchance. Lord Wrexton peered about. A smile of pleasure split his face. "Ha! That has claimed your attention, what?"

"I believe you can safely say that, sir," Garth said slowly.

"I tried." Aunt Clare sighed like a sad breeze. "I truly did."

"Meow." Percy concurred. Twelve pairs of cat eyes studied Julia intently.

"You cannot mean it." Julia gasped as his words finally settled into her psyche.

"I do."

"No!" Julia shot up from her seat. "You cannot do that."

"I can. It is completely within my legal rights."

"I mean, you wouldn't."

"Oh, yes, I would, Miss Contrary. And I will. Make no mistake. I want to see my grandchildren before I die. You need a man to settle you down and give you lots of babies. *Then* see if you have time to run about in your night rail. Or help other gels elope to Gretna Green while you sit on the shelf."

"You will see nothing." Julia clenched her fists. "I will not be forced into marriage. You may cut me from your will. You may withhold all funds. I shall live in penury before I give up my independence and permit myself to be shackled to any man. I shall beg in the streets before that."

"I would never be that cruel." Lord Wrexton smiled. To Julia's discomfort, his smile appeared more feline than that of the twelve felines present.

"Thank you." Julia lifted her chin and offered him a small, curt nod.

"I am not a monster." Her father actually rubbed his hands together. "If you fail to marry, you need only apply to Garth, my favorite, one-and-only godson. Because he will be my new beneficiary if you refuse to get yourself a husband. He will have the ordering of any moneys you might receive."

"What?" Garth sprang up, his expression appalled. "Good God, sir, no!"

Julia gurgled. She could not muster a word, she was so furious. She glared with loathing at Garth. He did not notice her brimstone glance, for he persisted in staring at her father as if he were actually terrified.

Balked of satisfaction, Julia turned the furnace of her fury back to Lord Wrexton. Her sire was overly occupied with laughing. The devil had played his trump card well, and he knew it.

Julia drew in a ragged breath. Galled to the very depths, she could not consider anything except escape. "Very well, Father. You wish me to be wed and quit from this house. So be it. I am still an heiress for these next six months, am I not?"

"You are," Lord Wrexton nodded benignly.

"I will become engaged within the week, married within the month." Julia eyed her father narrowly. "Will that be expedient enough for you?"

Her father grinned. "I believe it will be."

"Bendford, please," Aunt Clare begged. "Do reconsider . . ."

"So be it!" The words seethed through Julia's clenched teeth. She picked up her skirts, or rather, Betina's night rail, and swept from the room. She tripped over Alexander the Great, which took the edge off of her grand exit somewhat. It did not, however, slow her momentum down one wit.

Two

Julia sat at the breakfast table, staring down at the paper before her. The meager light of dawn muted the cheery tones of the room. Julia took a sip from her tea and set it down with precision as a heavy sigh sounded from behind her. "Do stop reading over my shoulder, Ruppleton."

"Yes, Miss Julia," Ruppleton said.

Julia turned in her chair. Ruppleton, the family butler, teapot held at a tilt, loomed over her, his tall frame cantilevered over her in order that he may peruse the paper in front of her. "I repeat, stop reading over my shoulder."

"Yes, Miss Julia." Ruppleton obediently rocked back upon his heals.

"Thank you." Julia turned back to her work. A breath of exasperation escaped her. Percy, who had been sitting staring at her from a distant chair, now lay squarely upon her paper. The cat was magical in his ability to move his mass in a flash. She glared at him. "Do get off my paper."

Percy glared at her. "Meow."

"If you think to make a statement, forget it." Julia reached over and pushed at the huge cat. "I will do what I wish, thank you."

Percy refused to be brushed away. "Meow."

Julia glared at the cat with extreme displeasure. He

merely rolled over on the paper, his back legs inelegantly stretched out, while he licked his one front paw.

"Percy! My goodness!" Aunt Clare entered into the breakfast room, a gentle look of reproach upon her face. She floated over and sat in the chair next to Julia, settling the skirts of her morning dress of lace net worked in stripes over ecru satin. Long ribbons of coquelicot dangled from her cap of point lace. "What are you doing upon the table? How very ungentlemanly of you."

"Meow." Percy laid his ears back in apology. He did not budge, however.

"He refuses to get off my paper," Julia accused, her anger rising.

"For shame, Percy," Aunt Clare admonished. "Do move from Julia's paper, dearest."

"Meow." Percy flipped his girth over and flattened himself to the paper all the more.

Aunt Clare blinked. She looked solemnly at Julia. "Percy is clearly determined upon this head. What exactly is on the paper, my love?"

"What does it matter?" Julia asked, ruffled. It was galling to be forced to defend one's actions against those of a cat. "It is certainly no business of his." She flushed. She sounded rather childish, even to her own ears. "Very well, it is a list of the men I will consider marrying."

"Oh, dear, no." Aunt Clare's sweet face grew alarmed. "Percy is quite right, dearest. You must not do this."

"I have no choice." Julia looked away. She had remained awake all night, pacing the floor, attempting to make a decision. It had not helped to remember how she had boasted just hours before to Garth that she was thankfully not one of those unfortunate women who must marry and curry to a man's whims and megrims. Now it seemed she was, indeed, one of those poor women.

How a few short hours had changed everything. No, how her father had changed everything. His vow to hand Julia's fortune over to Garth was the clincher. Lord Wrexton loved Garth as a son. He would feel no guilt in giving her money to *him*.

A shudder ran through Julia. To be compelled to apply to Garth for funds over the years would be unbearable. She envisioned herself pushed to chase him down at his mistress's to beg for pin money. She never doubted she would be wearing glass ear bobs, while his mistress sported rubies and diamonds. Resolutely, she reached for the paper underneath Percy. Percy batted her hand away. "Accept it, Percy, the jig is up. I must marry."

"Please, dear," Aunt Clare pleaded. "Permit me some time before you take such drastic steps. Perhaps I will be able to sway your father from this course."

Julia's heart warmed. Her aunt was so very sincere. "How long have you known about father's plan, Auntie?"

"He has been considering it for over two months now." Aunt Clare leaned forward. "Please do not be angry I did not tell you, dearest. I had hoped you would never need hear of his plan. It surely cannot help but make one feel . . . pressed."

"Pressed? That is rather an understatement."

"But you must not give up hope, dearest. I shall continue to do everything within my power to sway your father."

"Thank you," Julia said gently. "But if you have not stopped Father before this, I doubt you will now. He knows he has me at *point non plus*. I will not wait to lose my fortune to Garth. How father could have devised such a Machiavellian plot is beyond me."

The guiltiest of expressions crossed her Aunt's face. "I fear it was me who gave him the notion."

"You! You thought this frightful plot up?"

"Oh, no. I do not believe you can ever force love. You can nudge it, perhaps, guide it, assist it, but never force it. Never. No, your father mistook something I said."

"Of course," Julia said, relieved. Her world was spinning out of its natural orbit as it was. She was not sure she could have tolerated the news that her sweet, dithering aunt was a mastermind of deception. "What did you say?"

"Your father declared he would leave your fortune to charity if you refused to marry in the next months. I begged him to reconsider, for he surely would not wish to leave it to strangers." She looked down. "Then I suggested he ask Garth to come home."

"Oh, Lord." Julia rolled her eyes. What a bumble-broth. She could very well see how it had transpired. Aunt Clare's mention of Garth at that fatal moment had given her father the one missing weapon he needed.

"I thought if Garth came home he could talk reason to your father."

"Oh, indeed. As if Garth would do anything to assist me."

"Now dearest, Garth cares for you . . ."

"Fiddlesticks!" Julia was so unladylike as to snort outright.

"And you care for him . . ."

"What? I do not care for him. Why, I do not give a rap for that . . . that bounder! That rake . . ."

"Hello." Garth strolled into the breakfast room. His gaze was bright and quizzing. "Bounder and rake, Julia? Whoever could you be talking about?"

Julia glared. "What are you doing here?"

"I do not know. I rather thought to indulge myself in the decadent custom of breaking fast." He sat down beside Aunt Clare. "Who were you talking about?"

"No one," Julia snapped. "It is early. You never breakfast early. You—"

"Ha! You were talking about me." Garth winked at Aunt Clare. "She loves me, you know?"

Aunt Clare beamed. "I know!"

Garth's face took on an alarmed look.

"I love him as much as he loves me," Julia interjected maliciously.

"Exactly," Aunt Clare smiled benignly. "And that is the reason I thought Garth should be summoned when your father decided to force you to marry."

Garth looked at Julia, confused defeat registering within his gaze. "What is she talking about?"

Julia shook her head, biting her lip to maintain her composure. "You do not want to know."

"But he just said he knew," Aunt Clare frowned. "And you said so, too. Since you both admit you love each other—"

"What!" Garth looked appalled. "I was merely roasting Julia. I was not serious, Aunt Clare."

"You weren't?" Aunt Clare's face fell.

Julia lost the effort. She broke into delighted laughter. "Gracious, let us drop this discussion. I do not have the time for it." Julia slapped lightly at Percy. "Now do give it over, you beast."

"What is he lying on?" Garth asked.

"It is Julia's list of the men she thinks she can marry," Aunt Clare whispered loudly.

Garth's brows rose. "You are gammoning me, are you not, Aunt? For shame, I never knew you to be such a tease before."

"No, dear, I am not." Aunt Clare's sincerity could not be mistaken. "You know I have always tried to teach you honesty. What a sad example it would be if I lied to you . . . excessively, that is." She frowned. "Though I am beginning to wonder if sometimes it isn't necessary to fib a jot. The . . . the grander scheme of things is more important once in a while."

Garth smiled, but it was to Julia that he turned his intent gaze. "You are actually making a list?"

"She has twenty names at present," Ruppleton said from behind.

"You are truly going through with this, then?"

"Of course." Julia glared at him. "What else am I to do?"

"I do not know." Garth shrugged. "Though I did not expect you to meekly roll over and do your father's bidding."

"Yes, you would like me to defy him, wouldn't you? You'd gain a fortune from it. And me, I'd be out in the streets."

"No, dearest," Aunt Clare said. "You would only have to apply to Garth for funds."

"I promise you, I would take my chances upon the street before that ever happened."

Garth's eyes flared. "Gads, but you are shrewish in the morning. Who are the poor chaps on the list? I best warn them of your vile morning temper."

"I have no doubt you will." Julia sugared her tone.

"That is right," Garth said, his words clipped. "There is a fortune at stake here. I am a bit low in the water these days. I ran through my funds while in France. Punting on tick is what I am doing, don't you know?"

"Garth!" Aunt Clare cried. "Never say so."

"Wine, women, and song, Auntie, are expensive. Even more so on the Continent." Garth's smile returned to his face.

"Garth." Aunt Clare frowned severely. "You really

should stop shamming it so. You will make Julia think
you are a rake."

"I know he is." Julia rolled her eyes. "It is a shame
I did not know what Father had in mind. I would have
let that man shoot you through last night. It would
have settled matters most charmingly."

"Julia!" Aunt Clare gasped. "For shame!"

Sheer deviltry rose within Garth's eyes. "You say you
have twenty names on the list? Do you *truly* think there
are that many men willing to marry you?"

Julia shrugged. "I am an heiress. I am passably at-
tractive. Yes, I do. Indeed, I am sure I am overlooking
another twenty or more. However, I must set my stan-
dards."

"Such sweet modesty."

Julia narrowed her eyes. "I have no time for modesty.
I intend to become engaged within the week, and I
must decide which man is to be my first choice. If for
some odd reason he does not wish to marry me, then
I will need to have other choices prepared."

Garth lost his smile. "Your father was right. You lack
any feminine sensibilities."

Julia forced a laugh, even as his barb sunk deep
within her. "Indeed. I have no doubt you wish I were
some silly, crying, sighing chit who did not know what
to do. How feminine not to have the gumption or the
wherewithal to save oneself from penury. Or worse."

"And I am the 'or worse'?" Garth stared at her hard.
Julia returned an equally brittle look. He shook his
head slowly. "I pray to God your 'marks' turn you
down, all twenty of them. It would serve you right."

"Pray all you want, but don't turn too religious. I
will get a husband, I assure you." Julia batted her lashes
and offered him a demure smile. "I am not that paltry,
if I do say so myself."

An odd sound came from Garth, something suspiciously like the grinding of teeth. "Let me see the list."

Before Julia knew what he was about, he leaned over and slid the list out from beneath Percy with neither a tear nor rent. Indeed, Percy gave him not one bit of complaint.

"Traitor," Julia hissed to the cat.

"Hmm." Garth leaned back to survey the paper.

"Give me my list!" Julia demanded.

"List?" Lord Wrexton asked as he entered the breakfast room. "What list?"

"Good Lord." Julia clenched her teeth. "You, too?"

"What list?" Lord Wrexton persisted. He all but bolted to the table and sat down, his gaze trained upon the paper in Garth's hand.

"It is a list of the men Julia intends to stalk and trap into matrimony," Garth said, his tone dry.

"Blast and damn." Lord Wrexton hooted and clapped his hands together. "There's the spirit, my girl."

A severe headache was developing behind Julia's left eye. "You never breakfast with us, Father. Why are you here?"

"I wanted to see if you were sulking over my ultimatum," Lord Wrexton admitted with very little of the diplomacy he employed when in the House of Lords. His face broke out into the widest of smiles. "I never thought you'd ride to hounds with such speed."

"And crack the whip with such cold blooded intent," Garth voiced.

"Who do you have on the list?" Lord Wrexton's face brightened. "Have you got Sinclair's on it? He should be the first, in my opinion. One of the finest young speakers I have ever known."

"No." Julia's voice tightened. "You told me I must

marry, and so I shall, but I will decide who the man is to be."

"Here, now, put Sinclair on the list. He is a good candidate."

"For the speaker of the house, perhaps," Julia said frigidly. "But not for my hand. I refuse to put him on the list."

"My lady"—Ruppleton spoke softly—"I do beg of you not to consider Baron Fulton who is number eighteen on your list."

"Why?" Julia asked.

"He . . . he has the most unsavory reputation amongst the maids." Ruppleton frowned. "He is not kind, and I would not have that for you."

"Thank you, Ruppleton." Julia smiled warmly. "Scratch him from the list."

"Here, now," Lord Wrexton complained as Ruppleton jumped to perform the task. "Why do you listen to him when you will not listen to me! He is a servant."

"No, he is Ruppleton." Julia lifted her chin. Many times as a child she had run to Ruppleton for advice rather than to her father. "He loves me."

"I love you, too, blast it." Lord Wrexton's face displayed deep hurt. "Look what I am doing for your sake."

"Really? For my sake, you say?"

"Yes, confound it. It is for your own good. And why Ruppleton should have a say about the list and I don't is beyond me. It's bloody . . . democratic. Why, it is something a Whig might do."

"Indeed." A slow, wicked grin crossed Julia's face. "It *is* bloody democratic. And Ruppleton is free to cross off any man he wishes and add anyone he wants in that place." She looked to the butler. "Do ask the other servants for their suggestions, Ruppleton."

"Yes, my lady." Ruppleton bowed. He spun and took off at high speed; his coattails flapping.

"Here, now," Lord Wrexton exclaimed. "You cannot do that."

"Why? It is perfectly within my legal rights." Lord Wrexton looked so very astonished that Julia laughed. "What is the matter, Father? Are things not working out the way you want them to? Do not feel so bad. Life is like that."

"I wish it were not so." Aunt Clare sighed. "I have never understood why it is so. I wish I might figure it out."

Aunt Clare's perplexed expression restored Julia's good humor.

"I think it is because everybody always *says* it," Aunt Clare murmured.

"Says what, for God's sake?" Lord Wrexton asked, frowning.

"Why, that life must be like that." Aunt Clare looked at her brother as if she had just experienced an epiphany. "It is because everyone *says* it. Life never works out the way we want it to because we *say* it must not."

"Oh, Lord." Lord Wrexton shook his head. "Clare, try not to think. It only confuses matters."

Aunt Clare looked penitent. "I am sorry, Bendford."

"I know you mean well." Lord Wrexton sighed. "But you are not equipped for it. You only end up causing us all sorts of difficulties when you try to think."

Julia smiled and sighed. She had heard this conversation more times then she could remember. Ever since she was a little girl, in truth. Or even as a baby, no doubt. Her mother had died giving her birth, and Julia's memory only consisted of Lord Wrexton and her aunt Clare, who had come to take care of her. "Auntie, I quite agree with you. Someone should make this world better than it is. I would not object."

"Thank you, my love." Tears welled in Aunt Clare's eyes. "You are the sweetest child. You should have only the best."

"Miss Julia!" Ruppleton entered the room. Wilson, the chef, followed behind him. "Wilson would like a word with you."

"Yes?" Julia frowned. "What is it, Wilson?"

"My lady," Wilson approached. He was all of four feet and five. His girth equaled his height. Ruppleton and Wilson were not only the backbone to the running of the Wrexton establishment but were fast friends as well. It was said that opposites attract. Ruppleton's tall, lanky frame next to Wilson's short, rotund form proved it. "Please, I beg of you, scratch the earl of Torrence from your list."

"Hey, hey," Lord Wrexton exclaimed. "I was just about to suggest the man should be on the list."

Julia studied Wilson. "Why should he not be on the list?"

"He refuses any manner of sauces," Wilson whispered lowly, looking about and beading up with sweat as if he were divulging the most heinous of crimes. "You would never be able to have a hollandaise at table again. Or a velouté. Or a crème de tartar. Not even a demiglace! Or . . . my own special sauce."

"Oh, no!" Julia gasped with the appropriate amount of horror. "I never knew that. Heavens, he must be crossed from the list this instant."

"Yes," Aunt Clare agreed. "What a dreadful thing. Even I am more adventuresome than that. And look at Percy." Cats were placed on the planet in Aunt Clare's estimation to teach poor unenlightened humans how to go on. "He is always demanding in his taste and never accepts simple fare. Which reminds me, Wilson. We must consider the kitties' menus for the day. Alexander the Great has made it clear that he wishes fresh

Scottish salmon today. I think a nice dill and cream with it."

"Confound it!" Lord Wrexton cried. "Do not talk about what the infernal cats are to have when I do not even have one blasted beefsteak set before me. And I like the earl of Torrence. Blast it! Who gives a rap whether he likes a sauce? Now will you let me look at the list?"

"No." Julia stood. Her head pounded behind both her right and left eye now. "It is my list, and I will make the decisions." She jerked the paper from Garth's hand. "Now, if you will excuse me, I have work to do. If everyone will give me peace, I will post my final choices for inspection."

Julia delivered her words with vitriolic bitterness. That should certainly shame them.

"How very kind you are," Aunt Clare exclaimed.

"Thank you, Miss Julia." Ruppleton beamed. Wilson wore even a broader smile.

"Heh? What good will that do me?" Lord Wrexton grumbled. "I want to see the list now."

"Oh!" Julia clenched the paper and fled. Garth's laugh was the last thing she heard as she ripped out of the breakfast room.

Julia all but staggered from her bedroom. Wadded balls of paper littered the high four-poster bed and the Aubusson carpet. She walked down the stairs elated. She had done it! She had a final list, and all on one sheet. Granted, it had taken her a full day, but deciding upon one's future husband at such short notice required extensive consideration.

Glancing at the grandfather clock in the foyer, Julia immediately made her way to the back of the house, toward the kitchen. She entered. Aunt Clare, Ruppieton, and Wilson were huddled in deep discussion at the large table. The maids were at present lifting various trays and forming a queue.

"Excellent!" Julia said. "I have caught you before you go to feed the kitties."

"Julia, love." Aunt Clare looked up from the table. "What do you desire for this evening's dinner fare?"

Julia smiled. Now that all her four-legged friends were to be fed their special diets, Aunt Clare would attend to the family. It was the pattern every day. "It is of no significance to me, I shall not be home for dinner." She waved her sheet. "I am going to attend the Monteiths' dance tonight and make certain my future husband knows he is to come and propose to me tomorrow morning."

"Oh, dear, you have decided, then?"

"I have the final list right here." Julia walked over and proudly laid the list down in the center of the table. All three heads bent over it as Julia ticked off the names on her finger. "Number one is Charles Danford, the marquess of Hambledon. Then number two, Lord Mancroft. Lord Beresford is three. Lord Redmond, four. Viscount Dunn is number five. The earl of Raleigh, number six. And the earl of Kelsey, number seven." Julia laughed. "Despite what Garth believes, I do realize I may not get my first choice or even my second. After all, they may have prior commitments of which I am not aware. But surely out of seven, one will come up to scratch."

"Oh, dear." Aunt Clare sniffled. "I-I had hoped never to see this day."

"Aunt Clare, please do not cry. We simply must make the best of a bad situation."

"I-I cannot help it." Tears welled up in Aunt Clare's blue eyes. "This is wrong, very wrong. Bendford is wrong. You are wrong. You should marry the man of your dreams. Not . . . not somebody on a list."

"It is fortunate I have never dreamed of any man, then." Julia forced a smile. Aunt Clare's tears were dampening her elation and scuttling her hastily crafted resolve.

"Of course you have not." Aunt Clare sobbed. "You have never had to dream of him."

"What?" Julia blinked. Her headache was returning. "Why not?"

"Because you have known him all your life. Dreams are for what you have not seen yet."

"What . . ." Julia pursed her lips. Then the realization struck her. "Oh, no. You are not talking about this morning again. No! You cannot mean . . . You do not think . . ." She shook her head. "You do not mean Garth!"

"Indeed I do." Aunt Clare nodded.

"No, Aunt Clare, no." Julia pointed at the paper with a stern finger. "There is the list. Garth's name is nowhere on it. Even when there were twenty names on it, Garth's name was not on it. If there had been a hundred names on the list, Garth's name would still not be on it." She drew in a deep breath. "Now, there is the list. It is final. You may post it anywhere you wish. Post it for Father. Post it for Garth. Post it for the entire world to see, for all I care. I am not going to change it. Not one wit."

Julia spun and marched from the kitchen. She reminded herself that her aunt had always been a little crazy. Rarely would she permit anyone to say such a thing to her. For the sake of loyalty and love, Julia avoided employing the term in conjunction with her aunt even within her own thoughts. Now, however, she could no longer deny it. Her aunt was crazy, totally unhinged, and without the slimmest tether to reality.

Garth was not the man of her dreams!

Garth strolled through the hall toward the breakfast room. He had purposefully come late this morning, hoping to avoid the type of scene of yesterday morning. Indeed, he had remained away all yesterday, enjoying a reunion with old friends, sharing drinks and reminiscences.

He admitted to himself, and only to himself, that he also wished to avoid Julia's waspish sting. He sighed. How had matters disintegrated so between him and Julia? She, orphaned of her mother, and he, of both parents, had been each other's confidant while growing up. Even when he had first gone to boarding school, they still lived to see each other again.

He frowned. When had it changed exactly? Sometime when he arrived upon the town, he realized. He was a young sprig just learning the ways of the world. That is when he suddenly had little time for Julia. He was busy gaining town bronze. She was just preparing to be introduced to society. He was involved in gaming and horses and wenching. She was investing her attention on the dance master, her modiste, and a gaggle of giggling girls just let out from the schoolroom.

He shook his head. At that age he had expected Julia to adore him. As an eligible, handsome blade with a title, all the other girls had. Even older women had cast out lures to him. Matrons. Widows. Paphians. But not Julia. She only cast his youthful indiscretions in his face. And she'd disdained his offer of support upon entering society, her insinuation being that she didn't need him or his tarnished reputation.

Yes, that is when it had all started. And it had only

grown worse. Julia had grown into a completely unapproachable woman. Into the woman they now called the Citadel. A woman who turned the same famous coolness upon him that she did other men, as if he were the veriest stranger.

He halted as he discovered Ruppleton standing outside a closed door, a torn expression upon his face. His entire body leaned toward the plank of wood as if drawn, but fighting it.

"Gads hounds, Ruppleton." Grinning, Garth approached the butler. "Give in to it. Put your ear to the door and have done with it."

Ruppleton jumped. "My lord, forgive me."

"You know I will, old man." Garth lifted a brow. "Just what is transpiring in the library of such import to lead you to eavesdropping?"

Ruppleton sighed heavily. "Number one has arrived, my lord."

"Number one?"

"Yes. The first suitor upon Lady Julia's list."

Garth's eyes widened. He ignored the anger that assaulted him. There was no reason for it, surely. "She is going through with it, then?"

"I am afraid so, my lord." Ruppleton reached into his pocket and drew out a paper. He offered it to Garth, his expression melancholy. "Here are the finalists."

Garth waved it away. "Why would I wish to see that? It is none of my business, and I intend to keep it that way. I will not be drawn into this inanity."

Ruppleton's gaze was far too knowing. In the kindest manner possible he said, "She is closeted with the marquess of Hambledon."

"Gads, she cannot want that poker-faced Puritan."

"He is the first on the list. She invited him to see her this morning. I believe she does want him."

"Do not concern yourself." Garth feigned a nonchalance. "I doubt Julia will succeed the first time out of the gate."

"Do you think so, my lord?" Ruppleton seemed cheered.

"Julia won't be able to reverse her manners as easily as she thinks she can. Changing from the Citadel to Please-Gallop-Me-Down-the-Aisle will not happen in a day."

"I do not know, my lord. Miss Julia can be persuasive when she sets her mind to it." Ruppleton looked longingly at the door. He then bowed. "I better go and supervise er . . . something."

"That's the ticket." Garth smiled bracingly. "Do not become blue-deviled. Even if Julia can change overnight into a siren, the marquess of Hambledon is a famous trencherman when it comes to avoiding marriage."

Garth kept his smile in place until Ruppleton departed the hall. Then he eyed the door. His code of honor was not as strong as Ruppleton's. Knowing full well that he was behaving like a schoolboy, he leaned his ear to the wood. How many times he had done it when he was young, he would never confess. Then again, Julia had been a master at it herself.

He frowned. The door was far too thick to hear through. He adroitly clicked it open. It would be a test to see how alert Julia was now. When they were young, it had been a game to them, one they would call each other upon.

Hearing no voice of discovery, Garth widened the crack.

"My lady, I have come as you requested." Charles Danford, the marquess of Hambledon, was speaking, his voice subdued and evenly paced.

"I thank you. Do you know why I invited you here this morning?" Julia's voice was soft and breathless. An instinctive male shiver coursed through Garth. This was a voice of sweet, luscious promise, one he had never heard come from Julia. Without thought or conscience, Garth opened the door farther and peeked around it. He simply must see Julia's face. Could it possibly match her voice?

"No, my lady," Charles Danford said. "I do not. That is why I came."

Garth had gained a view. It could not have been better. Danford and Julia stood well across the library, in front of the fireplace. They were far enough away not to notice the door, yet positioned exactly where he could see them both. Faith, the way they stood in front of the large, ornate fireplace, they looked like actors standing before a proscenium arch.

His heart lurched. Julia's face matched her voice. It was soft and flushed, her look sweetly dewy-eyed. She clasped her hands in front of her in the demurest fashion.

Garth shook his head. *Coming it too strong, Julia.*

"I-I have been . . . been noticing you for quite a while," Julia murmured softly.

"I was not aware of this." Danford frowned.

Probably because she hadn't ever glanced at you before, that is why.

"No." Julia hid her eyes by looking down. *Good ploy, very good ploy.* "I . . . a lady should not be so forward . . ."

Julia, you hussy.

"But . . ." Julia lifted her gaze once more. Her eyes were golden brown pools of yearning. "I can no longer pretend. I-I believe we would suit very well, my lord."

"Suit?" Danford asked.

The man needs an anvil taken to him.

"Yes. I would be pleased to accept a proposal of marriage from you, My lord."

Ouch. I said an anvil, Julia, not a boulder. He'll bolt for sure now.

Danford stared at Julia. He stared long and hard. She met his gaze, unflinching. He then bowed, his own face unflinching. "Madame, would you do me the honor of offering your hand to me in marriage?"

My God!

"Yes, my lord, I would." Julia smiled graciously. She held out her hand. "You may speak to my father upon the morrow. He is engaged at the House of Lords to-day."

"Yes, I know." Danford took Julia's hand in his and, bending, brushed his lips to it.

That was it. Without one hair out of place, Julia Wrexton had become engaged. No commotion. No passion. No anything.

Damn you, Julia. What have you done?

Three

Julia smiled in triumph as Danford bowed over her hand dutifully and promised to call upon her father the next day. She had succeeded. Furthermore, he was her first choice! The marquess was such a gentleman. He had been so easily maneuvered, so ordered in behavior.

She wished Garth could have witnessed her adroitness. Indeed, she was quite pleased with the élan she had displayed and regretted that Garth could not have been there. He had scoffed at her. He had held she could not make a man propose to her. Well, she had, and it was a shame he would never know with what skill she had done so.

The soft sound of a door shutting came to her. Julia's head shot up. Her eyes widened in consternation. "No!"

"What is the matter, my lady?" Danford frowned in confusion.

Oh, Lord! Julia harbored no such confusion. Blast, Garth! She was out of practice. He had succeeded in spying on her. How dare he!

"Nothing." Julia forced a smile as red-hot rage flooded through her. This should have been a private moment. Her wishes of just moments before faded in that blaze. "Permit me to walk you to the door."

"Er, yes." Danford nodded his head perfunctorily.

"May I say that you have made me the happiest of men."

"I am so glad," Julia murmured. Faith, but she would make Garth the unhappiest of men when she was done with him.

She led Danford to the front door. They confirmed his visit to her father the next morning at ten o'clock sharp. She said goodbye once more. She shut the door on her new fiancé with far more force than necessary.

She stomped back into the library. She wasn't surprised to discover Garth awaiting her there. "How dare you! How dare you spy on me!"

"Got one over you, Jules." Garth strolled to a chinoiserie cabinet built into a wall of shelves, swinging open its doors. It was what they use to say to each other as children. "You have certainly lost your skill."

"Of course I have." Julia clenched her jaw. "I was mistakenly under the impression that we were adults now. Adults do not eavesdrop or peek."

"I didn't peek." Garth hefted a brandy bottle up and uncorked it. "I simply opened the door and watched."

"You drink this early in the morning?" Julia watched in astonishment as he poured himself a liberal bumper.

"I must celebrate your engagement." Garth lifted the glass toward her. The look in his eyes was unsettling. "Congratulations."

A fiery blush rose to Julia's face. "You were no gentleman to watch. It was a private moment."

"Private?" Garth raised his brow. "Forgive me, my dear, but I must have missed something, after all."

"I beg your pardon?"

His smile was grim. "I did not see anything which could not have transpired upon an open street without drawing attention or censure."

Julia stiffened. "What are you implying?"

"I am saying that the performance was definitely

lacking. And since you are intending to have my head for the washing, I only wish there had been something of more interest to take the punishment for."

Hurt slashed through Julia. "I am sorry to have rendered such a dull performance. I did not know that I needed to entertain a . . . bystander. As far as I am aware, this is my home, not Drury Lane."

"Oh, no. Your performance was most excellent." Garth shot back a gulp of brandy. "Stellar. Outstanding. Why, you had old Danford netted within minutes. No, no, I do not fault you whatsoever."

Julia bit her lip. Had she actually been mad enough to want Garth to observe her skill with Danford? Watch what you ask for, to be sure. When Danford had proposed, triumph had filled her. Now she felt somehow small and a failure. "Thank you."

"Now Danford's performance . . ." Garth shook his head and pulled from his brandy. "It definitely fell flat. Forgive me, I know I should not insult your future husband so."

Julia blinked in confusion and consternation. Faith, he was right. He had insulted her future husband, and for a moment she hadn't even realized it. In truth, it was hard to imagine. She flushed. "I saw nothing lacking in his performance . . . I mean, his proposal."

"What? Come, Julia, even for you, didn't you think Danford's proposal too cool, too formal. Too readily given without emotion or concern?"

"I see." Julia tilted her head up. "The marquess failed to propose as you would, I assume? That is the problem."

Garth snorted. "Me and any other red-blooded man."

"Red-blooded?" Julia narrowed her eyes. "You mean hot-blooded and randy, do you not? I make no doubt your proposal would be so heated as to insult a genteel woman."

"No, damn it!" Garth slammed his brandy glass upon the bar.

"Cursing at the beginning of a proposal would be good," Julia taunted. "It is certain to demand a woman's attention."

"I am not proposing to you, confound it, and you know it!" Garth's eyes were dark and feral.

"Thank God!"

"If I were," Garth said softly, "I would never give my name and future to a woman who held out only her hand for me to kiss. I would also demand that at least one strand of her hair was overturned before I left."

The oddest tingle coursed through Julia. "You are disgusting."

"No, Julia, I am not." Garth stepped from behind the bar. "Or I would not be . . . if I were proposing to the woman I loved."

"In-deed?" Julia's heart caught. Worse, it showed in her voice, and she didn't know why. She thought it had to do with how Garth's voice had lowered and his eyes had deepened to an arresting teal.

"Yes, indeed." Garth approached to stand towering over her.

Julia's lips suddenly turned dry. She licked them. "Just . . . just how *would* you propose?"

"What?" Garth paled.

"I am curious?" Julia looked away, striving for nonchalance. Her heart raced, and the emotion building within her was anything but mild or polite. How would Garth behave toward the woman he loved? How? "It-it is easy for you to denigrate the marquess, but are you sure you could do better?"

"Yes, I can!" Garth spun away from her. Julia's eyes widened as he paced back to the bar and, picking up his glass, gulped from the brandy. He set the glass down with a definite crack. When he looked up at Julia, his gaze was grave. "My lady, Julia?"

"Yes?" Julia realized her words were breathy and far too nervous. She swallowed. Lifting her head, she tossed it in a flirtatious manner. "Yes, my lord?"

The solemnity disappeared from Garth's face. Instead, a most provocative smile traced his lips. "My beautiful, wild Julia."

"Wild?" Julia forgot her pose. "I am no such thing. Why, what an infamous thing to say when you are proposing!"

"Ah, but I have not proposed yet." Garth shook his finger at her.

A laugh escaped Julia. "Very well, proceed. But calling me wild, as if I am a hussy and no better than I ought to be, is not my notion of an appropriate beginning."

"Hussy," Garth repeated with a warmth and approval to his voice as he stepped closer to her. "You are, you know? You play with men's hearts."

"I do not." Julia crossed her arms in both denial and frustration. "Gracious, I said *propose*, not attack."

"You play with men's hearts and do not even know that you do so." Garth stepped even closer. Julia's mouth dropped open. "You *are* wild, Julia. You are brave and free. And, the devil confound you . . . unobtainable. The hellish Citadel. No man can own you and thank God."

"Garth?" He had moved so close that Julia uncrossed her arms swiftly and put out a staying hand. "I—"

"I do not need to own you." Garth clasped her hand tightly. "I only need you to love me. I only need to have your spirit and body beside me day and night."

"Garth, you—" Julia halted. Her heart actually

melted. Such words had been spoken to her only in secret dreams.

"Marry me, Julia," Garth whispered.

A knot welled in Julia's throat, making it difficult to breathe. "You . . . you may stop now."

"No. I am afraid I cannot."

"Wh-what do you mean?"

Garth's thumb massaged the palm of her hand. "You told me to propose to you."

"Yes, I did. But I expected—"

"What?" Garth's eyes, so very seductive and warm, flared with the amusement which was so very innate to him. "You expected platitudes from me, perhaps? Or poetry? An ode to sweet Julia's little toe?" He shook his head. Julia shivered as Garth drew her unrelentingly closer. "Wrong, Julia. Remember, I know you. I have always known you. Like no other man knows you."

"I s-said you may s-stop now," Julia stuttered, and placed her one free hand upon his chest.

"I will not let you turn me away." Garth's voice was fierce.

Julia jumped. His gaze was a mix between teasing and earnestness. "But . . ."

"I must have your hand!"

"You have got it," Julia squeaked. She tugged away, nervous and frightened for some reason. Her breath wheezed out heavily, and her heart pounded erratically.

"No, sweet liar." Garth smiled. "You have not given anything. You hold it all back. Your love. Your fire. Your loyalty and faith. Give me your hand, your heart, and your love."

His lips were mere inches away. Julia closed her eyes. "Er, ah . . . Garth?"

"Yes?"

She frowned. "I . . . I forgot what I was going to say."

"Good."

Her eyes flew open. "Beast!"

She swallowed. It was impossible. His lips were now but one inch away. They stood frozen.

"Just say *my love.*" Garth murmured. His lips covered hers.

Julia moaned and sagged into him. His arms tightened, and he kissed her with open passion. He tasted of brandy and man. Never had Julia been kissed in such a manner. She responded with a sudden and natural fervency, her growing desire the teacher. Or perhaps Garth was, for he molded and smoothed her curves with his hands, just as his lips and tongue drew and demanded, taunted and gave.

Julia felt awash with heat. It was insanity. Perfect insanity. This is what she needed. It was what she had been missing all her life. "Garth!"

"My love," Garth whispered. Or Julia thought he had whispered it. She was so lost in emotions, she could not be certain.

"Yes." Julia sighed. "My love."

Garth tore his lips away from her and buried his head on her shoulder. "I have never felt like this."

"I never knew at all."

Garth straightened and suddenly pushed Julia away. Julia could only stare at him in breathless confusion and wonderment.

"Do not look at me like that," Garth groaned.

"Like what?" Julia panted. Then she blushed and lowered her eyes. Her hungry and needing eyes, she knew. She licked her lips.

"Like that!" Garth jerked her back into his arms.

Julia went willingly, so willingly that it was a crashing of bodies and lips. The strength and passion coursing through them rocked them and at the same time weakened their knees. Or perhaps only Julia's. She could not say as they fell to the floor. Garth pushed her back and covered her. Julia greeted his weight. She was shivering.

"My Julia." Garth's voice was worshipful as his hands explored the curve of her breasts and his lips slid to nuzzle her ear.

"Hmm." Julia breathed in pleasure. Tingling and heat. And Garth. The most perfect, irresistible blend.

"Now is when you say you will marry him, dearest," Aunt Clare's voice directed from out of nowhere.

"What?" Julia gasped in astonishment.

Garth's lips and body stiffened. "Oh, God, no!"

Julia, his horrified words ringing in her one ear, forced herself to look past him. Aunt Clare stood over them, her blue eyes alight with approval. Flushing hot with mortification and anger, she shoved at Garth. "Indeed not!"

"*Ooff!*" Garth rolled to the side from the onslaught of her attack.

"I am sorry, Aunt Clare." Julia sprang up, lurched slightly from too swift a change to her equilibrium, and righted herself. "We . . . ah . . ."

"Grew carried away." Garth said from his position on the floor.

Julia trembled. Those were the words he had used when they had been pretending for Jason that first night. This time, however, they were true.

"That is all right, I believe, since you are to be married." Aunt Clare clearly attempted to look wise and sagacious. She only looked pleased and happy.

"No, no." Garth rose stiffly from the floor. "We are not going to be married."

"Indeed not." Julia bit her lip. Garth's avid fear of Aunt Clare's assumption was insulting. Well, she would wipe that look from his face, as well as Aunt Clare's happy one. "I am engaged to the marquess of Hambledon."

"What? But how . . . ?" Aunt Clare blinked.

"H-he was just here, before Garth," Julia said quickly. "He proposed, and I accepted."

"But then what were you and Garth—?" Aunt Clare gurgled.

"Er, yes, that." Julia blushed. "Well . . ."

"That . . . that was all playacting." Garth said. "It was not real."

Aunt Clare's eyes glazed over with confusion. "I do not understand? What do you mean it was not real? It looked excessively so to me."

"But . . . it wasn't," Julia said even as her heart wanted to shrivel up and die. "It was merely playacting."

"I see." Aunt Clare nodded. Then she sighed and shook her head. "No, I fear I do not see. Not at all. Just what play were you performing?"

Garth shifted. "It—it wasn't from any particular play."

"From a book, then?" Aunt Clare asked.

"No." Garth's voice was strained. "I believe I said it wrong. What we were doing was playing make-believe."

"Oh." Aunt Clare only appeared more confused. "Then what I just saw was not real, only make-believe?"

"Yes," Julia and Garth said in unison.

"And Julia is now engaged to the marquess of Hambledon?"

"Yes," Julia nodded.

She frowned. "Did you play make-believe with him as you did with Garth?"

"No," Julia admitted.

"Thank heavens. I am glad to know that you behaved properly in public." Aunt Clare's look held reproach. "I am your chaperone, after all. You shouldn't have received the marquess without me. It was most improper of you."

Julia's eyes shuddered wide open. Aunt Clare was indeed her chaperone, but rarely did either one of them take notice of that role or duty. "Forgive me."

"And see what has happened. You became engaged to the marquess." Aunt Clare shook her head. "I fear that is what I cannot believe is real."

"Well, it is," Julia said stoutly.

Aunt Clare sighed. She trod over to Julia and, standing upon her tiptoes, kissed her. "You know I love you, dear. I will always want the best for you."

"Yes, I know." Julia nodded.

Aunt Clare turned and stepped over to Garth. She crooked her finger at him. "Bend down, please." Garth bent obediently, and she kissed him. "You know I love you, too? Julia is the daughter I never had, and you are the son I never had."

"Yes, Auntie, I know that." Garth smiled gently.

"I am so glad." Aunt Clare beamed at them as if they all had come to some kind of deeper understanding and agreement. "I am going to leave you two now. Please remember. Love is the most important thing in the world. I know this because I have never found my own true love and I still await him. I know I should not be impatient, but the years *are* passing, and one would think that he—" She halted and looked wide-eyed at them. "Gracious. I digress, do I not?"

"No, Auntie." Garth grinned. "Do, do proceed."

Aunt Clare giggled, and she shook a minatory finger. "You two are adults now, and you must know there is no such thing as playing make-believe for you. Children play make-believe because they are dreaming of what they want to do when they are grown. Adults, since they are already grown, are only doing what they really want to do and calling it a dream."

With that comment, Aunt Clare traipsed from the room.

"Good Lord." Garth stared after her. "Is she really your chaperone?"

"Oh, do be quiet." Julia spun from him, for she could not look him in the eye. Her gaze fell upon the bar. Like a man lost in the desert and seeking water, she hurried over. Grabbing up Garth's half-finished glass, she drank the contents swiftly. The brandy burned her throat and brought tears to her eyes. Worse, the taste of it reminded her of the taste of Garth's kiss. She slammed the glass to the counter.

"Julia, forgive me . . ." Garth stepped toward her. His gaze was confused and rather hesitant.

"Bounder!" Julia spat. The very tone of his repentant voice infuriated her. She'd be blasted if she would permit him to pretend an apology.

"What?"

"Cad!" Julia rolled the word swiftly off her tongue. Gracious, but that felt good to say. It eased the turmoil of her emotions.

"Cad?" Garth drew himself up to his full height. "This is all my fault, then?"

"Of course it is," Julia said hotly. "You had to play the lover to the hilt, didn't you? You pulled out all the tricks in your nasty little seduction book just to—to make a May game of me."

"No, I—" Garth halted. Something passed through his eyes, a realization of some sort that made him jump as if shot. He lifted his chin. "What if I did? I'd say the boot is quite on the other leg. What of your behavior?"

"Do not try and turn the tables on me, sirrah. I am not accustomed to such forthright seduction. I was not prepared."

"Not prepared?" Garth stalked over to her. "Gammon!"

"I beg your pardon?"

"It seems to me you were very well prepared for it.

If I overplayed the scene, so did you." Garth eyes narrowed. "Just where did you learn . . . ?"

"How dare you!" Julia couldn't bare to hear the rest. Wounded, her hand instinctively flew up.

"Confound it." Garth caught it in its descending arc toward his cheek. His brow shot up in the most astonished look. "How dare *I*?"

"Fiend. Let me go." Julia jerked her hand back. She rubbed it, trying to ignore her sheer embarrassment. She had never lifted her hand to anyone.

"Shrew," Garth retorted. "Faith, but I pity Danford. He best have quick reflexes if he intends to survive marriage to you."

"He will not need them." Julia lifted her nose in haughty disdain. *"He* is a gentleman."

"More the pity to him. If he were smart, he would be hightailing it out of London, and leave you to your father tomorrow morning."

"You would like that, wouldn't you?" Julia, shaking with rage, narrowed her eyes. "Well, it won't happen. You can denigrate Danford all you want. You can taunt me and make me look the fool. But it won't help you. I am going to marry Danford, and you are not going to get my fortune. You will just have to remain at low ebb for the rest of your life."

"You—you think that I—?" Garth halted. He stiffened, and whereas his eyes had been a steamy gray, they now turned a cold coal. He shrugged. "I thought it was worth a try. When a fortune is in the balance, one should make a push for it, you know?"

"Of course." Julia swallowed hard. "But you have failed. I am going to marry Danford. As quickly as I can."

Garth stared at her. Something flickered in his eyes, a need or a regret, but it disappeared. His lip curled into a derisive smile. "Do not say I have failed . . . yet.

There has often been a slip between lip and cup. You managed to command a proposal out of Danford, but don't' count your chickens before they hatch. You're not down the aisle yet."

"You are odious."

"Tsk, tsk." Garth wagged a finger at her. "You really should be nice to me. After all, you never know. Fate might be with me, and six months from now you will be applying to me for funds."

"Never! I will never be under your thumb. Ever!"

"What is that all about, Rolly?" Garth frowned and waved briskly for a servant to bring him yet another drink. Considering the lateness of the hour and how many he had already partaken of during the day and night, it was not very wise.

However, wisdom was not Garth's goal. He watched Charles Danford from across the suitably refined rooms of White's, and for that he needed another drink. Indeed, he had watched the man for over an hour now. Why he did so, he would not consider.

Charles Danford played at cards as he had for apparently the entire evening. He appeared to not have a care in the world. Men often approached him discreetly. He would nod to them, never turning his gaze from the cards. They would then smile and leave in haste.

"They are pretending to congratulate him." Rolly, a passable acquaintance for the moment, laughed. "In truth, they are attempting to gauge the validity of the engagement. Who would win Lady Julia's hand has been upon the betting books forever, don't you know? Danford is a dark horse. If the engagement is official, many are going to lose a bundle."

Garth stifled a growl. Danford had already let the

tôn know of the engagement, even before his meeting with Lord Wrexton on the marrow. Rolly had told him that it wasn't Danford who had leaked the news. Danford was honorable. It was his youngest sister who had set it about to her friend. Of course, after that, it had spread across the *tôn* far quicker than the plague. "It does not seem to interrupt Danford's game."

"Charles is a cool customer." Rolly shrugged. "He is winning tonight. Indeed, young Rendle went down heavily to him an hour ago. The halfling went out of here looking like death. Whose, though, I would not place money upon."

"Made a friend, has Danford?" Garth accepted the drink the servant brought. He gulped from it.

"That is a life of the true gambler, and Danford is the truest of them all, old man." Rolly's lips twisted. "No one can deny that it is Danford's day. He won Lady Julia's hand in the morn and Rendle's manor in the eve. As for what he will win when the final wedding vows are spoken? Well, I am already considering my wager."

Garth's gaze narrowed. He wondered if Julia knew her perfect gentleman of a fiancé was such a gambler. Though it clarified Julia's easy conquest of the morning. The man was accustomed to making an instant decision according to the cards laid before him. Julia had been the queen of diamonds dealt to him from the bottom of the deck. He forced himself to look away from Charles. "Gads, let us talk of something more interesting than the latest betting."

"Certainly, old man. What do you think about the prime minister? Did you hear him speak last Tuesday?"

Rolly dutifully rambled on about politics. Garth didn't notice as he downed his brandy. His anger flared higher. Julia did not need a gambler for a husband. She did not need a man who would not flinch at passing a thousand pounds over for the mere turn of a card.

A sudden vision of Julia's future reared before him. She would be neglected as the marquess left her on her wedding night to play cards with his cronies. Years later, when he had finally performed his duty by Julia and she had her children, he would lose her entire fortune at play. Julia and her children would be out upon the streets. Garth gritted his teeth. "Captain Sharp!"

"What, old man?" Rolly blinked. "Zounds, is that what you think about the minister?"

Garth's eyes narrowed as he watched the marquess stand. "Thinks he is a smooth one."

"True, true." Rolly nodded. "He's one of the best speakers I've ever known. Can slide them words in there, but always thought him one of the staunchest supporters of England."

"Blast it!" Garth sprang up as he watched the marquess pick up his winnings with a swipe of a white hand. "He will bankrupt her!"

"I say! Surely you cannot believe that. Where are you going?"

"To stop him, confound it." Garth stalked away.

"Garth, you cannot mean it!" Rolly called. "You can't knock the minister up at this time of the night, for God's sake! Think of what you are doing!"

Garth did not even hear Rolly. The marquess was already far ahead of him. It was as if the man knew his reckoning was at hand and made a dash for it. Of course, Garth's speed was impeded by his three-bottle evening and its resultant altercations with a table, two chairs, several misfortunate servants, and even one hat rack.

He panted heavily as he broke out of White's. He looked both ways, gritting his teeth. "Aha."

The marquess was to his right. Strolling in the night air, mind you, as if he'd not a problem in the world. As if he had no consideration that he was going to leave Julia and her future prodigy begging upon the streets.

Biting back an angry curse, Garth started toward the retreating marquess. He feared he would not catch him. Suddenly, the marquess stopped. He turned toward an alley. Hope spurred Garth onward. He sprinted toward the marquess.

"Danford," Garth shouted.

The marquess of Hambledon spun. Garth skidded to a halt. Alcohol befuddled, he blinked to discover that the marquess had drawn a small sword from his cane and was brandishing it at him. Garth smiled grimly. "Ah, you wish to fight, then."

It was Danford's turn to blink. Indeed, he blinked rapidly four or five times. He then passed his free hand across his eyes. "Who are you, sirrah?"

"I am Garth Stanwood," Garth announced. "Er . . . friend of Lady Julia Wrexton."

"Oh." Danford lowered his dagger. "Forgive me."

"Forgive you?" Garth frowned. He was raring for a fight, and now Danford clearly withdrew from it. "Why should I?"

"I thought I heard something from the alley," the marquess said. "I thought I saw shadows. Mohawks, most likely."

"Mohawks?" Garth stiffened. He looked around blearily. All was quiet, not a glimmer of a movement anywhere. "Are you bosky, man?"

"Yes." The marquess nodded his head vehemently. "T-tap-hackled, s'fact."

"Gammon!" Garth stepped closer, squinting as he studied the marquess. Regardless of his own condition, or perhaps because of it, he realized that the marquess spoke nothing but the truth. "Gads, so you are. Never noticed it until now. Y-you are . . . are impressive, old chap."

"Thank you." Danford puffed out his chest. "That is . . . is one of my rare talents. Th-that and cards."

"And you are engaged to Julia," Garth said, trying to regain focus and purpose.

"Yes, this very day." The marquess nodded. He crooked his finger in a beckoning way.

"What?" Garth stumbled forward.

"I-I am engaged to the Citadel." Danford's voice was low. "And . . . and I don't know how it happened. Been drinking and thinking all day. Still don't know how it happened."

"You—you don't know how it happened?" Garth stared. Then he lifted his gaze to the heavens and howled with laughter. The marquess was drunk because he was engaged to Julia and didn't know how it had happened. Worse, he, too, was drunk because the marquess was engaged to Julia and *he* didn't know how it had happened. Moreover, he would lay both his and the marquess's last monkeys on the fact that Julia didn't know how it had happened, either.

"What is so amusing?" Danford asked solemnly.

"Us, old man." Garth slapped the marquess on the shoulder. "Us."

The marquess did not respond. He merely toppled over, capsized like an axed tree.

Garth stared down at the fallen man. "Danford?"

He knelt. Confused thoughts raced through his mind until he heard a trace of a snore escape the marquess. He rose, shaking his head. "Drinking's a talent of yours, is it?" He grinned. "Wait until I tell Julia."

A sound came from the alley. Garth blinked. It was his turn now to think he heard noises, but more like whispers. He stalked farther into the alley, peering into the dark gloom.

A shriek of a dog, definitely a dog, rent the air.

"Faith." Garth sighed. He was tap-hackled as well. To be frightened by a stray dog no doubt fighting for its dinner that night, was past foolish. He turned, shaking his head at his own stupidity. Then he frowned. The marquess still lay prone upon the sidewalk, his snores rising loudly toward the heavens.

Garth meandered over to the fallen marquess. "Suppose I can't leave you to the dogs, no matter what I think." Bending, he reached down and hauled the man up over his shoulder. He shifted his weight and rather wove his way down the street.

The marquess did not really wish to wed Julia. He had become tap-hackled because he didn't even know how he had become engaged. A slight smile tipped Garth's lips. "Minx." That was his Julia. He was not the only one who had been vanquished by her that day. Laughing, he began to sing loudly an old battle song. Noble carriages passed, and Garth waved cheerily. He marched pass a street cleaner and nodded amiably.

Only when he saw a hackney driving past did he shout and wave his hand. He stepped into the street as it stopped. "Take this fellow home. The marquess of Hambledon's residence. Relay him to his servants, please. They shall take care of him. He is . . . an engaged man."

The driver was a good fellow. He climbed down and assisted Garth in depositing the snoring marquess into the hack. He grinned all the more when Garth paid him not only sufficiently but handsomely, very handsomely. After watching the hackney disappear, Garth turned to make his own way home.

Things were becoming blurred, extremely blurred.

Four

The midmorning sun beat down on Julia. Relentlessly. She tightened the jonquil satin ribbons that held the wide, flat crown of her gypsy bonnet down around her face, shielding her complexion from the sun's rays. Why must it be an unseasonably hot day?

She clipped a withered branch from the rosebush in the beautifully designed, lush town house gardens. Antonio, the gardener, had suggested that she need not concern herself with the pruning. She had assured him she would like to tend the gardens this morning. He had resisted, but she had held firm. Indeed, he had almost gone away in tears. Honestly, those Italians, they could be so very emotional. They would cry at the drop of a pin, or a shears in Antonio's case.

Julia snipped at a branch as odious tears stung her eyes. Unlike Antonio's, her tears were not spent upon that yellow-leafed branch that fell to the ground. Rather, they were tears of rage. At least that was what Julia could define. Julia felt the sting of a thorn penetrate through her glove. It was nothing. Inside, deeper yet, the nastiest spur dug into her. It was the suffocating sensation of being trapped, held, imprisoned.

"How did they know about the engagement?" Julia snipped her shears in punctuation. A beautiful yellow rose toppled from the bush. "Oh, dear."

She gazed in regret at the rose. Even with as short

a stem as it had, she vowed she would find a perfect arrangement for it. She also tried to tamp down her anger. She may have become engaged yesterday, but it was never to be official until her father and fiancé had discussed the settlement, until it had been posted correctly within the *Gazette*. Till the bans were read. It was never to be official, drat it!

Yet the steady stream of well-wishers and meddlesome inquirers that had arrived upon her doorsteps this morning had made it far too official. Indeed, it had been as busy as any posting house and well before any proper hour.

"Well-wishers? Ha! They can take their insincere blessings and go to . . . drat." Guilt consumed Julia. She had just cut another perfect bloom down in its prime. She gazed at it, a strong sympathy welling within her. She herself felt too young to be cut down in her youth.

"What are you doing out here?" Garth's voice asked. "I have never known you to concern yourself with horticulture before."

"There are many things you do not know about me." Julia said before she drew in her breath, pinned on a smile, and turned. Her eyes widened.

Garth stood a few feet away from her. He wore a jacket of superfine, a pristine white cravat tied in the four-in-hand, bespeaking his acceptance into that club, and buff unmentionables. Indeed, the perfect attire of a London buck except for the raffish shadow that covered his chin and eyes possessing a sleepy crankiness. "What on earth happened to you?"

"Nothing," Garth growled.

"Shot the cat, did you?" Julia laughed. Indeed, his miserable state lifted her spirits. "The signs are highly evident."

Garth lifted a bleak brow. "If you knew, why did you ask?"

Julia lowered her gaze demurely. "I just wished to hear you confess it."

"I will confess it when you confess why you are out here mowing the roses at this hour." Garth's voice was deep and husky, no doubt from his revelry of the night before. He strolled up to her. "Are you hiding, perhaps?"

Julia's gaze flew up to his. For a moment she was lost in the depth of his dark, tired eyes. She experienced the strongest desire to lift her hand up and soothe his cheek, to feel the scratch of the shadow upon it.

"You could have shaven, at least." She quickly turned back to the rosebush. "I am sure you did not appear like that last night to your . . . your *cher amie.*"

The lowest, masculine laugh sounded from behind her. She vowed she could feel the very breath of it, for a shiver ran up her spine, lifting the very hairs at the nape of her neck. "You would be positively shocked to know who I 'appeared' to last night. It rather shocked me, I own."

"I do hope it was not the wife of that unfortunate man with the pistol and cravat. If it was, I vow I will invite him to tea and introduce myself—and you to him properly."

"No. I tarried with someone far different last night. Someone who, I must warn you, snores atrociously."

Julia started. Heaven forefend, that man was actually going to tell her about his lascivious doings. "It is no business of mine, I assure you."

"Come, Julia, do ask me who it was."

"I do not care to know who it was or what you did with them." Julia rounded on Garth. "I am an engaged woman. Your *petite* affairs do not concern me."

"Of course not. Only your grand passion for Danford matters, does it not?"

Julia would have kicked Garth right then and there, only for the fact that his eyes were no longer lazy. A banked fire glowed in the back of them. He was as agitated as she was. An unworthy satisfaction filled her. "That is quite correct."

"And that is why you are out here massacring the flowers when you should be within accepting callers and their congratulations, in high alt as any other newly engaged miss would be."

Julia flinched. Blast the man, he was far better at the game, even with a wicked head from dipping rather deep. "I am gathering flowers . . . to make arrangements."

Garth peered past her. By the amused look in his eyes, he had seen the poor buds astrew on the ground. " 'Fess up, Julia. You are out here to escape the consequences of your impetuous actions."

"I am not." Julia was proud of the lightness within her voice. She laid down her shears and quickly scooped up the roses. "I am sublimely happy. Delirious, in fact."

"Oh, confess it, Julia, and be done with it." Growling, Garth grabbed her by the shoulders and shook her. "You do not like all those well-wishers. You wish them at perdition. You are not happy."

"No," Julia gurgled.

"Confess!"

"No." This time Julia's gurgle rattled so much that it ended in a squeak.

"Confess." Garth's voice had turned from a growl to a chuckle.

"Never. I adore it . . . all."

"Confound it, confess, woman. Before I become nauseous and mortify myself by casting up my accounts."

"I confess," Julia squealed. "Drat you, Garth. I confess. Don't you dare do such a thing!"

"Thank God." Garth stopped shaking her and drew her close, laying his chin to the top of her head. His sigh was loud.

"Garth?" Julia drew in a nervous breath. "Are . . . are you going to be all right?"

"Hmm, what?"

"Y-you are not going to be sick, are you?"

"No." His deep chuckle vibrated through her. "I am feeling surprisingly well all of a sudden."

"What? You dastard." Julia pushed him away. She buffed his chest. "Flirt. Womanizer."

"Stop, vixen." Garth captured both of her hands in his. "Forgive me. I could not resist you. I mean . . . teasing you."

Julia stilled and stared up at him. The light expression in his eyes disappeared. It seemed they darkened at the very moment the very wicked memory of his kisses crossed Julia's mind. "You must resist. I am an engaged woman."

"Are you? Are you truly?"

"Y-yes."

"Are you positive you want Danford?" Garth's look was intent, as if he wished to see through to her very soul.

"Of course." Flustered and embarrassed, Julia looked down. Her gaze fell upon the shears. She dived for them, grateful for a purpose. She turned to the rosebush and attacked it once again. It was fairly thin of branches by now, but she found a stub to snip. "Why should I not?"

"Julia . . ." Garth halted.

"What?" Julia lifted a brow and stared at him.

"Nothing." His face grim, Garth strode over to where a wheelbarrow lay, a shovel set against it. He grabbed up the shovel and stalked away a goodly distance from her.

"What are you doing?" Julia asked, exasperated.

"Digging." Garth drove the shovel into the ground.

"Why?"

"I think a rosebush should go here."

"Really?"

"Really."

"Julia!" Lord Wrexton's voice bellowed.

"Yes, Father?" Julia tore her gaze from Garth, who refused to look at her. She promptly began clipping away at her bush.

"Where the devil are you?"

"Here in the garden."

Lord Wrexton finally appeared. Perplexity and a bit of awe stamped his features. "Ruppleton said you were here. I did not believe it."

"You can believe it, sir," Garth said, throwing a shovelful of dirt back.

"Garth, you here, too?" Lord Wrexton exclaimed. He frowned. "What the devil are you doing?"

"He thinks a rosebush would be nice there," Julia said sweetly.

"Hmm, perhaps," Lord Wrexton said with due consideration. Then he rattled his head like an angry terrier with game trapped between its jaws. "Confound it. This is not the time for you two to turn bucolic."

"Isn't it?" Julia asked. "I thought it a famous time to do so."

"She's bamming you, sir." Garth warned. "She is hiding from all those well-wishers wearing the steps thin."

"Apparently her fiancé is doing the same." Lord Wrexton's indignation could not be missed. "Too bad he is not out here . . . hoeing the . . . the rhododendrons."

"What do you mean?" Julia halted her rosebush slaughter and frowned.

"Well?" Lord Wrexton looked at her as if her wits had gone a-wondering. "Did not you tell me that he would call at ten o'clock?"

"Yes, I did." Julia gasped. Oh, Lord, her wits *had* gone somewhere, but she didn't care to consider the exact place. "Gracious, is it already ten o'clock?"

"It is a blasted hour past that already," Lord Wrexton cried. "Does no one care about time? Punctuality? What type of fellow are you marrying, young lady, that he is tardy to the most important appointment in his life?"

"I do not know," Julia said, stunned.

"An understatement if ever there was one," Garth muttered.

Julia glared at him. "I meant, I do not know what could have detained him. Something of dire importance, I make no doubt."

"Yes, to be sure," Garth twirled his shovel. "He must have realized that he had a pressing engagement. Out of town at that. Or better yet, out of the country."

"What are you insinuating?" Julia snapped.

"Digging your own grave there, son," Lord Wrexton observed.

"Nothing, nothing at all." Garth returned to flinging dirt in every direction.

"I suppose you are insinuating that Danford has run off?" Julia, in turn, renewed her pruning.

"Er, Julia . . . ?" Lord Wrexton said. "That was half the shrub."

"I did not say that exactly," Garth muttered. "But what if he did? You are here in the garden. He might have decided to take it farther afield."

"Garth, my boy! You just dug up a—" Lord Wrexton shook his head and backed away. "Never mind. I do not think I want to see this. Julia, watch that you don't cut off your nose to spite your face."

"Danford would never cry off," Julia persisted, ignoring her father's wise words and his wiser departure. She was too intent upon finding new blood. She swooped over to a fatter bush. "And that's that."

"That's that," Garth mimicked. "Of course. Queen Julia's decree."

"Danford would never bolt," Julia avowed. "He is a man of honor. Something dire has transpired to keep him from seeing Father. He . . . he must have fallen ill."

"Ill? More likely he is too h-hu—" Garth stopped.

Julia narrowed her eyes. "What do you know about this?"

"Nothing." Garth quickly returned to the hole he had dug.

"You know something. What did you do?" Julia marched toward him in fury. "You did something to frighten him off, didn't you?"

"Of course I didn't," Garth thundered. "Why should I want to do something like that?"

"Because you want to gain my fortune and lord it over me." The worse thought blinded Julia. She gasped. "You warned me about the slip between lips and cup."

"Oh, for God's sake!"

"You probably killed him," Julia accused him. "That is what happened."

"Why would you say something so totty-headed?"

"Only death would keep Danford from my side." Julia waved her hands dramatically, and with it the shears.

"Watch it, Julia," Garth jumped back. "It is clear I am not the dangerous one here."

"That is right," Julia cooed, snapping her shears. "I am the dangerous one, and do not you forget it."

A sudden gasp sounded. Julia spun. Antonio, the gardener, stood frozen except for a tremble that appeared somewhat epileptic.

"Murderer," the gardener croaked. "Murderer."

"What?" Julia asked, blinking. A chill ran down her spine, as if someone had walked upon her grave. She looked at Garth and swallowed hard.

"He means you, widgeon." Garth rolled his eyes.

"I beg your pardon?" Julia asked.

Antonio stumbled forward to the rosebushes that had received Julia's "tender" attentions. He fell to his knees, a great sob racking him. "Murderer."

"Oh, dear," Julia murmured. Flushing, she dropped the shears as if they were a bloodied knife instead.

"Murderer," the gardener sobbed, rising. Now he stumbled over to the large hole Garth had dug. He fell, and pushing the dirt aside, unearthed crushed impatiens. "Murderer."

"Hmm, yes." Garth immediately dropped his shovel. He took Julia by the elbow. "Come. Let us leave him to his grief."

"Yes, I agree." Julia fell swiftly in step with Garth.

They left the garden silently. *Murderer* rang in Julia's ears.

"There, there, dearest Julia," Aunt Clare said in a soothing tone. "I think you should be happy. It is clear the marquess is not the man for you."

"Thank you, Aunt," Julia murmured as she lifted the china cup to her lips. They then twisted wryly. Tea and sympathy. From her spinster aunt, no less. Gracious, how she had fallen.

"Yes," Garth said from his chair. "Any man who can

not meet your father to talk about a fortune within four days is clearly not the man for you."

No sympathy there. Julia's temper, which was admittedly raw from the past tense days, flared. "Odious creature. I still think it is your fault. Did you pay him off? No, wait I forgot. You couldn't. Your pockets are to let. You must have done away with him then directly."

"Julia!" Aunt Clare gasped. "What a thing to say."

"Well." Julia flushed in embarrassment. "He—he drives me to say those things."

"Indeed. I await your abuse." Garth put his hand to his chest and looked soulful. "I must have a good scratching from you every day or my world is dim. And you actually think I would need to lift a finger in any way to cause Danford to take French leave?"

"Garth!" Aunt Clare exclaimed.

"I am sorry, Aunt Clare, but Julia is bird-witted to say the least."

"Stop it, both of you," Aunt Clare ordered in one of her firmest voices. "Gracious, you two were never so difficult as children. Thank heaven you openly loved each other then instead of pretending otherwise."

"*Urugh.*" Julia sputtered on her tea.

"S'death." Garth growled into his.

"Now *that* is the truth." Aunt Clare nodded her head and sipped from her cup calmly. Percy meowed from his position on her lap as if in concurrence, cleaning his paw complacently.

Julia's gaze caught Garth's eyes. His consternation clearly equaled hers. Indeed, he was so evidently appalled, as she was, that a chuckle escaped her. He smiled then and actually blew her a kiss.

Against Julia's will, hot blood rushed to her face. She was not sure if it was their shared laughter or the memory of their real kiss, but it sobered her swiftly. Garth sobered as well. They stared at each other. Julia's heart performed a somersault.

"Hello, I have news," Lord Wrexton's voice called. He fairly promenaded into the parlor and took up a chair. Indeed, his look was full of import.

"Do you, Bendford?" Aunt Clare leaned over to prepare his tea with a dollop of cream and one spoonful of sugar. "I do hope it is good news."

Julia gratefully tore her gaze from Garth and looked at her father. "Yes?"

"It depends upon how you look at matters." Lord Wrexton shrugged as he received the cup from Aunt Clare. "Personally, I would say it is very good news. I drove around to Danford's house and talked to the servants. The man never came home the night he proposed to you, Julia."

"What? Impossible! I—!" Garth froze and quickly snapped his mouth shut. He sipped his tea then, slowly and precisely.

Julia eyed him narrowly. "You had something to do with his disappearance, after all, didn't you?"

"No, damn it!" Garth flushed and looked at Aunt Clare. "Forgive me, Auntie."

"Certainly." Aunt Clare looked at Julia. "Julia, dear, you really must stop accusing Garth of such deeds. No matter how you two scrape and wrangle, you know Garth would never be so ungentlemanly as to do something to drive your fiancé away."

"He did something." Julia knew it instinctively.

Garth glared at her. Then he shrugged. "Very well. I will confess. I was so nefarious as to pour your drunken fiancé into a hackney that night. That is what I did, fiend that I am."

"You lie," Julia said angrily.

Garth threw up his hands. "God give me patience and Julia a mind." Lord Wrexton hooted. Aunt Clare tsked her disapproval. "No, I do not lie. He was drunk as a wheelbarrow. I just happened to be leaving when he was. I caught up with him to offer him . . . my congratulations."

"Now you lie!" Julia exclaimed in triumph.

Garth grinned wryly. "Very well, I was going to offer him my condolences. Are you happy now?"

"Yes," Julia said, regardless of the inanity of it. "Now I at least know you are telling the truth."

"Thank you." Garth nodded. "As I said, when I went to offer him my condolences, he . . . he passed out, right there upon the open street." Garth's look to Julia was potent. *"He* is the one who snores atrociously. I did attempt to tell you that, if you care to remember."

Embarrassment welled up in Julia. "Oh."

"I could not very well leave him lying upon the street for some footpads to overtake. Therefore, I picked him up and found a hackney for him. I ordered the driver to take him to his home and turn him over to his servants. That is all, I swear it."

"See, Julia." Aunt Clare clapped her hands together and sighed. "Garth was the hero, and not the villain. He saved your fiancé."

"What did you two speak about before he passed out," Julia asked, unable to let loose of her rancor.

Garth shook his head. "You simply will not allow it to rest, will you?"

"Well?" Julia persisted.

"Julia, the man was in his cups." Garth's voice gentled. She saw the truth enter his eyes and had a quick presentiment that she was not going to enjoy what he was about to say. "If you must know, Danford had become royally foxed because he was having difficulty understanding how he had become engaged to you."

"My goodness," Aunt Clare exclaimed, her blue eyes

round in astonishment. "The man *was* befuddled. Julia, he asked you to marry him, did he not?"

Julia bit her lip. "Yes, Aunt, he did."

"Then how could he not know how he became engaged? He asked you."

Julia flushed. She understood Garth, and now Danford, far too clearly. "That is why you have been so positive that he left town."

"Yes. But I did not wish to say it in case Danford's disappearance was for another reason altogether."

"What does it matter why he disappeared?" Lord Wrexton said in exasperation. "The important thing is that we know he decamped that night. I also circled around all of his clubs. He's not been seen these past four days. That is enough proof."

"Proof?" Julia asked.

Lord Wrexton grinned. "Proof that he has run off and has yielded any claim to your hand. You are a free woman, Julia."

"Free woman?" Julia blinked, then blinked again. She was not a free woman. She was a scorned woman. Even worse, Garth had known of her failure well before she had!

"Yes, dear." Aunt Clare's smile was sweet. "It has clearly worked out for the best. Things like this always do. Now you may forget all this nonsense."

"Good Lord, Clare," Lord Wrexton exclaimed. "Are your attics to let? That is not what it means. It means Julia can go out and find a different husband. She does not need to wait for Danford any longer. I made sure every man in London knew I had not yet approved Danford's suit and that no settlement had been made."

"You did?" Julia's cringing pride sighed in relief. "Thank heaven."

"I have been thinking, Julia," Lord Wrexton continued. "And I know where you went wrong."

"Bendford," Aunt Clare said with reproach. "She did not go wrong anywhere. The marquess simply was not the right man for her. She should marry for love."

"Where?" Julia asked, looking at her father.

"I should have talked to Danford before he proposed. Marriage frightens a man. That is why the settlements should be drawn up first. Then, when a fellow wants to cut and run, he has something stable like a fortune to keep him trained on the mark."

"I see." Julia said. It was not flattering. But then again, having had one suitor already bolt was not flattering, either. The need to retrieve her pride and position goaded Julia. "I am sure you must be right."

"So then." Lord Wrexton leaned back in his chair, his eyes snapping in anticipation. "Whom do you wish me to approach?"

Julia frowned in concentration. "I do not know."

"Thank heaven." Aunt Clare sighed. "Do not let Bendford force you into this again, Julia."

"It is her wounded pride driving her, Aunt Clare," Garth said wryly. "Nothing else."

Julia stiffened. "It is not. I have a fortune at stake here."

"B'gads, she does." Lord Wrexton's tone was just as defensive. "Julia has a right to recoup."

"I believe you should wait a bit, Julia. Truly I do." Aunt Clare wrung her hands. "After all, perhaps the marquess did not desert you. Something dreadful might have happened to him, as you first thought. Perhaps he truly wants to marry you but has been detained."

"Zounds, Clare," Lord Wrexton exclaimed. "Do get off that hobbyhorse. The man bolted on Julia. But that doesn't matter. There are plenty more out there. We will find one with bottom yet."

"Yes," Julia said. "I forgot who was next on my list. Was it Lord Mancroft or Lord Beresford?"

Aunt Clare all but moaned. "It was Lord Mancroft."

"Lord Mancroft? Aha! I am going after our man, Julia." Lord Wrexton set his cup down and was at the parlor door in a flash. He glanced back. "You will be ready to accept his proposal tomorrow morning?"

Julia swallowed and nodded. "Yes, certainly."

"Tallyho," Lord Wrexton cried, his voice rising high like a hound's bay upon finding the scent.

Garth and Aunt Clare sat in the breakfast room, both lingering over the last rack of toast and last drop of tea. Both seemed to ignore the fact that Julia had not attended breakfast and this morning should see the arrival of her new suitor. According to Lord Wrexton, he would surely be there with bells on, since Lord Wrexton had been extremely generous with the settlement terms.

Garth continued to dally, attempting a nonchalance. Aunt Clare, bless her dear, skitter-witted heart, never noticed his partaking of a fifth cup of the stiff-brewed Irish tea.

"My lady! He has arrived." Ruppleton dashed into the breakfast room. He skittered to a halt when he discovered Garth still at the table. "Forgive me, my lord."

"Of course." Garth smiled. "I assume Julia's number-two suitor has arrived?"

"Lord Mancroft, dear." Aunt Clare frowned. "You must try to remember his name. You do not want to be discovered in public calling poor number two . . . well, poor number two."

"She has already taken Lord Mancroft into the parlor." Ruppleton delivered this fact like a dirge.

Oh, my!" Aunt Clare bolted up. "Then I must hurry. I am Julia's chaperone. I am to be present in these instances, you know. Truly I am."

"Indeed, Miss Clare." Ruppleton's face lit with relief. "You *should* be present."

"No doubt about it." Garth nodded, hoping he did not appear as avid. It was shameless, but if he must ride upon Aunt Clare's coattails—or skirt train, rather—he would. "You really should be there. Julia is often too trusting and lax in propriety."

"Gracious, yes. We do not want her playing make-believe with total strangers, even if they *do* propose marriage." With the look of a crusader with the Holy Land in sight, Aunt Clare picked up the skirts of her lilac muslin gown and dashed from the breakfast room, a froth of petticoats and stockings displayed. Ruppleton legged it after her. Due to those long appendages, Garth found himself very much left in the dust. He was forced to run at full tilt to catch up with the two. He pulled in, a panting third, at the parlor door.

"Julia, dear?" Aunt Clare rapped smartly upon the door. "It is me. Your chaperone, remember? Do let me join you."

The door opened so swiftly that Aunt Clare jumped and squeaked. Even Garth was startled.

"Aunt Clare. Here you are." Julia's voice was dulcet, but her eyes were alight with deviltry. A sandy-haired gentleman approached to stand behind her. "Permit me to introduce you to my fiancé, Lord Mancroft."

"Already?" Aunt Clare asked, her face bewildered. "How *could* you be so fast, Julia?"

"Aunt Clare!" Julia gasped.

"Oh, my stars!" Aunt Clare blushed red. "That did not sound right, did it? You know I meant how could the *proposal* be so fast, and not you yourself, my dear."

"I fear that must be laid at my door." Lord Mancroft

laughed and offered Aunt Clare an audacious grin. "I do beg you to forgive me for my rough-and-ready tactics."

Aunt Clare's eyes widened in alarm. "Dear, dear me. What were you two children doing in there?"

"No! Now I fear *I* said it wrong." Lord Mancroft said. "The only rough-and-ready tactic I employed was my haste to propose to my darling Julia."

"Thank goodness." Aunt Clare's hand fluttered upon her chest. "I thought— Well, we should not discuss those things in company. Pray, do go on."

"When Lord Wrexton informed me that the marquess of Hambledon was no longer in the race, I knew I dare not wait one minute more . . ."

"That you didn't." Aunt Clare nodded vehemently. "Not even a second, I would say."

"Er . . . but to propose immediately," Lord Mancroft finished, definitely put off his stride. He recovered swiftly, however. He turned a fatuous gaze upon Julia. "I am the most fortunate of men."

"And I of women." Julia returned that silly look.

"I will leave for my estates posthaste to inform my parents of the good news. I shall return, however, within two days." He reached out and took Julia's hand in his. "I shall miss you."

Julia smiled. "And . . . I you."

"Farewell, my love." Lord Mancroft, bowing, placed a kiss upon Julia's knuckles. He then turned her hand and openly placed a kiss in the palm of it. Julia's eyes shuttered wide. Garth ground his teeth. The bounder.

"Ah, hello," Aunt Clare said in a small voice. "I am here. I-I am the chaperone."

Lord Mancroft straightened. His gaze was guileless as he smiled. "I know. Do take care of my Julia for me."

"I will see you to the door, my lord." A quiver passed through Julia's voice.

"So will I!" Aunt Clare said stoutly.

Ruppleton and Garth did not bother with such niceties. They openly escorted Julia and Lord Mancroft to the door. They presented a silent vanguard as the newly engaged couple made their goodbyes and Lord Mancroft finally departed, whistling merrily as he took the town house steps two at a time.

There was only one smile left in place when the door closed. It was on Julia's face as she turned to them. "Well?"

"Well, what dear?" Aunt Clare's voice was cautious.

"What do you think of my future husband?"

Aunt Clare's face scrunched from her concentration. "He is very—"

"He is brash beyond forgiveness and took blatant liberties that he should not have." Garth refused to pussyfoot around the issue.

Julia's mouth fell open. "What? You told me Danford was too formal and without passion. Now you say Mancroft is too brash and fault him for taking liberties. You cannot have it both ways."

"Yes, I can," Garth said, blatantly ignoring logic. "Because I am right in both instances."

"You are not!" Julia then smiled like the cat who'd eaten the canary topped with caviar. "Though it is clear he is eager to wed me. You heard him; he will miss me while he is away. Unlike the marquess, I can trust that his affections will not waver, can I not?" She pranced up to Garth and chucked him under the chin. "Perhaps *you* should go and find an heiress to wed yourself, because *this* one is keeping her fortune."

Laughing, Julia picked up her skirts and waltzed away, humming Mendelssohn.

Five

"It is teatime, and Aunt Clare is not here? Nor Sir Percy?" Garth raised a quizzical brow toward the only other occupant in the parlor, Lord Wrexton. The two men were the sole proprietors of a silver pot of tea and a rapidly disappearing mound of biscuits with jam.

"Julia took her out this morning." Lord Wrexton frowned and appeared terribly confused. He was not a man who wore confusion well.

"Indeed?" Garth tried to keep his voice calm.

"Thought the same." Lord Wrexton nodded. "It is not a common occurrence. Clare does not care for the social affairs, and Julia never demands her to attend with her. She did this morning. In fact, she chose Clare's dress and supervised her dresser. She would not tell Clare where they were going. She said it was a surprise. She would not tell me, either."

"Really?"

"Yes. I have to own I'm as nervous as you. I am worried about my little girl. These past seven days have been hard on her. I hated like the devil to tell her yesterday that Lord Mancroft never went to see his parents. The best my man could tell me was that he stopped at an inn. He met up with a buxom wench, a *very* buxom wench, and he took her to his room. Seems they slipped out in the dead of night. Shot the crow. At least that is what the landlord said. Packed his bags but didn't take the time to pay his shot." Lord Wrexton heaved a sigh like a bellows puffing out air. "I cannot understand this younger generation. Does not a fortune and a beautiful woman count for anything anymore?"

"I thought Julia took it well." Garth mildly sipped his tea.

Lord Wrexton pinned him with a sapient eye. "I am an old man. Do not bother to try and bamboozle me. Julia took it too well. Quiet-like. Reposed. Gentle."

A chill ran down Garth's spine. "God, I know."

"I hate to admit it, but it frightens me down to my boots. I would rather face the cut direct. Or even a cannon direct. Could it really be that my little girl has accepted defeat? Folded? Left the table?" Lord Wrexton swiped three biscuits up in his one large fist.

"Julia is strong; she'll come about yet." Garth pushed back his feeling of guilt even as he offered Lord Wrexton those comforting words. In truth, he had been secretly relieved when Mancroft went the way of Danford. That was figuratively speaking, of course, since one had merely gotten drunk and taken a hack out of town, while the other had not only taken out of town but had taken a buxom piece of Haymarket ware with him. Yet, by no stretch of imagination, could Garth see Mancroft as a worthy mate for Julia.

"Julia must truly be in the doldrums." Lord Wrexton shook his head. "She actually took Clare along with her. Meek as you please, she reminded Clare that she must come as her chaperone. She then said Sir Percy could be the true judge."

Garth was sipping tea at the moment. He spit out the entire mouthful. "God!"

"What?" Lord Wrexton frowned. "Is the tea too hot? I thought it rather tepid myself."

"Blast and damn! Who in blazes is the next poor chap on her list?"

Lord Wrexton blinked. "I do not know."

"Number three?" Garth snapped his fingers imperiously. "Lord Beresford?"

"Yes, now that you mention it, I believe you are correct." A wistful expression crossed Lord Wrexton's face. "Not a bad chap."

"You had best like him," Garth growled. "He is Julia's new target."

"Target?"

"Her next fiancé." Exasperation shot through Garth. "Confound her. She has not given it up, after all. I vow she'll break her neck before that."

"Never say you think she is going out after another husband?" Lord Wrexton dropped his paw of biscuits as he leaned forward. "I thought surely she had lowered her flag."

"I will lay you a monkey she has not." Garth snorted. "In fact, I will double that bet. At this very moment she is out commandeering some poor fellow into proposing to her."

"Deal!" Lord Wrexton shouted and slapped his knee. Then he looked bewildered. Bewildered was another expression he did not like to wear. Therefore, it was brief. "Blast it all. What am I saying? The man would not be a poor anything if he married Julia. And, gads, I should not be betting against the very thing I have been wanting."

"I will triple it."

"Done!" Lord Wrexton bellowed. "You are on! What say you we add something more spirited to this demn tea!"

"Meow. *brrrr!*" Sir Percy darted through the open parlor door and leapt to a chair. His yellow eyes blinked dissatisfaction. *"Brr—mr."*

"Hello, Percy," Lord Wrexton said. "Where is Clare?"

"I am here." Aunt Clare staggered into the salon, her pace much slower. She was pale and wan. She toppled into a chair. "Tea. Yes, tea would be lovely. Thank the Lord for tea. Sometimes it is the only security in the world."

She did not move, however, merely gazing at the tea with longing. Garth, concerned, rose and prepared her a cup, thankful they had not made the pot into a gentlemen's brew. "What happened today?"

"Where is Julia?" Lord Wrexton asked.

"She will be arriving shortly." Aunt Clare's hands trembled as she took the cup and saucer from Garth. *"Pon rep,* I am exhausted."

"Just what did you two ladies do?" Lord Wrexton asked. "You look haggard."

"I did nothing." Aunt Clare shook her head as if in a daze. "I did nothing."

"Then what did Julia do?" Garth returned to his chair. He rather thought he'd like to hear Aunt Clare's news sitting down.

"Did she get a proposal?" Lord Wrexton asked bluntly.

Aunt Clare's teacup snapped to its saucer. "How did you know?"

"I knew it the minute I heard she had asked you to attend her as chaperone," Garth said.

"You are such a clever boy." Aunt Clare shook her head morosely. "How I wished you had warned me of it, though. I had no notion."

"You never do, Clare." Lord Wrexton chuckled. He rubbed his hands together. "Julia is engaged to— Who was number three?"

"Lord Beresford," Aunt Clare supplied. "He does have the loveliest establishment."

"I win the bet," Garth said through clenched teeth. "Remember that is triple the odds."

"You knew that as well?" Aunt Clare gasped. "Gracious, you are very clever."

For some reason Garth tensed. "Know what as well?"

"That it was tripled." Aunt Clare's brow wrinkled. "Or is it quadrupled?"

"What are you dithering about, Clare?" Lord Wrexton's tone was impatient.

"Why, that Julia has had four proposals, not one." Aunt Clare said, blinking.

"What!" Lord Wrexton cried.

"Do not say it," Garth said.

"She accepted proposals from—" Aunt Clare's face crumpled. "Forgive me. I fear I have all their names confused. They are number three, four, five, and six on the list. She stopped by to get seven as well, but his servants did not know his direction."

"I cannot believe it," Garth murmured.

"I can." Lord Wrexton grinned. "That is my Julia. She could have been a general. B'gads, but she has performed a full-out, rousing advance."

"Advance?" Garth stared at Lord Wrexton. "She has accepted proposals from four men. That is not an advance. It is a decline. A decline into sheer insanity."

"Here, now." Lord Wrexton objected. "Julia is not insane. She is—"

"Simply playing the odds," Julia said in a calm voice as she entered the room. She was decked out in a fetching capote à la Russe. The lavender silk mantle trimmed in gray squirrel was fastened jauntily on the right shoulder with a carnelian clasp. Pulling off her russet kid gloves, she sat down and flipped the gloves carelessly to the delicate enameled table beside her. She shrugged out of her mantle, revealing a peach muslin frock, and sat back with a gracious smile.

"Which should please you no end. Your triple bet has been tripled again."

"Wait, now," Lord Wrexton objected. "That is not how it goes. Garth laid odds that you were out getting a proposal. That you got four is only a surplus. It doesn't increase the original bet."

"Come, Father, you should pay him for all four." Julia's eyes glittered. "Since it will be the only money he is going to receive from you."

Garth gritted his teeth. "Julia, if you went and received four proposals merely to spite me . . ."

"I did not!" Julia's retort was hot. "I merely decided I might as well roll my dice all at once."

"Your dice?" Garth asked, his tone bitter. "I thought we were talking about men."

"I am." Julia flushed. "But I do not want to have to face what I have in the past few weeks. So I have four proposals now instead of one. Surely out of the four there should be one man who will not be fickle. One man who will prove to be true."

"And what if they all prove to be true? Then what will you do?"

"I-I will choose the one I care about the most."

"Good God! You do not care about a single one of them."

"I might be able to if I am ever given a chance. They seem to disappear on me before I can even discover if I care about them or not." A desperate, wounded look passed through Julia's eyes. It was gone within a moment. She looked at her father. "I have sworn all the men to secrecy. I also have given them morning appointments and afternoon appointments in which to visit you. Two each day."

"Excellent," Lord Wrexton nodded.

Garth in turn looked to Aunt Clare. "Do you not think this insane? Or am I the only one?"

"I think it extremely exhausting." Aunt Clare sighed. "I am completely burnt to the socket."

"You are leaving now, I presume?" Julia asked coolly to Garth as she and Aunt Clare left the breakfast room. She tried to hide her tension with a smile. Garth had been urbane throughout the breakfast, yet Julia could not help but be on tenterhooks. Lord Beresford was due to arrive soon to discuss the settlement with her father. She did not trust Garth to behave properly. He would throw a spanner into the works if he could.

"Yes, Garth?" Aunt Clare asked. "What do you have planned for the day?"

"Nothing at all." Garth's voice was quite innocent. "I thought I should remain here to help support Julia in this nerve-rending time."

"It is not a nerve-rending time," Julia snapped. "Or it would not be if you were not here."

"Tsk, tsk." Aunt Clare clucked absently. She frowned. "Why should Julia be nervous, Garth?"

"Only consider it." Garth wagged his brows. "The question looms. Will suitor— I cannot remember . . . Which one is this?"

"Suitor number three, dear," Aunt Clare supplied kindly.

"Lord Beresford." Julia gritted her teeth. "He has a name."

"Yes, but why should I take the trouble to learn it? After all, out of the four contenders, only one will take the pennant. No, I refuse to become attached until you choose the final one."

"As if you would become attached, anyway." Julia didn't bother to hide her disdain.

"Indeed, that will be *your* duty, will it not?" Garth's smile tightened. "I may continue knowing them as suitor number two and suitor number three. While you will have to learn their names, and once you've settled, much, much more."

Julia's heart twisted in the oddest way. For once she was at a lost for words.

"What is the question which looms, Garth?" Aunt Clare was clearly in a brown study.

Garth laughed, though his look let Julia know that he knew he had scored a point. "Why, that is simple. Will suitor number three come up to scratch? Or will he—"

"Be quiet," Julia ordered tersely.

"Children, children," Aunt Clare said. "Why you must continue to pull caps when—"

"Miss Julia," Ruppleton whispered from across the foyer. He was just then closing the door to the library. He hurried over. "I fear we are in the suds. Lord Redmond arrived, and your father assumed he was Lord Beresford and took him directly into the library before I could do aught to correct him."

"Good gracious," Julia exclaimed.

"Who is Lord Redmond?" Garth asked.

"Number four," Ruppleton and Aunt Clare replied in unison.

"He was not scheduled to come until tomorrow." Julia clenched her fists in frustration.

Garth hooted with laughter. "You mean number four has stolen a march on number three without even knowing it?"

"Lower your voice." Julia looked desperately about. "It is in no manner amusing."

"It is to me."

"I am to bring them the best port. Lord Redmond favors port." Ruppleton's face paled. "What should I do?"

"Exactly that." Julia ordered. "Then, in the most unobtrusive manner, tell Father I must speak with him a moment out here."

Ruppleton's face grew alarmed. He swallowed hard. "I will get the port now."

"No tippling of it beforehand, Ruppleton," Garth called as the butler sped away.

"Oh, dear." Aunt Clare said. "This is a tangle."

A knock sounded at the door. Julia jumped and stared at it.

"I wonder who that could be?" Garth said in an innocent voice. Julia refused to answer. Aunt Clare appeared absolutely paralyzed. "Very well, I imagine I best answer it, since Ruppleton is busy elsewhere." He strolled to the door and opened it. "Hello, Lord Beresford . . . is it? How are you this fine and bustling morning?"

Julia's breath wheezed out. She couldn't seem to move.

"I am fine." Lord Beresford's voice responded, confusion clear within it. "Er, do I know you, sir?"

"No, no." Garth's tone was jovial. "I am an old friend of the family. Lord Wrexton is my godfather, in fact."

"I say," Lord Beresford said. "How very interesting."

"It is, is it not? Garth stepped back. "Do come in, my lord."

"Thank you." Lord Beresford entered.

"Lord Beresford." Julia, knowing she could no longer remain invisible, rushed forward. She cast Garth a lethal glare before smiling at her fiancé. She held out her hands effusively. "It is so good to see you again."

"Er, yes, it is good to see you, too." Lord Beresford, a man of medium height, took her hands in his. His smile was wary. "Er . . . was this not the time I was to arrive?"

"Yes, it was." Aunt Clare rushed forward as well.

"Certainly, old man." Garth withdrew his watch fob and studied it. "In fact, you are here upon the very minute. Impressive."

"Father is detained, however." Julia managed a shaky smile. She waved her hand. "D-do let us go to the drawing room."

"Yes, yes, a good notion." Aunt Clare whirled about and dashed toward the room. Julia followed with Lord Beresford. She noticed that Garth had closed the front door and now followed them. He clearly intended to join them.

Her mind roiling, Julia shepherded Aunt Clare and Lord Beresford into the drawing room. Once they were within, she halted, effectively blocking Garth's entrance. "I wish to order tea for us. I will only be a moment."

Aunt Clare's face was one of shock and alarm. Lord Beresford's, fortunately, was one of complete unawareness. Julia spun and shoved Garth back into the foyer, closing the door behind them.

"Julia, really!" Garth shook his head. "You should not throw yourself at me in front of your fiancé, or one of them, that is."

"Hush, I have no time for your teasing!" Julia flushed. "Please remain here and explain to Father what is transpiring when he comes out."

"Ah. *Now* you wish my company and help!"

"Garth!" He quirked a brow. Julia knew defeat. "Very well, yes. I do wish for your help and . . . and company. Please."

"But of course I will help you." Grinning, Garth stepped back. In a perfect imitation of Lord Beresford, he took both her hands in his. His eyes glinted. "Anything for the sake of true love."

Julia jerked her hands out of his. "Thank you."

"Hmm? Though I do have a poser. Just which one is your true love? The one in there?" Garth pointed toward the drawing-room door. Then he spun and pointed to the library door. "Or the one over there?"

A knock sounded at the front entry door.

"Aha! But wait." Garth held up a staying hand. "Or could it possibly be the person behind door number three instead?"

"No. It could not be," Julia moaned. "Could it be?"

"Only if fate is against you, sweetings." Garth strode toward the door. "Ready?"

Julia scurried over, cravenly hiding behind Garth's large frame. It was unworthy of her, she knew, but she was suffering enough by just speaking the next word. "Yes?"

Garth opened the door. His tones were sepulchral. "Yes? May I help you?"

"Hello," A male voice asked. Julia bit back a groan. "Is Lady Julia Wrexton receiving?"

"*Fate* is with you, sirrah," Garth said. He stepped so quickly to the side that Julia blinked, feeling like a deer exposed to a lantern's light. "She is indeed receiving. Her just desserts, I would say."

"What?" Lord Dunn frowned. Then he smiled when he spied her. "Lady Julia, forgive me. I do hope you are not angry with me for coming here so early. Only, I could not wait to see you again."

"That is what they all say." Garth said. "All horses to the starting gate, lad."

Lord Dunn blinked. "I beg your pardon?"

"What?" Garth appeared confused. "Did I say anything?"

"He said nothing," Julia glared at Garth. "Nothing of significance, that is. It is his tendency to mutter and mumble."

"I see." Lord Dunn stepped directly past Garth to

stand looking down at her. His voice was low. "Who is
that fellow? The butler?"

"Who is he?" Garth asked from behind. "Is
he . . . ?"

"He is my father's friend . . . Lord Dunn." Julia
grabbed hold of Lord Dunn's arm and drew him forward.

"Number five, then?" Garth asked.

"Yes." Julia gritted in exasperation. Lord Dunn stiffened and looked at her inquiringly. She offered him
the most brilliant of her smiles. "Yes, er . . . five o'clock
will be fine Gar . . . Er, Lord Stanwood. Father will be
pleased to visit with you. Now, Lord Dunn, do let us
go into the drawing . . . um . . . no, the . . . the parlor."

"I see," Lord Dunn said. "You say he is a friend of
your father's?"

"Indeed. Ah, here is the parlor."

Julia drew Lord Dunn into the seventh door on the
right. Garth might have followed. At least the look
upon his face read that. Julia slammed the door quickly
between them before she could ascertain his true expression. Nodding to herself in satisfaction, she turned
with a smile, only to discover Lord Dunn but three
inches away from her. "My lord!"

"My lovely Julia." His voice was worshipful. Before
she could divine his intentions, he pulled her to him
and gave her a smacking kiss. Indeed, smacking was
the nub of the statement. Unprepared for such vigor,
Julia jumped. Her lips and teeth clashed with Lord
Dunn's.

"Ouch, ouch!" Julia's hand flew up to her wounded
lip.

"My dearest, forgive me. What an abysmal accident."
Lord Dunn reached out with his hand to smooth her
hair. His cuff link promptly caught within her curls.

"Ouch! Ouch!"

"Forgive me!" He swiftly and rather unwisely jerked his hand away. It flipped Julia's hair into her face while sending streaks of pain shooting through her.

"Ouch. Ouch. Stop!" Julia shouted.

"Oh, I say . . . forgi—"

"Please move slowly." Julia dragged in a breath and her temper. Indeed, she had to be somewhat polite. He was one of her prospective fiancés, after all. "We are tangled."

"So we are," Lord Dunn said as if confessing a secret. He reached with his free hand to work at the strands of hair. "Permit me."

"Certainly." She really had no other choice, did she?

"There! You are free."

"Thank heaven!" Julia pushed her tousled hair from her face and then winced.

The mortification upon Lord Dunn's face was supreme. "Can you forgive me?"

"Yes." Julia offered the concession, though her hand on its own accord flagged upward to ward him off. "Th-think nothing of it."

"No, I behaved far too forward by half. It is only . . ." Lord Dunn's eyes lighted. "I have been in love with you ever since I laid eyes upon you. When I discovered yesterday that you wanted me like I did you and that you were so brave as to come to my house to tell me . . . well, it is enough to drive a man to all kinds of impulsive behavior."

Julia flushed, looking down. Was there such a thing as a female cad? If there was, she was top on the list. Lord Dunn's sincerity and heartfelt emotion, compared to her lukewarm one, was shaming. "Yes, I-I know what you mean."

"We are to be married, after all. Never would I have

had the courage to act like this before. It is the first time we are alone, you know?"

"Yes, it is, isn't it?" Julia tensed. Regardless of his sincerity, she did not wish for any more snatched kisses. "But we shouldn't be! Permit me to find my aunt directly."

"Indeed." Lord Dunn nodded solemnly. "Now that we know the dangers of our ungovernable passions when not chaperoned, it is best."

"Yes," Julia choked out. She whirled toward the door. Then she halted. Frowning, she turned back. "Why did you come here in the first place?"

His eyes gleamed in anticipation. "I wondered if you would care to go riding with me in the park."

"Certainly." Julia's mind raced. She forced a smile. "I must have time to change into my habit."

"Indeed. I know that it takes time for you ladies to change. I am prepared to wait."

"Good." Julia said, so relieved that his condescending tone did not even irritate her. She sped from the room. Once she closed the door, she leaned against it, squinting her eyes shut against the situation.

"Tsk, tsk, this is not the time to rest." Garth's voice whispered into her ear. "You have more company. Guess who?"

Julia bit back her moan. She refused to open her eyes. "I do not care. Unless it is Prinny himself, I refuse to see them."

"Oh, but you must." Garth's tone was positively gleeful. "It is suitor number six, if I am not mistaken. The earl of Raleigh. I put him behind door number four."

"It cannot be!" Julia snapped her eyes open in consternation. Her breath whooshed right back down her throat. Garth was a mere three inches away from her. His one elbow rested against the door, and he leaned upon it in the most negligent fashion.

"I know you do not wish for my opinion," Garth smiled lazily at her. "But if I were you, I would sack the entire lot of them. Suitor number seven is still out there. This group does not know how to listen to orders, and you should never marry a man who cannot take orders."

"I am not that demanding!" Julia snapped.

Garth's lips twitched in a most irritating manner. "No, indeed not."

"I . . ."

"Hell-o-o?" Aunt Clare's voice called.

Julia looked up as Aunt Clare sneaked out from door number two. Julia winced. Garth's joking would make her out a Bedlamite yet. "We are over here, Aunt Clare."

Aunt Clare let out a small squeak. Then she turned, and her face brightened. She hurried over. "There you are, my dear. Is Ruppleton bringing the tea?"

"Gracious!" Julia started. She bit her lip guiltily.

"I am quite concerned for Lord Beresford." Aunt Clare reached out and clutched onto Julia's arm. Her face had an odd greenish cast to it. "No doubt he is a delightful man, but he is pacing so dreadfully that I am feeling a certain amount of . . . water sickness. I have been upon the seas only once, and I felt the same way." She frowned in contemplation. "Or does he remind me of Newmarket?"

"It is of no significance." Garth chuckled. "Here is Ruppleton now."

Ruppleton approached them with a laden tray in hands.

"Thank heaven, Ruppleton." Aunt Clare dashed over to him. "We are in need of the tea most frightfully."

"Tea?" Ruppleton halted. His face worked in alarm. "I was to bring the port, was I not?"

Aunt Clare looked over to Julia, her eyes pleading. "Did not you tell him tea, Julia? I am sure you said tea. That is what Lord Beresford is expecting. Surely he will notice the difference?"

"I am sorry, Auntie. I did not order tea," Julia confessed, stepping over to her. "I was distracted."

"Lord Wrexton ordered the port," Garth clarified. "Poor Ruppleton is two suitors behind."

"I beg pardon?" Ruppleton gasped, looking appalled.

"Do not take it to heart, old man." Garth strolled forward with the most cheerful of looks. "If I am not mistaken, Aunt Clare is actually three behind."

"I am?" Aunt Clare exclaimed. "Heavens."

Garth grinned. "And Julia needs to pick up her pace, too. She is four suitors behind."

"Really?" Aunt Clare looked around in fright. "Where are they all, then?"

"Very well, here is the lay of the land for the moment. Watch carefully." Garth raised his hand and pointed to the library. "Suitor number four is behind door number one with Lord Wrexton." He spun his finger. "Suitor number three is behind door number two."

"The drawing room," Aunt Clare nodded eagerly. "That is where I am."

"Yes." Garth swung his finger. "Suitor number five is behind door number three at this moment." He sighed in a feigned exhaustion. He spun his arm once more and pointed. "Suitor number six is, of course, behind door number four."

"The sewing room!" Julia gasped, appalled. "You put him in the sewing room?"

"Is that what it is?" Garth inquired. "I would not know. I merely opened the door and had the fellow toddle on in."

"Oh, Lord," Julia muttered. "Surely you could have done something else."

"Really?" Garth lifted a brow. "Just where would you have put him?"

"I think you very clever, Garth," Aunt Clare patted his arm. "Indeed, that you can remember where anyone is at all amazes me."

"Ohh! Never mind." Julia clenched her teeth. She needed to keep her mind clear. "I must change."

"You have seen the error of your ways, then?" Garth quirked a brow.

"No." Julia glared at him. "I must change into my riding habit."

"Julia, dear, I do not mean to be difficult," Aunt Clare said. "But this is not the time for a ride. I own, if I cared for horses, I, too, would wish to—to climb on its back and take off *ventre a terre*. However . . ."

"No, Aunt." Julia flinched. "I promised to go riding with Lord Dunn."

"Is *that* what you promised?" Garth quirked a brow.

"Yes." Julia glared at him. "Why?"

Garth looked at her in steady silence. His gaze seemed to physically touch her bruised lip and her disheveled hair. Julia blushed. She had completely forgotten how she must look after her painful interlude with Lord Dunn. "It is not what it seems."

"What?" Aunt Clare asked, blinking. "What is not what it seems?"

Julia shook her head, refusing to look at Garth now. "We do not have time. We cannot afford to have any of them stepping out of their rooms to look for us."

"Heaven forbid." Aunt Clare's hand flew to her chest to thump there loudly.

"I doubt heaven has that much to do with this. This is definitely in the nature of a mortal coil." Garth's tone was dry. However, he winked at Julia and then clapped Ruppleton upon the shoulder. "Ruppleton, be a good man. Pour out a glass of port."

"Yes, my lord." Ruppleton walked to a pier table. He proceeded to set the laden tray down and poured a stem of port.

"Thank you," Garth said, and took the glass of port from him. He held it in midair, preparatory to drinking it. "Ruppleton, you must still enter and inform Lord Wrexton that he must settle with suitor number four and then go to suitor number three, who awaits him at door number two. Julia, you will go to suitor number six at door number four and entertain him."

"I do not know." Julia sagged. "I am supposed to return to Lord Dunn . . ."

"I know!" Aunt Clare clapped her hands together in excitement. "He is suitor number five, isn't he?"

Garth nodded. "In door number three."

"I am beginning to follow this." Aunt Clare's eyes widened.

"Good for you, auntie." Garth's smile was warm. It cooled when he looked at Julia. "You need to attend suitor number six. After all, he *is* one of your prospective fiancés as well."

"Very well." Julia sighed. "You are right. I will see him first."

"Aunt Clare, you will go see suitor number five instead." Once again Garth's gaze flicked over Julia. "He is in strong need of a chaperone, I believe."

"One moment." Aunt Clare ticked on her fingers. She broke into a smile. "Suitor number five. Lord Dunn. Door number three."

"You have it." Garth nodded. "And instead, I will keep suitor th—"

"Lord Beresford!" Aunt Clare exclaimed.

"Yes, him. I will try and keep him calm." He lifted

the port glass to his lips and then halted. He held it out instead. "Does anyone require a bracer?"

"Most certainly not." Julia said instantly.

"No, thank you." Aunt Clare shook her head. "I do not imbibe."

"I believe—" Ruppleton halted, appearing conflicted.

"Not until lately, that is!" Aunt Clare reached out and took the glass swiftly from Garth. She took a strong sip. Coughing, she returned it. "Thank you, Garth."

Ruppleton smiled gratefully. "I-I could tolerate a dose myself."

"Good man. Gird yourself for battle." Garth held the glass out.

Ruppleton took it and lifted it. After one hearty swig, he sighed and handed the glass back to him. "Thank you, Master Garth."

Garth held it out, his gaze challenging upon Julia. "You are positive?"

"Yes." Julia lost her dignity as she looked at it with longing. "I dare not smell of port when I meet my fiancé."

"So be it." Garth shrugged. He swiftly quaffed the rest.

Every last bit of it, Julia couldn't help but notice with regret.

Garth's eyes flared with amusement when he caught her glance. He laughed and strolled over to the tray. "Sorry, Ruppleton. I am commandeering this for the anxious suitor number three and me. Let us hope he favors port as suitor number four does. You may inform Lord Wrexton if you like."

"Yes, my lord." Ruppleton nodded with understanding. Then he jumped. "I mean, no, my lord. I will bring him another tray. I fear he will have need of it."

"And tea?" Aunt Clare pleaded over a last cough.

"Yes, Miss Clare." Ruppleton bowed.

"Now!" Garth clapped once. "Everyone to their post."

"Oh, my, yes," Aunt Clare squeaked. She darted forward, halted, then scurried back. "I beg your pardon, Garth. But where am I going again?"

"In there," Garth said, pointing. "Remember?"

"Oh, yes!" Aunt Clare tripped on over to the door and opened it. "Yoo-hoo. It is me. The chaperone."

"Suitor number four . . . door number one," Ruppleton muttered, pacing across the foyer to the library door. He opened it and disappeared. "Lord Wrexton . . ."

"Now it is your turn, Julia." Garth lifted the tray.

"I know. I know." Julia winced. Even to her own ears, she sounded reluctant. "I am going to see suitor number six. Door number four . . . the sewing room."

"Cheer up." Garth grinned. "If the man still wants to marry you after being put in the sewing room, you might have your husband."

Julia forced a smile. Somehow it did not cheer her. She moved toward door number four. "Yes."

"Julia. Stop."

"Yes?" Julia turned.

Garth held out the tray. "Could you come and take this a moment."

"Certainly." She walked back to him and took the tray. After all, any excuse to tarry would help.

Garth shook his head. "I vowed I would not lift a finger in this regard."

"What regard?"

"Your hair is definitely messed." Garth reached out and ran his hand through her hair, smoothing it back.

"Oh." Julia almost dropped the tray. A tingle ran down to her very toes.

"I also noticed . . ." Garth grasped one sole curl between his thumb and froze. His gaze lowered to her lips.

"What?" Julia nervously ran her tongue over her lips. Then winced.

Garth's smile was soft. "That you have a cut."

"Yes. That." Julia quivered. "I—he . . . it was accidental. He startled me so, you see. I jumped just when he was trying to—" Julia stopped. She simply could not finish the story.

Garth's eyes lighted. It was clear he understood without her finishing. "Really?"

"Yes." Julia smiled. A giggle actually escaped her.

"Poor Julia." Garth dropped the curl. Before Julia realized that she felt disappointed, Garth ran his finger gently across her lower lip. "I am sorry. There is nothing I can do to rectify that."

"Of course not." Julia whispered. Her heart pounded wildly. The strangest, glowing feeling invaded her. "I mean. W-what c-could you d-do?"

"Right." Garth gazed at her solemnly, his finger settled upon the corner of her mouth.

Julia's lips trembled. The rest of her, weak, glowing mess that it was, could not be budged.

"Confound it." Garth leaned over and kissed her firmly. The tray rattled, and Julia almost dropped it, so blinded by sweet sensations was she. She felt Garth's large hands cover hers on the tray. He did not draw back. Not until he had drawn two more earthshaking kisses from her.

"Why?" Julia's voice squeaked. She cleared her throat and lowered it. "Why did you do that?"

"You could not have the port." Garth shrugged with a wry grin. "It looked like you needed a bracer."

"Oh."

He lifted a brow. "Now, if you would tell all these fellows to take themselves off and forget their proposals, we could settle down to a glass of port very comfortably."

Julia lowered her gaze. It sounded far, far too tempting. She shook herself. "You would like that, wouldn't you?"

"Yes." Garth eyes glinted. "It would save me a deuce of trouble later."

"Wh-what do you mean?" Julia heart raced madly.

Garth studied her until Julia blushed. Smiling wryly he shook his head. "I only meant that I would not be forced to direct traffic for the next hour. But if you are still set on this perilous course, so be it."

"Ah, yes." Julia blinked.

Garth withdrew his hands from the tray. He then took Julia by the shoulders and spun her. "Now go. Door number four. Suitor number six. Remember?"

Remember? Julia moved toward the sewing room in a daze. The only thing she seemed to recall was those kisses. They were supposed to have acted like a bracer. The only thing they had done, as far as she could tell, was to have knocked the wind out of her. She found it very difficult to focus as she opened the door and discovered the earl of Raleigh sitting between a stack of rent linens and a pile of ripped petticoats.

Six

Julia, plate in hand, moved alongside the glittering buffet table. Such delicacies as lobster patties, petite poupettes of veal, oyster sausages, and powdered almond cakes, ladened the table. Lady Sefton, upon the advent of her celebrated annual ball, did not curb her chef's culinary whimsies or spare any expense in that direction. No one of the *tôn* ever missed her *fête*, not only because of the fare but because of the woman's political power.

Julia felt no excitement, not even interest, in the array. Indeed, the thought of food turned her stomach, an organ that had been feeling very much as if someone had delivered a windmill punch to it. Within a course of two days she had successfully become engaged to four men, all with her father's blessings. Within the course of two weeks she had become unengaged due to all her fiancés fleeing forthwith. With their own blessings, no doubt. They never left notes of apologies, begged audiences to explain, or even sent flowers in regret. They simply vanished.

Indeed, the findings of her father's discreet inquiries indicated that her fiancés had employed every means of transportation across or out of England to escape her. The earl of Raleigh had taken a merchant boat to France. He hadn't even waited to take his own sleek sailing vessel harbored at Portsmouth. Lord Redmond had defaulted on the very race he had personally arranged, turning about his curricle midway, as it were, and headed toward Scotland instead. Lord Beresford had forgone his intended visit to his mistress, who had been left quite wroth. Lord Dunn had merely bypassed his tailor.

If anything could shake a woman's confidence, losing four fiancés in two weeks should do the trick. In truth, it made a total of six now. Not only had Julia's confidence deserted her; the rejection had all but sunk her.

"They say that foul play is most certain." Lord Fensworth was talking to Lady Terrel directly behind her.

Lady Terrel was Julia's acting chaperone for the evening. Julia would have preferred not to come to the ball, but her pride would not permit her to hide away. The sympathy she was receiving from Garth was like proverbial hot coals being heaped upon her. Even worse, if possible, were Aunt Clare's supportive efforts. Each of her avowals that Julia need *only look to her heart and her true love* drove Julia to gnash her teeth.

"Gracious," Lady Terrel said. "How dreadful. What is the world coming to when a powerful man like the earl of Kelsey is abducted directly from his house?"

"It will be fortunate if that is the case," Lord Fensworth said. "It may very well be out-and-out murder, you know?"

Julia froze. Her eyes widened and she gasped. "Number seven?"

"What, Julia, dear?" Lady Terrel asked.

Julia whirled upon the couple so fast that the two lobster patties on her plate flew. "What happened to seven?"

"Julia!" Lady Terrel jumped back to avoid the launched patties. "What *are* you doing?"

"I-I mean, the earl of Kelsey?" Julia stammered. "What happened to him?"

"He was taken from his house late last night." Lord Fensworth withdrew his handkerchief and bent to scoop up the patties. Lord Fensworth was a very particular and neat fellow. "Servants said he was in the library having a nightcap. They heard him cry out. When they arrived, he was gone. There was a pool of blood by the fireplace. The windows were wide open. They say the dogs outside were howling to wake the dead." He stood and shook his head as he folded the patties in the linen square and neatly tucked them beneath an enormous silver epergne holding trailing ivy. "Pity. It was probably for the poor earl they bayed."

"Please, Horton, let us not speak of it anymore," Lady Terrel pleaded. "It makes me positively shiver."

Shivers coursed through Julia, too. Actually, they were more like tremors—of outrage. Possibly fear was mixed within it, but rage was the overall emotion. Suitor number seven had just vanished. It could be a coincidence, but Julia did not accept that notion, not by a long chalk. Not after six other men who were on her list had disappeared.

Foul play? Oh, yes, indeed. The entire thing stunk to the high heavens, and she very well knew who the perpetrator was. Garth had just overplayed his hand by taking the earl of Kelsey before she had even had a chance to bring him up to scratch. Faith, she had intended to do so within a week, being slow in the chase due to her fit of blue melancholy. Her melancholy lifted like steam off of water. Eyes ablaze, Julia scanned the room, looking for the felon.

"Julia?" Lady Terrel's voice asked. "Are you all right?"

"Hmm? Oh, yes." The shameful man. The blackguard. He had offered her feigned sympathy, had let her think herself the most unwanted woman alive, and all the time it had been of his design. She drew in a strong, new breath. "Oh, yes. I am most definitely fine . . . now!"

"Lady Julia," a female voice said directly behind her.

Julia turned. She stiffened in astonishment. The marquess of Hambledon's mother actually stood before her, as bold as you please. How the lady could do so when she and her son had embarrassed Julia before the *tôn* by leaking the story of their engagement was beyond Julia. Not to mention that her son had then humiliated her by leaving her in the lurch. Julia realized now that Garth had had something to do with it, but it made very little difference to her. The marquess should have possessed more backbone than to permit Garth to persuade him otherwise.

"I can no longer refrain from speaking!" Lady Danford, a petite and frail woman, had turned even more deathly pale than was her want. Her lips twitched erratically.

Julia nodded in sudden understanding. Lady Danford wished to apologize to her. "Yes?"

"I must know." Lady Danford stopped. She drew in a breath. "What have you done with my son?"

"I beg your pardon?" Julia's mouth dropped open. "You dare to ask me that?"

"He is all I have." Lady Danford lifted a clenched fist to her mouth, sobbing. "I beg of you, tell me what you did?"

"I did not do anything to him." Julia flushed. "It was he who deserted me."

"You lie."

"I do not." Julia stiffened. Those around her had quieted and now watched closely, especially those directly in the buffet line behind her. Julia purposely stepped from the line. Regardless, no one moved. "He promised he would meet with my father. He never did."

"You lie!"

"Why do you persist in saying that? It was your son who bolted on *me*." Julia strove to reign in her frayed temper. The lady before her clearly suffered under the weight of strong emotions. She trembled and shook as if close to a fit of apoplexy. Alarmed, Julia looked hastily around. The crowd about them was increasing unreasonably as they scented tomorrow's *on-dit*. She lowered her voice. "It is not something I care to admit or vaunt, I assure you. He had but to talk to my father and explain that he had reconsidered and did not wish for my hand. Instead, he took off to parts unknown."

"He did not!" Lady Danford pokered up. Her eyes turned fervent. "My Charles is a man of honor. The servants vow he never returned home that night. I have not heard from him since. No one has! What did you do? It must be your fault."

"It is not," Julia said more gently. Lady Danford was obviously desperate and grasping at straws. Unfortunately, Julia did not particularly enjoy being a straw. "I am totally innocent."

"No, you are not!" Another woman's voice cried out. The crowd rumbled and then parted. Julia swallowed hard. If she were not mistaken, the mother of suitor number four, Lord Redmond, now stalked toward her. "Harry has vanished as well."

"I beg your pardon," Lady Danford objected. "I am talking to Lady Julia. We are speaking about *my* son."

"And mine, too!" Lady Redmond nodded. "He was engaged to Lady Julia."

"What?" Lady Danford staggered back. "Impossible."

"They were secretly engaged." Lady Redmond's tone

was a cross between pride and anger. "Harry told me so just last week."

"Not true!" Yet another voice cried out. Lady Beresford, the mother of suitor number three, stomped forward. A large woman, her voice was a bellow, and her sails were in full mast. "It was my son, Reginald, she was engaged to last week. Not yours."

"No. That I will not credit!" Another female voice called out. Lady Dunn, suitor number five's mother, advanced. "It was my son Herrington to whom she was engaged. He vowed me to secrecy. But now I must speak! I have no choice."

"Oh, Lord." Julia stared, aghast. It was a nightmare, an absolute nightmare. Never would she have imagined there were so many men who still confessed their private affairs to their mothers. She must have chosen the only four in the entirety of England. Could anything be worse?

"She's engaged to my son, Giles!" A female voice shouted from within the crowd. "He sent me a message."

Yes, things could be worse.

"You are all wrong. The woman is engaged to my son, Matthew!"

Much worse!

"Explain yourself, Miss Wrexton, if you can." Lady Danford swayed like a sapling in the wind. "You were engaged to my son. Now these ladies claim that you were engaged to their sons. Just who were you engaged to?"

"Er, all of them." Julia bit her lip. "In a manner of speaking, that is."

"Bigamy!" Old Lord Lathan's gruff voice was heard to say. "Ain't that bigamy? The gel should be clapped up."

"No. She would have had to marry them for that,

and it would be polygamy" answered Lady Clivedon. Her voice was condemning. "She didn't even do *that much.*"

"Jilt!" One voice called out. The word hissed around the room. Jilt. Jilt. Jilt.

Julia drew herself up. She doubted she would make it out alive, as ugly as the crowd was becoming, but she'd be hanged if she would cower. "I was not the jilt. It was the other way around. Lady Danford, your son never met with my father. Therefore, nothing was official."

"What about my son?" Lady Redmond cried. The following echoes of the same question were mortifying. "He did meet with your father! You were engaged to him."

"Yes! My Herrington, too."

"And my Giles."

"Reginald as well."

Julia waited for the chorus to die down. She drew in her breath. "Very well, yes. I had a mind to marry, plain and simple. I accepted all your sons' proposals." Everyone took a collective gasp. Even though that is what they had all accused her of, they still acted astonished. Julia clenched her teeth. How delightful it was to be forced to admit in front of the entire *tôn* that six men had fled from marriage with her. Granted, Garth, that beast, had something to do with it, but it still was lowering. "However, none of them, and I repeat none of them, stayed to see an engagement through to the end and officially claim my hand."

"That is because you did something to my poor Charles," Lady Danford shrieked. "I know you did. You are a Black Widow!"

"I have not seen my son for a week now." Lady Redmond's eyes widened. "Gracious. What did you do? I never thought . . ."

Julia flushed. Her painful confession had been for naught. Indeed, it had exasperated matters. Now they truly desired her blood.

"I thought Reginald had merely—" Lady Beresford halted. "But it was you! He has disappeared."

The gasps and cries of the responding mothers down the line were gruesome as each joined, all maternal loyalties rising to the forefront.

"I had nothing to do with their disappearances!" Julia was forced to raise her voice over the clamor. What Garth had to do with it, she would find out later, and heaven help him when she got through. No, it would have to be the nether regions to come to the rescue of one of their own. "I assumed your sons jilted me!"

"Not *my* son," Lady Danford cried. "*My* son is honorable. He would never jilt a lady."

"And what of my son?" Lady Redmond squared off against Lady Danford. "Do you insinuate that it was different with him?"

"Your son is well-known for philandering." Lady Danford sniffed. "You will most likely find him safe in . . . Well, I will not say, since we are in public. It is obvious she accepted my Charles first before anyone else. He was by far the best choice."

"Then why did she do something to get rid of him? Hmm?" Lady Redmond sneered. "She most likely decided she could not tolerate him."

"What?" Julia gasped, appalled. "Truly, I did not do anything to your sons. I merely became engaged to them. They . . . they disappeared through their own devices."

"I could believe that about Lady Redmond's son," Lady Danford said coldly. "But not *my* son."

Lady Redmond snorted. "At least my son can pass a gaming table without sitting down directly."

"That is not true." The fury in Lady Danford's eyes

was frightening. Enough so that Julia pedaled backward swiftly when the small woman stepped toward her. Unfortunately, the banquet table behind her impeded her escape. "Tell them, Lady Julia. Tell them Charles was your first choice and that none of their sons mattered to you."

Julia resolutely maintained her silence. Agreeing with the rabid Lady Danford would surely be swift suicide. The other mothers were now moving to flank about her ominously. They had lost all semblance of ladies of the peerage. Harpies with talons open and ready for rending described them far better.

Julia gripped her plate. Perhaps she ought to throw it at them. Or something. "I . . ."

"Ouch!" Lady Danford's head bobbed to the left.

Julia blinked. Could desperate thoughts have physical power? She could have sworn a small plum had pelted Lady Danford and had bounced off her head. Impossible, of course.

"How dare you!" Lady Danford spun around to glare at Lady Redmond. "How dare I what?" Lady Redmond asked, her face belligerent.

"You struck me," Lady Danford said. She took her brisé fan and rapped Lady Redmond upon the arm.

"Ouch!" Lady Redmond's face turned grim. "That was uncalled for. I did not strike you. You imagine things."

"Lady Redmond is right." Lady Beresford stepped forward. "You have lost all sense of reality, Lady Danford. It is my son who would have been the perfect husband to Lady Julia."

Stunned at the change in conversation, Julia almost missed the orange that pelted Lady Beresford in the small of the back. However, that lady surely did not.

"Gracious!" she shrieked, jumping. She turned to

glare at Lady Dunn, who stood close beside her. "Why did you do that?"

Suddenly, a rain of well-placed grapes boinged off the irate ladies. Each shied grape caused considerable anger. The wroth ladies did not turn their temper in the fruits' direction, those little missiles falling swiftly to the floor beneath skirts and shoes. No doubt, believing, like Julia, that it was quite impossible for fruit to be flying willy-nilly about Lady Sefton's ball, they turned their ire upon the lady beside them. Though it might have simply been their favored choice. Quashing a grape could not be as exhilerating as attacking a contending mother. Manners, for the sake of motherhood, could justifiably be cast aside, and no portside fishwife could outwail a mother whose offspring had been wronged.

Since it was still Lady Sefton's ball, the fight that insued was *bon tôn*. It was a force majeure. Even the smallest of the protective mothers held their own against a barrage of slapping fans, trounced hems, and a cannonade of the most cutting barbs. Lace and feathers flew.

Julia could only stand and watch in awe. The pelting fruit had been manna from heaven, for the ladies had quite forgotten her.

A heavy hand gripped her arm. Julia jumped and then sighed in relief. Her father stood grinning down at her. "Time to go, Julia."

"But . . . woof!"

Her father was a strong man. Rather than answering her, he dragged her along, a helpless tow behind him. He steered her unerringly between bystander and gawker. Only when they cleared the crowd did he rest, peering back. "Gad, but that boy is brilliant."

"Who?" Julia strove to catch her breath.

"Garth." Lord Wrexton chuckled. "Look."

Julia followed his direction, narrowing her eyes. Then they widened. Garth stood unobtrusively to the side. With a flash of his hand he threw a grape. Immediately his hand was tucked into his vest, his expression innocent.

"I feared those mothers would hie you off to Bridewill, or worse, lynch you themselves." Lord Wrexton shook his head grimly. "Then Garth devised this plan."

Garth's hand slipped from his vest, and he pelted a grape. Only this time someone noticed. They pointed at him. A woman's voice shrieked. Another howled. Then four more bayed.

"Blast, he has been discovered." Lord Wrexton

"Oh, no." Julia lifted up her skirts, ready to charge back into the melee. "We must help him."

"No, Julia," Lord Wrexton commanded. "You go home. Leave this to us men. Those biddies are savage. Garth did not save you so that you could get yourself killed."

"But . . ."

"No. You would only draw their fire."

"But . . ."

"You can only hurt us, girl, and you know it."

Julia dropped her skirts and lowered her head. She did know it, as galling and unfair as it was.

"Leave us." Lord Wrexton's eyes gleamed. "We will rally yet!"

Julia paced the parlor floor. She had lit but one candle. The rest of the household remained asleep, and that is the way she wished it. She was grateful to discover she could slip in the back kitchen door without Ruppleton's notice. Since Lord Wrexton's command that Ruppleton not assist her, Ruppleton had deserted his post. It had hurt Julia slightly, that desertion. Tonight she was grateful for it. She needed time to compose herself, and if Ruppleton saw her tonight, the fat would be in the fire.

Guilt washed over Julia. It was all her fault.

She gritted her teeth and took another spin about the room. No, it wasn't her fault. She must remind herself of that. It was Garth's fault. Her father had said Garth was brilliant, but she doubted he expected Garth to be so very clever. Julia crossed her arms and tried to control her shaking. Garth was involved with the disappearances of her grooms. Heaven only knew what had happened with the seventh suitor, the earl of Kelsey.

Julia shook her head without knowing it. Something must have gone wrong. Garth would not have hurt someone on purpose. In truth, the deepest part of her could not believe that he had lent himself to any of it. Regardless of their fights, despite everything, her heart did not want to accept it.

Her head, however, could not permit her heart to keep its blinders on. It rolled out the hard, cold facts. With those mothers' accusations still ringing in her ears, Julia was forced to conclude that her suitors were missing. They had not just jilted her; they had truly disappeared. Only Garth would have a reason to drive her fiancés away or pay them off, or whatever he had done. It was also Garth, and Garth alone, who had known who would be her next choice of fiancé.

"You may cease your pacing." Garth's voice teased. "I am quite safe."

Julia jumped and then skittered to a halt. She had been so involved with the nervous exorcising of her thoughts, she had not heard him enter. Her heart pounded. "You should not sneak up on a person like that."

"I did not sneak up." Garth smiled warmly. "I was excessively noisy, I thought, but you were too busy pacing. Worried over me?"

Julia noticed that Garth vaunted a bruise beneath his eye. She did worry her lip but firmed her resolve. She must remember what Garth had done. "Not a wit."

The smile left Garth's face. "Of course not." He spun and walked from the room.

"Where are you going?" Julia picked up her skirts and followed.

"To the kitchen."

"You wish to eat at a time like this?"

"No. I believe I have had enough of food for the evening. Even if I *was* throwing it rather than eating it."

After that Garth fell silent. Julia did the same, determined not to be the one to break. Her emotions were too confused. Guilt, gratitude, anger, and betrayal fought with each other. Unable to speak, yet unable to retreat and let sleeping dogs lie (since the dog was Garth), Julia followed him into the kitchen. She coolly watched him as he lit the lamp and moved about the room, setting the water on to boil, finding liniments and bandages as well as a stout brown bottle of Blue Ruin hidden in the larder behind a half-barrel of onions. Garth glanced at her periodically. She presented a stoic countenance.

Sighing, he set his collection down upon the table. He then sat himself. "All right, Julia, what is it?"

"What is what?" Julia frowned as Garth uncuffed his shirt.

"What burr do you have under your saddle?" Garth rolled his sleeve up to his bicep.

Julia gasped and hastened forward. Garth's wrist and arm were welted badly, and small spots seeped blood. "Good Lord, what happened?"

"I never knew ladies had such a talent with their fans." Garth's tone was wry as he picked up the bottle of gin with one hand.

"Here, I will do it," Julia murmured, still frowning. She took the bottle from him and picked up a cotton cloth.

"I intend to write the War Department and inform them of a secret source of infantry we are missing." Garth grimaced as Julia liberally daubed it on. "Gads! Are you enjoying yourself, Julia?"

Julia flushed. It was far from it. Her heart was aching in a most unnatural way. "You are positively riddled with these small punctures."

"Pins." Garth nodded. Julia halted and stared at him. His eyes flared with amusement, and he shook his head. "Do not ask me from where those pins came. I can only imagine they took their broaches off and employed them. Rather diabolical. Give me a good sturdy blow any day. That I can see coming."

"Faith," Julia said weakly. "I would never have thought of pins."

"No." Garth grinned. "You are far more like us men. You attack straight on without subterfuge. It is something I have always admired in you."

Julia looked down, pretending to be focused upon her work. She could not meet his gaze. "How did you escape?"

"Your father."

"My father?" Julia did look at him.

"He is amazing. He harangued the men until they rallied with him and pulled the women off me and each other. He then set up an oration that should be written in history. By the time he was done, you looked like the poor, put-upon heroine, and the other ladies looked to be in the wrong."

"I am glad to hear that." Julia bit her lip.

"Cut line, Julia." Garth's hand swiftly covered Julia's hand. "Out with it."

"With what?"

"I asked you what burr was under your saddle." Garth gazed at her intently. "And I ask again. You should be far more glad about this than you are."

"I do not know what you are talking about."

"You do not?" Garth's eyes flared with anger. "For starters, why not be slightly more grateful to your father and me for saving you?"

Julia stiffened. "I beg your pardon!"

"You may and should." Garth dropped her hand and stood. "Confound it, woman, why must you always be so headstrong and irrationally independent? You will never accept your loved ones' support and their efforts to save you from yourself. I mean . . . your father gave his best for you tonight. You would have been in a regular fix otherwise."

"Save me from myself?" The damn burst open. "Forgive me. It is not myself who pitchforked me into this situation."

Garth expelled an exasperated breath. "Very well, your father started this entire fiasco. But it is you who continued it. He wanted you to find one husband in six months. Though heavy-handed and demanding, that was not ridiculous. But no, you had to get your dander up. You must find one within a week and marry him within a month. When that did not work out accordingly—and why in blue blazes you expected it to, I'll never know—you had to tether in five more. I can only guess such an escapade was because you are accustomed to having the world at your feet."

"I am not!"

"Yes, you are. Else you wouldn't have been so obstinate and hell-bent as to keep bagging more fiancés. My apologies, but yes, you do need saving from yourself and no one else. Do not blame your father for this."

"I do not blame *him.*" Julia sprang up. "I am not such a fool. I know who is to blame. I have learned all!"

Garth reared back at her vehemence. Then his hazel eyes twirled to teal in amusement, and he quirked a brow. "You have learned all? Forsooth, what does that mean?"

"It means . . ." Julia drew in a shaky breath. The moment had come. "It means that I know it is you behind everything."

"That it is me?" Garth shook his head, his face still showing what looked like innocent confusion. Then it changed, but only to mild irritation. "Oh, good Lord. Not that again. Are you cracked?"

"I heard about the earl of Kelsey tonight."

Garth shrugged. "So did I. The gossips say that he was murdered. What does that have to do with me?"

"He is number seven," Julia said. "Number seven on the list. It is too much of a coincidence by far to believe his disappearance has nothing to do with me. Nor, after I heard those ladies tonight, do I believe any longer that those six men left me without some sort of persuasion being applied. And you are the only one who would gain from my fiancés disappearing."

Garth stared at her long and hard. "Can you truly believe that? My God, the earl of Kelsey was most very well murdered. You believe *that* of me?"

Julia fidgeted. Her mind told her not to back down, but her heart begged her otherwise. "I do not believe you would have murdered him. Some kind of accident must have occurred. Something . . . beyond your control."

"Something beyond my control?" Garth shook his head, his voice low. "No, Julia, the only thing beyond my control is you and your distrust. I would never do anything to hurt you or your father, and you should know that."

Julia trembled from the condemnation in his eyes. "Why should I believe you? All you have done since you've arrived is to jest and mock me, but now I should know better?"

"No, I suppose not." Garth turned from her. "Believe whatever you wish. It is of no significance to me."

"I know. You care for nothing." Julia watched as he strode to the door. It was totally unreasonable, but she felt as if she had just destroyed something and as if her heart were breaking because of it.

Suddenly, Garth stopped. He whirled around. "Fiend seize it, I am not going to accept this."

"What do you mean?" Julia asked, blinking as he stalked back, an angry panther.

"I am going to prove you wrong, Julia Wrexton." His eyes had darkened to stormy gray. He grabbed her by the shoulders and shook her slightly. "Do you hear me?"

"I-I hear you." Julia's heart leaped with an emotion akin to pleasure. "How?"

"I will find the true culprit, and that is a promise." Garth stilled then, and his fingers gripped into her shoulders. "I will find him, and then you will be forced to take back every disbelieving word you have ever said."

"Fine." Julia kept her tone pugnacious. Secretly her heart lightened.

"What?" Garth's brows rose.

Clearly he had not expected such an easy capitulation from her. Julia tossed her head and sought a quick retrieval. "And I will help you. After all, it will benefit me the most to discover who is behind this all. They are destroying my chances of marriage."

"Fine." Garth retorted. "Because once we find the culprit, I myself will gladly assist you down the aisle and give you away to whichever poor fellow you finally alight upon."

"Excellent!" Julia said.

"Famous!" Garth nodded.

"It is a deal, then?" Julia held out her hand. His warm hands upon her shoulders were causing havoc.

"It is a deal." Garth removed his hands from her shoulders and clasped her proffered hand with his. "You will believe in me in the end, Jules."

"I want to," Julia said before she realized she had.

Garth's eyes lit. "Do you?"

"I mean . . . I want us to find the culprit."

"I see. That is what you meant." Garth's lips twitched.

"Yes." Julia employed the primmest of tones. "The *tôn* believes I am the perpetrator . . ."

"As you believe I am." Garth shook his head and stepped closer. "We will just have to save each other, I am afraid."

"I guess so." Julia gazed up at him, unable to hide her smile any longer.

"There is no drawing back, mind you. I have my reputation to clear."

"So have I." Julia tried to infuse as much indignation into her voice as possible.

"However, if you are going to assist me in this, there are certain rules."

"Rules?"

"Yes, rules. You, Lady Julia Wrexton, will have to stop pulling caps with me at every turn. You will need to cooperate with me rather than fight against me."

"That is your rule?" Julia lifted her brow. Garth nodded. "Then my rule is that you must cease pinching at me so until you cause me to loose my temper."

"I do not know." Garth raised his free hand and brushed a strand of her hair from off her face. "That will be hard to resist."

"I do not understand why it should be so." Julia frowned.

"Either do I. There is just something which makes me—" Garth halted.

"Makes you what?" Julia encouraged.

Garth's smile twisted. He drew his hand back and clearly drew in his breath. "Makes me think it is time for us to both retire."

Julia blinked. "Retire?"

Garth turned swiftly and walked across the room. "We will have a long day of it tomorrow, no doubt, trying to discover the culprit. It is definitely time to retire."

"Very well." Julia scurried to pick up the candle and follow him from the kitchen. She controlled a shiver. In truth, she didn't wish to tarry alone. She would far prefer Garth's escort through the darkened house, the thought of what might have happened to her grooms unnerving her. Just as the thought that she and Garth would be working together in unison did.

The sound of tinder against a box could be heard within the kitchen. From the butler's pantry, to be exact. That door swung open. Aunt Clare tiptoed out from the pantry. In one hand she held a candle. In the other she held a bottle of the best Bordeaux.

Seven

Clare sat in the parlor alone. The pomona-green drapes were released from their gold-braided-ribbon ties to fall loose across the enclosures of the floor-to-ceiling, bowed windows, shutting off the storm without. However, it did not help the storm within. Her stomach was fighting an upheaval, and her head was warring against a persistent throb.

She had abstained from breaking her fast. In truth, she had awakened very late and had taken even more time to make it to the breakfast room. When she arrived, she had discovered it completely vacant. Julia and Garth had already left the town house. Ruppleton had imparted that Julia had departed to her modiste and that Garth had actually accompanied her.

A heavy sigh escaped Clare as she stroked Percy, who draped across her lap, his tail touching the floor on one side of her and his forepaws brushing the floor on the other. He lay so still he gave the impression of a lap robe rather than that of a dignified feline. Percy, dozing, never bothered to even open his eyes.

"Oh, Percy. I vowed to be courageous and not turn away from adventure, but I am most disappointed. All these years Bendford has boasted about his fine wine, but I fear it is not good, not at all. Not if it makes one feel like this. There is so very much I must do. So much that requires concentration. How can I concentrate when my head hurts so much?" She stroked his back. "They say men are the stronger of the sexes, and indeed they must be if they can withstand such every day. I own, though, that I wonder if they are not simply want-witted." She jumped and looked around. She peered at the snoozing Percy, then nodded. "You will not repeat that, thank goodness. We ladies must have our secrets, you know?"

The thunder rolled again. It took on a different patter, more like a rapping. Aunt Clare blinked. "Percy, is that not the oddest thunder?"

At this Percy did open his eyes. "Meow."

"Is it, now?"

"Meow." Percy slowly stood up. He arched his back in a lazy stretch, still balanced upon Clare's lap. Then he leapt down and padded from the room.

Clare rose and with a mystified expression followed him into the foyer. The thunder was tattooing a beat at the entrance door.

"You are right. We do have a visitor." Clare turned to fetch Ruppleton. Then she halted with a weary sigh. It would be such a long and taxing trek at the moment. He would be in the kitchen seeing to the preparation of the kitties' meals. She would not wish to divert him from that most important duty, to be sure.

The beat at the door persisted. "Oh, yes. Very well."

Clare flitted to the door, Percy circling to stand beside her skirts. Percy was one of the finest of cats, not only a strong protector but also a reliable attack cat upon occasion. She opened the door.

Lightning flashed. A tall, dark figure loomed within its hot light.

"*Eeks!*" Clare jumped. Percy howled.

"Forgive me." The tall, dark figure bowed. "Is this the residence of one Lady Julia Wrexton?"

Clare squinted her eyes and leaned forward. The fig-

ure who had at first appeared to be the grim reaper
was merely a tall, sober gentleman. Embarrassment
overcame Clare. She had screamed in fright, and it
could only offend. The poor man before her surely
could not help it that he looked like an undertaker.
"No, no. Forgive me. Do come in from out of the rain."

"Thank you, madame." The man nodded gravely
and entered the house. A puddle of water immediately
pooled about him, trespassing onto the smooth marble
floor.

"You are here to see Julia, you said?" Clare bustled
to help the visitor with his wet coat. "Are you a suitor
of hers, then?"

"I am fortunate enough not to be, madame."

"I beg your pardon?" Clare froze with his dripping
coat in hand.

The man's lips cracked. Apparently, it was his form
of smiling. "I have heard it is quite hazardous to be a
suitor of hers."

"Gracious," Clare exclaimed, instantly disapproving
of the man. Indeed, his calm, smug look riled Clare as
she rarely was riled. "Why that is . . . poppycock!"

"Meow." Percy abandoned rubbing Clare's skirts
and prowled over to the stranger, shoring himself up
against one spindly leg. Clare blinked. Percy was a loyal
cat, and his sudden desertion was most shocking.

"Is it, madame?" The man, already stiff, pokered up
to an even greater degree. Percy dipped and rubbed
his chin on the man's boot. He sniffed. "We shall wait
and see."

"We, sir?" Clare cocked her head, frowning. "I already know that Julia is not hazardous in any fashion.
Why should I wait to see what I already know?"

"Madame, I only meant . . . *ah . . . choo!*"

"God bless you," Clare said, more from duty than
honesty.

"Meow." Percy stood up on his hind paws and patted the man's knee.

"I meant . . ." The man unbent enough to try and push Percy down. "That . . . *ah* . . . *choo!*"

"God bless you." Clare looked at her favorite feline this time in understanding and gratitude. Percy, the dear kitty, had not deserted her. Indeed, he was engaged in a very clever and devious attack. True to cat instinct, Percy must have divined that this man did not tolerate cats either emotionally or physically and was using it against the annoying human as only a cat can.

The man stood, coming to what appeared attention. "I am Inspector Bloodsoe, officer of the law."

"I see. That is very nice for you, I am sure." Clare smiled and nodded, wondering what else she should say to a man of the law, especially one whose eyes were reddening and tearing so swiftly. Regardless of her disapproval of the man, she could feel slightly sorry for him.

"I am here to interrogate Lady Julia Wrexton."

Maybe she could not feel slightly sorry for him, after all. "Well, Mr. Bloodsoe . . . I am sorry, but Lady Julia is not at home. You will need to interrogate her another time."

"I shall wait for her, madame, if you do not mind." Percy promptly rolled over atop both of the inspector's sodden shoes and squirmed.

"Percy, you shameful cat." A giggle escaped Clare. She then tried for a stern tone. "Do leave the gentleman alone."

"He-he is . . . quite affectionate, is he not?" Inspector Bloodsoe asked.

"Yes, he is." Clare's spirits rose. If there must be an inspector wanting to see Julia, it would be best if he were a slow top. She smiled kindly. "Pray, do come into the library to dry off. There is a fire there." Bendford always enjoyed a fire on chilled or wet days. In that manner he was very much like the cats he so abhorred.

Clare turned away. She did not fear if the inspector followed her. She could hear his pained voice directly behind her. "Nice kitty, nice kitty, nice kitty."

Clare did glance back once to see just what made Percy a nice kitty. The feline had wrapped himself like a muff about Inspector Bloodsoe's one leg. The undertaker-cum-inspector was doing his best to drag him along with proper form and dignity.

Clare turned away quickly and opened the library doors. She drifted into the room. "Bendford?" A snore arose from the large chair by the fire. "Bendford?"

"*Grr—humph.* What? What?" Lord Wrexton started up from a doze, the daily newspaper spread across his knees. He squinted. "For God's sake, what is it, Clare?"

"This gentleman needs to dry beside the fire. He is quite wet. I thought you two could enjoy each other's company. Perhaps you two might share a brandy while he waits for Julia to return. He wishes to interrogate her. He is under the impression that Julia is hazardous."

"What!" Lord Wrexton's brows snapped down at a fractious slant. He rarely awoke from a nap in a good humor. "What did you say?"

"Er, I do not drink." Investigator Bloodsoe said in a stifled voice as he trailed in, his furry anchor still attached to his boot.

"He is not one of her suitors." Clare added for clarification. "And he believes he is fortunate that he is not."

"Balderdash," Lord Wrexton growled. "Anyone would be fortunate to be Julia's suitor. The man must be dicked in the nob."

"No, he truly does not wish to be her suitor. It is strange, for Julia is so charming. But this is what he says." Clare was feeling better by the moment. The man was merely confused and needed Bendford to set him straight. "I see, that is why he wishes to interrogate her."

"Clare, this is rot." Lord Wrexton's voice was belligerent. "He does not need to interrogate Julia. She has done nothing wrong."

"I have already told him that. Only I said poppycock." Clare turned back to Inspector Bloodsoe. His pale skin had actually gained color; a tumescent blue shade. Percy had now unrolled himself and was performing a serpentine pattern around and between the man's legs. "Please, do sit down, Mr. Bloodsoe."

Mr. Bloodsoe, sniffing and wheezing, marched across the room. He lowered himself into a chair with precision. Except for a slight flinch, he did not respond as Percy pounced into his lap.

"No, blast it, do not sit down." Lord Wrexton slapped his paper and glared. "I do not want your company."

"Bendford," Clare said, concerned. "He is quite wet. Do share your fire with him. We do not wish for him to catch his death while he waits for Julia."

"Thank you, madame," Inspector Bloodsoe sniffed.

"Permit me to go and order Ruppleton to prepare tea for you, Inspector Bloodsoe, since you do not drink." After her own courageous but dismal foray into that arena herself, Clare could not help but respect the inspector in that one regard. Furthermore, no woman with a heart, and Aunt Clare had a large one, would not have it wrung by his puffy, red-eyed look. Leaving him with Bendford would be enough punishment.

"Come, Percy," Clare said firmly. Percy meowed. "I know, and I appreciate it, but do come with me." Percy stood and bounded from the man. "I shall return. It may take a moment. Ruppleton is preparing the kitties' food."

Clare drifted out of the library, intent upon her good intentions. She had not cleared the door, however, when some nagging instinct made her stop to listen.

"Why are you investigating Julia?" Lord Wrexton's voice was gruff. "She has done nothing wrong."

"I am here to investigate the allegations that Lady Julia Wrexton has been involved in the criminal act of . . . er, disposing of her fiancés. Whether by abduction or foul play to be determined."

"Balderdash," Lord Wrexton roared.

"That is to be determined as well, my lord."

"Leave my house! How dare you spew such . . . such . . ."

"Poppycock? *Achoo!*"

"Yes, confound it!"

"If it is, I will discover it, make no doubt." Inspector Bloodsoe's voice was calm. "I will await Lady Julia. Unless you wish to fall under suspicion of obstructing the Crown's investigation, you will permit me to do so. You will also oblige me by answering such questions as I will have for you."

Gracious. Clare's head pounded in double time, and the last vestiges of mercy fled her. Percy had read the situation far better then she. Things were grave indeed if an undertaker-inspector would dare order Bendford about. It would not do, not a bit.

"Very well." Lord Wrexton fell back into his chair. He had not navigated the political waters all these years for nothing. He had learned some patience. Still, the thought of a pale, weepy-eyed fellow with a Friday face daring to interrogate his Julia was the outside of enough. In truth, it was enough to make one split one's spleen. "Fire them off."

"Are you aware that your daughter was engaged to six men in a very short amount of time? And that they have all disappeared without a trace?"

"Of course I am aware that my daughter was engaged to six men," Lord Wrexton said tersely. "What type of hoyden do you think my daughter is that she would accept a proposal without my knowledge?"

"I do not wish to insinuate—"

"Good." Lord Wrexton cut the fellow Bloodsoe short. "My daughter's reputation is spotless and has always been so. She is not some romantic widgeon taken in by every town buck. Her character has always been upstanding and proper. Gads, I do not understand the brouhaha. My Julia finally saw the light, decided not to sit on the shelf, and went out to nab herself a husband. That ain't a criminal offense."

"My lord"—Inspector Bloodsoe voice held more than a tinge of surprise—"she nabbed six men within the course of a sennight!"

"I know what you are thinking." Lord Wrexton shook a finger at the inspector. "You think just because my Julia lost six fiancés, she is a jilt, but she cannot be one. Those fellows withdrew first." His tone was triumphant. "It is they who did not come up to scratch."

"My lord, they did not come up to scratch because they have disappeared. Vanished." Inspector Bloodsoe's puffy eyes slayed to the right as a cat entered the room and made its way over to him. "You have another cat."

"Yes, yes. That is another thing." Lord Wrexton continued his grievance. "Many girls get jilted, and it is not a nine-day wonder. None of *them* are branded as a Black Widow." He frowned. "Blast it, Romeo, stop licking the man's face. I am talking to him."

"Achoo!" Inspector Bloodsoe sneezed directly into Romeo's face. It made no difference to the feline. He licked him again. "My lord, it does not appear that they have disappeared of their own volition. The circumstances—" Inspector Bloodsoe lost his words for another moment. He pushed back into his chair as a Persian cat slinked into the room and slithered toward him. "Another one?"

"Ignore the creature. It is the best advice I can give."

"I shall try," Inspector Bloodsoe murmured as the Persian leapt to the back of the chair and began preening his hair. "The . . . the circumstances are too unusual. It cannot be a coincidence . . . *achoo!* Not another one!"

"Hmm, Doubting Thomas." Lord Wrexton frowned.

"If you wish to call me so, yes-*choo!*"

"No, no, that is the cat's name. Of course it is coincidence; that is what I am trying to tell you. Or human nature. Women lure men into proposing every day. The men do it, they lose their nerve, and they light out. There is nothing strange about that."

"But . . . *sniff* . . . six?"

"One? six? Why should numbers count? I am sure there are more than a hundred men every month cutting out on their promises. Ha. Go investigate that. And you are wrong. It shows what kind of investigator you are. Those men did not disappear in suspicious ways." Lord Wrexton's temper flared high. "Do you think I did not question around? I will have you know that I love my daughter. Of course I sent my man to inquire each time. The findings were all disappointing, but not uncommon, I tell you. The marquess of Hambledon got ape-drunk and lit out of town. Beresford met up with a straw damsel and took off to some love nest . . ."

"My lord, that information can only be considered speculation and hearsay."

"Hearsay? Rot. What I would call hearsay is you toodling out here on some poor demented woman's complaint." Lord Wrexton narrowed his gaze. "Because you do not need to tell me who began this totty-headed investigation. Mildred Danford got her nose out of joint last night and won't admit her son's a jilt, and that is that."

Inspector Bloodsoe did not appear impressed or surprised. "This is not based upon just one woman's complaint, demented or otherwise. There are women involved, plural. *Achoo.*"

"Women, then. That only doubles it as hearsay."

"*Achooo! Achooo!*"

"Ah! So you gentlemen are having a nice chat. Here is the tea." Clare bustled into the room. Ruppleton followed behind her, carrying a large silver service. Directly behind, Percy and a band of six other cats followed.

Ruppleton walked over to the table and set the tray upon it. He bowed and left. Clare found the chair next to the tea service and sat. The cats found positions around and upon Bloodsoe and did the same.

Lord Wrexton stared. "You have a way with the little monsters. I detest them myself."

"Bendford," Aunt Clare said, her face reproachful.

"Well, I do." Lord Wrexton shifted in his chair irately. "Is this not their luncheon time? What the devil are they doing down here?"

"I had Ruppleton delay feeding them in order that he could prepare Inspector Bloodsoe's tea first." Clare smiled beatifically. "I realized it was the only proper thing to do."

"It was . . . *sniff* . . . not necessary, mad—*choo*," Inspector Bloodsoe said.

"I thought it was," Clare said with sincerity. "Now, what part of the discussion have I missed?"

Lord Wrexton growled. "This blighter—"

"Inspector, dear," Clare corrected. "He told me so."

"Very well," Lord Wrexton said in exasperation. "He is calling me a liar." There was a sneeze. "And he has the brass to insinuate that Julia is a hussy . . ."

"Inspector Bloodsoe." Clare shook her head in reproach. "First you think Julia hazardous, and now you think her a hussy. You should be ashamed of yourself. You do not know her. She is a dear."

"He also thinks, for some demn fool reason, Julia did something criminal to make her suitors disappear." Lord Wrexton snorted. "As if any girl wants to be shown to be jilted that many times."

"My lord, I see that we are not making any progress in this direction." Inspector Bloodsoe shifted as Doubting Thomas burrowed to his left side. He sneezed and scratched at his neck, this while Romeo scratched in his hair. "Perhaps . . . perhaps I may look around the—the premises while I wait."

"What?" Lord Wrexton stared. "Do you take me for a looby. It will be a cold day in hell when I let you do that."

"My lord!" Inspector Bloodsoe sprang up. Two sneezes wracked him. "If Miss Julia is as innocent as you claim, it would not matter if I surveyed the premises."

"But it does matter." Enraged, Lord Wrexton stood slowly, his gaze black upon the inspector. "Because this is my house and I do not like you, sirrah. I do not appreciate your insinuations about my daughter and your insults to me. Survey the premises indeed. Just what for, I ask? Do you think Julia has hid her suitors in the wine cellar or someplace?"

"Oh, merciful heavens no, Bendford!" Clare visibly shivered. "What a dreadful notion. There are spiders and rats down there."

"According to Inspector Bloodsoe," Lord Wrexton said bitterly, "they would be dead, so what would it matter. And there better be no rats. My best wines are down there. I don't want them turning those bottles before its time."

Clare gasped and looked to the inspector. "Dead. You think they are dead?"

"I do not mean to alarm you, madame . . ." Inspector Bloodsoe began scratching himself.

"Then why are you saying such alarming things?" Aunt Clare asked, bewildered. "To suggest that anyone has been murdered is quite alarming and most unkind, I believe. It is important to always wish the best for people, do you not think?"

"I am sorry, madame." Inspector Bloodsoe had the grace to blush. Though it may have merely been the rash, which was forming on his neck. "It must always be considered when a person disappears and is not seen or heard from for an extended period of time."

"You mean, it must be considered when a person with power is hysterical enough to declare it so," Lord Wrexton said, his tone derisive.

"I am confused." Clare shook her head.

"Ha. I never thought I would say it," Lord Wrexton admitted. "But you are not, Clare. It is all nonsense."

"Thank heaven," Clare sighed.

"I cannot look at it that way. *Achoo.*" Inspector Bloodsoe's tone held the smallest hint of regret. His face settled then, however, into formal lines. "I must investigate this case."

"Well, do what you must do." Lord Wrexton grinned wickedly. "But do not think you will be poking your long nose about my house today. You will have to come back with someone higher in authority than you if you wish for that privilege. My title may not be marquess, but I have just as much political power, I warn you."

"Bendford," Clare murmured, biting her lip. "Perhaps we should permit the inspector to discover the truth for himself. We do not want Julia under suspicion."

"Balderdash," Lord Wrexton said stoutly. "She will not remain under suspicion for long. It is all just a brouhaha and nothing more."

"My lord, six titled men are missing and hold one thing in common. They are all connected with your daughter. It is not a mere brouhaha. I am considered the best there is. They do not send me out over brouhahas!" Inspector Bloodsoe sneezed. "Things will go much better for your daughter if you do not resist me."

Lord Wrexton drew himself up in anger. "I am not resisting you. I am simply telling you no."

"Inspector." Clare's face was diffident. "The kitties and I shall show you. I do not want Julia in trouble."

"Clare!" Lord Wrexton stared at his sister, shocked. "What the devil is the matter with you? I told the man no, and I mean it."

Clare visibly trembled, but she looked at the inspector with determination. "I am sorry, Inspector. Perhaps the kitties and I will show you about at another time, after you and Bendford cry pax with each other."

Bendford snorted. "Ha! Not bloody likely."

"I assure you we would not want you to think that Julia was hiding anything. Especially dead grooms. Isn't that right, kitties?" Aunt Clare asked. The cats chimed their sincerity.

Inspector Bloodsoe reared back. "Er, yes. Please inform Lady Julia that I must and will speak to her."

He all but bolted from the room.

"Well, would you look at that?" Lord Wrexton shook his head. "The man has no backbone."

"True, Bendford," Aunt Clare nodded. "But he does have allergies."

"Ha!" Lord Wrexton rubbed his hands together. "Did you see? I routed the old stick right properly."

Even Clare, who rarely was attentive enough to catch the nuances of life, smiled and nodded. "So you did, Bendford. So you did."

Julia and Garth entered the house. She felt like crying, which was ridiculous. She and Garth had debated all the morning over who might be involved in the disappearance of her grooms to no good purpose. That and the fact that Julia had refused to order a ruby dress he had taken a liking toward.

"Faith, we still do not have one single, solitary suspect upon our list." She fought down the panic. "This morning has been futile. Completely futile."

Garth grinned. "It wouldn't have been if you had ordered that ruby dress."

Julia clasped her hands together. They trembled. "Do cease about the dress. It was what a strumpet would sport. I refuse to be Haymarket ware for you or anyone else."

"What?" Garth's brows climbed high. Then he stilled, his gaze searching. "What is the matter, Julia?"

"Nothing. Nothing at all." Blinking rapidly, Julia looked away. She was exhausted. She had dreamed a nightmare for each of her seven grooms last night. "Only there are more important matters to attend to than fashion at the moment. I need no suggestions about my wardrobe. I need suggestions about who might have abducted my grooms."

Astonishment crossed Garth's face. "My God, Jules. You are frightened, aren't you?"

"What if I am?" Julia lifted her gaze and her chin in defiance.

"What if you are?"

"Yes. What if I am?"

Garth's eyes darkened. "You have nothing to be afraid of, Julia."

"Don't I?" Julia clenched her teeth. If there was one thing worse than admitting one was frightened, it was to have the platitude "that she had no reason" thrown at her. "Don't I, Garth? With the best of my heart I would like to believe that the seven men I became engaged to all went missing by coincidence. I would even prefer to believe that they all jilted me." She laughed dryly. "Two weeks ago I did not think I could live with that humiliation. Now I would gladly live with it. It would be better than thinking . . . that someone wanted to keep me from marrying so badly that they abducted my grooms. At least I pray to God they merely abducted them. If I thought that . . . that these men w-were killed because of me, I . . . I could not live with myself."

"Whatever happens, you will live with yourself." Garth placed his hands to her shoulders. His look was fierce. "You are strong and will survive. No, bedamn, you will overcome it, not just survive. What has happened, whatever it may be, is not your fault."

"Truly?"

"Truly," Garth said softly. "You do not need to be frightened. You will not be alone, Julia. I am here. We can face this together."

A knot formed in Julia's throat, choking her. How she wanted to believe that, yet her heart cried out that she could not. For too many years Garth had not been there. Too many years she had been alone.

"You can trust me, Julia," Garth said, almost as if he knew her thoughts.

Lord, the tears were going to fall. Julia looked away from him. "Forgive me. I am sorry for being such a . . .

a goose. But I do not know what to do. I-I cannot control this."

"No, you cannot. But Julia, you do not need to control everything."

"Don't I?" Julia forced a chuckle and stepped back. He was wrong. She did need to have control. As a young, motherless girl she had learned that. Fear and loneliness could overpower you. Especially when you had no mother, your father was a busy statesman, and the boy you trusted to be your confidant had grown up and left you. Then you learned that the only way to conquer fear and loneliness was to have control. Except then the need to control became overpowering.

Julia shook her head. She did not know from where that stray thought had sprung. She glanced up.

Garth stood still, a naked sadness within his hazel eyes. "Were did it go wrong, Julia? What happened to us?"

"We grew up?" Julia fought for a light tone. It took all of her effort. "That is all."

"There you children are!" Aunt Clare scurried forward from out of the library. She halted abruptly, her face hesitant. "Oh, dear. You are not fighting, are you?"

"No." Julia said quickly. "No, of course not."

"Thank heaven. We have no time for that." Aunt Clare's hands all but fluttered with alarm. "You will never imagine what has happened."

Julia forced a laugh. "I don't know. Right now my imagination is running amok quite handsomely, thank you."

"What?"

"Pay her no heed, Aunt Clare." Garth's smile looked as forced as her own. "We were not fighting. Honestly."

Aunt Clare blushed. "Honesty is a mysterious thing, is it not?"

"I beg your pardon?" Garth asked.

"You can say what is true, but it does not mean it is honest. Or you can say what is honest, but it can be quite untrue at the same time. It always confuses me. Is it better to be honest or tell the truth? Faith, it makes one's head hurt so frightfully, especially today." She gasped. "Oh, dear, forgive me. I am rambling. It just seems that so many things are happening at such a galloping pace. I do not know what I should do or not do. Like that visit from Inspector Bloodsoe."

"What?" Garth frowned.

"Inspector Bloodsoe." Aunt Clare nodded her head. "He came to interrogate Julia."

"What!" Julia exclaimed. "Why?"

"He thinks that you had something to do with your grooms' disappearance."

"No!" Julia gasped. "Impossible."

"I told him poppycock." Aunt Clare nodded. "Your father said balderdash."

"I quite agree." Garth's eyes were grim. "It is hogwash."

"Hogwash." Aunt Clare murmured, as if testing the word. "Yes. That feels good. Hogwash!"

"What happened?" Julia asked directly, fearful that her aunt would digress to something even more fanciful.

Aunt Clare jumped. Her gaze became refocused and very worried. "Inspector Bloodsoe wished to wait for you. Then he wished to search the house."

"Heavens." Julia paled. "He is that serious?"

"Is it so very bad?" Aunt Clare's hand rose to her heart.

"Of course it is not." Garth's tone was firm and comforting. "Do not worry so, Aunt Clare. This will all come about directly."

"That is what I keep reminding myself," Aunt Clare nodded. "One must merely be strong."

"Yes," Julia said. "That is so very true."

"And brave?" Aunt Clare asked.

"Indeed." Garth smiled. "And that is honest."

Aunt Clare looked down. She appeared to tremble. She dug in her pocket to help out an envelope. "In that case, Julia, I must show you this. It was slipped beneath the front door. I do not know how it appeared. Ruppleton at the time was not available. It is addressed to you."

Frowning, Julia took the letter and opened it. Aunt Clare stood upon tiptoe to see what was written. Instinct caused Julia to hide the words. When she read the missive, she knew why.

"If you wish to receive information in regard to your missing grooms, come to Vauxhall. The stone bench in Nimue's Grotto, off Druid's Walk. Ten o'clock."

Julia frowned. A crude map had been supplied showing her the exact bench she was to visit.

"Do read it aloud, dearest." Aunt Clare all but hopped up and down.

"What drivel is this?" Garth murmured.

Julia started. She had forgotten that with his height he had an eagle's eye view from over her shoulder. "I did not invite you to read this, did I?"

"No, you did not." Garth grinned unrepentantly. Then he shook his head. "It is clear someone is attempting to pull a prank on you."

"Prank?" Aunt Clare gasped. "Oh, no. Why do you think that?"

"This 'informant' wishes for Julia to go to Vauxhall Gardens." Garth laughed. "I assure you, Aunt Clare, a real informant would not suggest such a place."

"Indeed?" Julia asked cooly. She folded the missive swiftly. "I am sorry, but I think it is serious."

"Gammon," Garth frowned. "It is tommyrot, pure and simple."

"Why?" Aunt Clare actually slipped the letter from Julia. She unfolded it and read it, her lips pursing in concentration. "Why do you think it tommyrot?"

"I am sure you are not intending to go tonight, Julia." Garth's tone was so firm as to leave little room for argument.

Julia immediately advanced into that small space. "I most certainly am. You may be as derisive as you wish, but I am not going to pass up the chance to discover what happened to my grooms no matter how far-fetched it sounds."

"I do not think it sounds far-fetched at all," Aunt Clare said vigorously.

Garth rolled his eyes. "For God's sake, Julia, use your head."

"Thank you," Julia said, her voice clipped. "At least you concede I have a head; a moment ago you were insinuating I lacked that much."

Garth shrugged. "How can I not insinuate such? It is clear you are not thinking straight at the moment."

Julia stiffened. She had let her guard down and admitted her vulnerability. Now he was casting it back in her teeth. "I believe I am, sirrah."

"Do not lend yourself to this hoax, Julia."

"You do not know it is a hoax. I do not consider it unreasonable to assume that *someone* knows *something* about six men who have disappeared. If they wish to tell me, so much the better. It is not as if I have a plethora of ideas myself."

"Serious people do not draw maps and command an appointment at Vauxhall," Garth said curtly. "It makes no sense."

"Neither does my six fiancés' disappearance. I am going." Julia offered him a stolid look. She'd not show her weakness to him again. "You do not have to go if you do not wish to do so. I would not want you to tax yourself too much."

Garth stiffened and glowered down at her. "You do not want me to attend?"

Julia looked away. She would not lay herself open to the disappointment of his desertion. "I would rather go by myself than have you pinching at me all night."

"Very well." A cord stood out along Garth's neck. "Your wish is my command."

"What?" Aunt Clare exclaimed. "But Garth, you must go with her. You simply must."

"Why?" Garth asked. "She clearly does not need me."

"But . . . but it could be . . . dangerous." Aunt Clare blinked. "Very dangerous. You are supposed to be her protector."

"Protector?" Julia snorted. She conscientiously ignored the anger that flared in Garth's eyes. "I can very well take care of myself. I do not need a protector, especially one who is so much against the notion."

Nodding, Julia turned and marched away. She stopped when she was a short distance from them but out of sight. She needed to regain her equilibrium. Would Garth truly have come if she had said something else?

"Garth, dearest," she heard Aunt Clare say. "You must not permit Julia to go alone."

"You heard her," Garth replied. "She does not need me. Besides, it is nothing but a prank. If Julia wishes to waste her time wandering the gardens, she may. Nothing transpires there but liaisons and dalliance. Why would someone ask her to meet there of all places?"

"I do not know. What do you think would be a good reason?"

"It might be a thwarted lover," Garth's voice speculated.

"Good gracious!"

"Someone who wishes to lure her into a . . . secluded place to . . . have their way with her."

"Oh, dear, that is far too unpleasant a thought," Aunt Clare exclaimed. "Surely it might be for some other reason? Perhaps it is a friend who wishes to help."

"Asking her to meet them at night in Vauxhall? Not likely."

Julia shook herself and hurried away. Faith, but it never paid to eavesdrop. She could not stop the chill that ran down her spine. Wisdom told her to withdraw. Stubbornness demanded she go.

Stubbornness, unfortunately, had always been her long suit.

Eight

Julia hastened down the darkened path, her voluminous Spanish velvet cloak swirling about her, her hands buried in its deep pockets. Fortunately, there was a full moon tonight, and the silver of it spilled upon the path richly. It lacked but a few minutes to ten o'clock. The sound of the Vauxville revelers was distant. This secluded area of the gardens Julia had always refused to enter. The dark walks. The place for rendezvous and secret assignations.

She would meet her informant, to be sure, but he would be wise to be on his best behavior or he would regret it. She refused, of course, to believe she would be in any real danger. If she were, however, she was prepared.

"Julia!" A voice called from behind.

Julia froze. Relief flooded her, but she squelched it. Turning slowly, she widened her eyes in feigned innocence. "Garth, what on earth are you doing here?"

"You know very well what I am doing here." Annoyance stamped Garth's features. "I am here to assist you in this fool's errand."

"Indeed?" Julia cooed. "Thank you very much. But I do not wish you to assist me. It is my fool's errand, and you may stay out of it."

"No!" Garth strode up to her and clasped her arm. Julia tensed. "I have been thinking. Aunt Clare might very well be right. Faith, I cannot believe I just said that. But you might be in danger."

"How could that be possible? It is surely a prank; you said so." Julia lifted her chin. "Besides, I am perfectly able to protect myself." Garth's cynical look raised Julia's hackles. "Now, if you will release me, I have an appointment to keep."

"Not without me," Garth said grimly.

"Yes, without you." Julia waved a hand. "Now do go and find your own corner of the garden."

"Julia, try to be reasonable." Garth sighed out utter exasperation. "Let us not stand here all night arguing."

A shriek rent the night, high-pitched and definitely feminine.

"Agreed!" Julia jerked her arm from Garth's slackened grasp. Spinning, she dashed down the path toward the scream. If she was not mistaken, it was very close to the spot marked upon the map, the very spot where she should be if Garth had not waylaid her.

"Demn!" Garth's curse sounded directly behind her.

Julia broke into a small clearing. She was right! There was the stone bench marked on the map. Beside it was a woman, a woman screaming. There was also a man, his arms tight about her. Clearly, he was accosting her. Julia's heart raced. That might have been her instead.

"Release her, sirrah!" Julia whipped her hand from her pocket and raised the coach pistol she had been hiding. Her hand shook frightfully.

"Egads!" It steadied as the man jumped back, a horrified look upon his face. His arms shot up into the air. "D-d-on't shoot. P-please, don't shoot."

The woman, evidently of the slow-witted variety, did not seize her moment to escape. Instead, she gaped at Julia, clutching something to her.

"You may run," Julia said kindly.

"N-no!" Most unreasonably and inanely, the woman shrieked. She then spiraled to the ground in a dead faint. Julia shook her head sadly. Apparently relief had overwhelmed the poor soul. Some women were like that.

"Good Lord, Julia." Panting, Garth drew up beside her. "Do be careful with that, will you?"

"I told you I could protect myself." Julia leveled a piercing gaze upon the man before her, her informant, no doubt. He was short, balding, and dressed like a country squire. Gracious, but looks could be deceiving. "Now, sir, we are going to end this game."

"No. You'll not kill again!" A man darted from out of the shadows. Indeed, he appeared a shadow himself, a sickly shadow. He lurched at Julia, rapping her pistol wrist smartly. Julia cried out as the pistol flew from her grasp. She wished she could join the woman who had fainted as the pistol exploded its shot. The very woods shouted and screeched. The astounding crescendo actually winnowed down into a cat's howl.

"What?" Julia was greatly confused over the cat's howl.

"You are coming with me," the stranger declared. His painful grip on Julia's wrist made it a likely possibility that she would.

"Unhand her!" Garth sprang upon the stranger. The battle was uncontested. The cadaverous man's hold on Julia was broken so swiftly as to make her head spin. Garth pinned him to the ground in the next moment. He lifted his fist, and Julia closed her eyes tightly. Garth was known to be handy with his fives and had once floored Gentleman Jackson.

"Garth, dear, please do not." The voice came from another shadow to the right.

Julia's eyes snapped open. They might as well have been closed, for she was certain she was dreaming.

Aunt Clare stood there. She held Percy close in her arms. His ears were laid back, and he appeared very unhappy with the entire affair. Ruppleton hovered behind Aunt Clare, his face no more pleased.

Garth froze, staring. "Aunt Clare? What are you doing here?"

"I came to help, Julia. I was afraid you were not going to come." Aunt Clare bustled over. She beamed at him. "But you did, and my, what a wonderful protector you are. Though I think you should not strike Inspector Bloodsoe if you can resist it. I believe the poor gentleman is confused."

"He is not the only one." Garth shook his head as if to clear it.

"So that is who you are?" Frowning darkly, Julia stepped forward and bent to study the prone gentleman. "Did you write the letter, then?"

"Letter?" Inspector Bloodsoe wheezed, no doubt affected by the weight of Garth upon his bony chest. "I wrote no letter. I am here to apprehend you."

"What?" Julia exclaimed.

"Like bloody hell you are," Garth growled.

"Garth, dear, perhaps you could permit the inspector to stand." Aunt Clare cocked her head to an angle.

"I do not particularly see why I should."

"You are obstructing justice," Inspector Bloodsoe bleated.

"No, it is not that," Aunt Clare said. "It is just that I find it very difficult to converse with a man from this position, or might it be his position instead, but either way, it makes me quite dizzy."

Garth stared at her. He then peered at the inspector. A laugh escaped him. "In that case, of course, Aunt Clare."

Garth stood. Inspector Bloodsoe rose far more

slowly. He sneezed. "Madame, do you always bring your cats with you?"

"Indeed not. Except for Percy, that is. He is such a fine companion and generally of great assistance." An odd gurgling sound came from Julia's forgotten culprit. They all spun to look at him. He was crouched beside the fainted woman.

"You did not escape?" Julia's brows shot up in surprise. "Faith, but you are full of brass."

"Julia dearest." Aunt Clare reproved.

"I-I am s-sorry." The man paled but maintained his position. "I-I will not leave m-my wife n-no matter what you do."

"Wife?" Julia gasped.

"You are married?" Inspector Bloodsoe asked. "You cannot be."

"But I am." The man cringed back. "For a year now, in fact. Th-this is our anniversary."

"Oh, Gads!" Garth barked a laugh. "Julia, you spoilsport."

"But I did not know," Julia objected.

"No, no, it is I who must apologize." Aunt Clare walked over to the pale man. "Or I must apologize for Percy, that is, since he will not. It is against his code as a cat, you understand."

"What does Percy have to do with this?" Julia asked, bewildered.

"He was very naughty, I am sad to say. He pounced upon the poor lady and startled her frightfully."

A mortified flush rose to Julia's cheeks. She looked at her culprit, now turned victim. "That is why she was screaming?"

"Y-yes." Fear showed in the man's eyes. He absently lifted his wife's hand and began patting it. "Phyllis has a dread of animals. She—she becomes rather hysterical around them, I fear."

"I thought you were attacking her."

Garth grinned. "Julia is a strong believer in rendering aid to strangers at all times. Even if they do not need or wish it."

"Strangers?" Inspector Bloodsoe frowned so severely that his sneeze was barely audible. "Sir, who are you?"

"Archibald Billingsgate," the man said.

"Archibald Billingsgate, I am Inspector Bloodsoe. I am an officer for the Crown. I demand the truth." He pointed to Julia in a dramatic manner. It was similar to having the grim reaper signal one out personally. "Do you know this lady here?"

"No, I do not!" Archibald's look toward Julia made it clear that he did not wish to, either.

Inspector Bloodsoe cast Julia a suspicious frown. "You say you do not know him?"

"For goodness' sakes, of course not. If I had known him, I would not have thought he was attacking his wife, in which event I would not then have felt it necessary to save her. I do not go about drawing a pistol upon just anyone, I will have you know." Julia gasped. "My stars, but that is what you think, is it not? You thought *I* was attacking Archibald? You thought that I wanted to shoot him?"

"You little weasel," Garth growled. "You have been trailing Julia!"

Inspector Bloodsoe drew himself up with dignity, wounded dignity to be sure, but dignity nevertheless. "Sir, I attempted to meet Lady Julia in an open manner this very day. I was driven from the house for my efforts."

"Oh, dear," Aunt Clare worried her lip. "I had hoped you had not felt it to such a degree. Bendford cannot help his temper, I fear."

"Madame, it was not your brother who drove me

from the house." Inspector Bloodsoe delivered his words crisply. "It was your cats."

"Was it?" Aunt Clare's eyes widened. Percy snarled. "Oh, dear . . ."

"Do not heed the man, Aunt Clare," Garth soothed.

"Indeed not," Julia said, quite wroth. "He thinks that I would kill a man in cold blood. Here at Vauxhall Gardens, at that."

"Madame, you have had six fiancés, and all have disappeared under curious circumstances." Inspector Bloodsoe swung his finger toward Archibald. "I feared that he was your seventh prey."

"Prey!" Julia shrieked.

"Me!" Archibald squeaked. "No, no. I am married to Phyllis. I could not be anyone's fiancé now. Phyllis would never permit it." He flushed. "S-so you see, I cannot be anyone's prey." He ceased patting his wife's hand. He moved to pat her face, rather briskly in fact. "Darling. Wake up. Phyllis, wake up, now! We must go."

"Hmm . . . ouch!" Phyllis shot up as if rising from the dead.

"Hello, dear. Are you all right?" Aunt Clare asked kindly. Percy hissed. "Did your little rest make you feel better?"

Phyllis's blurred eyes widened. She cringed back into Archibald's arms. "That cat! There is that nasty, dreadful cat that attacked me."

"Yes, dear, I know." Archibald hauled Phyllis up as if she were a sack of potatoes. "Please do not ask questions. We must leave now."

"Madame, pray, do forgive me," Julia stepped forward.

"Archibald! There is that woman!" Phyllis cried out even more loudly. "That woman who held you up!"

"I didn't mean to," Julia objected.

"Yes, dear, now come," Archibald said. "I will explain later."

"Oh, oh, it is all too much." Phyllis appeared to crumble.

"Yes, dear, but come." Archibald ruthlessly pulled her up and dragged her away. "No time to faint now."

"But Archibald . . ."

"You may faint later, dear. I might join you."

Julia, flushing, looked down in embarrassment. Then she gasped, her eyes widening. Now she knew what Phyllis had clutched to her. The discovery was very lowering. "Phyllis! Archibald! Your champagne. You have left your champagne."

"No! No!" Archibald's voice drifted back.

"Archibald . . ." Phyllis's voice was plaintiff. "I could use . . ."

"Phyllis, dear, be quiet," Archibald was heard to say. "We are going back to Little Dippington . . ."

"But that cat . . ."

"We will never visit London again, I vow."

"And that woman . . ."

"It is a strange, wicked place."

"Dear me." Aunt Clare sighed. "I fear we have destroyed their anniversary night." She looked down at Percy. "And it was your fault, dear. I begged you to behave and to leave the matter alone." Percy's meow was rather satisfied. "No, you should have listened to me."

"As much as I do not wish to support a cat," Inspector Bloodsoe said in a stern voice, "I will say that it is not his fault as much as Lady Julia's."

"Mine?" Julia lifted her chin. "I will admit to some of it. But your attack upon me did not help matters, either."

"Madame," Inspector Bloodsoe said, "I was not attacking you. I was apprehending you."

"You're manner could have fooled me. Charging neck-or-nothing out of the bushes as you did." Julia said scornfully.

"You did fool *me*," Garth grinned.

"You were making threats upon a man with a firearm." Inspector Bloodsoe said stiffly. "My actions were well within the line of duty."

"So were mine." Julia smiled most sweetly.

"I beg your pardon?" Inspector Bloodsoe glared.

"I consider my duty to be the same as yours, Inspector Bloodsoe. You followed me in hopes of discovering what happened to my seven suitors."

"There are but six."

"Yes, that is what I meant. Six suitors," Julia corrected quickly. "And I came here to discover the same thing."

"Here?" Inspector Bloodsoe sniffed.

"Yes. I received a note that if I wished for information in regard to my missing grooms, I should present myself here at ten o'clock."

Inspector Bloodsoe stared. "My lady, I am no fool."

"I beg your pardon?" Julia gasped. "I am quite serious."

"It is far too ridiculous."

"Why should it be so ridiculous?" Aunt Clare asked. "I still do not understand why?"

"No one meets here in this particular place except for reasons of an unsavory nature." Inspector Bloodsoe sneezed. "I suspect that is exactly what you came here for, madame, a liaison. A lethal one, to be sure, for you carried a pistol. What a devious mind you have."

"Faith." Garth shook his head with awe. "You are beside the bridge on that one. Julia would never make up to a man so that she could shoot him. She does not hold with roundaboutation. If she wanted to shoot a man, she would do it point-blank, without dalliance."

"Thank you for your support," Julia gritted.

"Anytime."

Julia turned her glare upon Inspector Bloodsoe. "I carried the pistol because, like you, sir, I had decided the message I received might be a ploy. The writer of the message might wish me ill. When I heard Phyllis's scream, I feared her attacker might have been somehow involved with me."

"Madame, you cannot distract me with such a far-radiddle." Inspector Bloodsoe sniffed. "It is well known by all that Inspector Bloodsoe never follows red herrings."

"Meow!" Percy said.

"Yes, I know you like herring; we will get some later, dear," Aunt Clare murmured. "But do let the inspector talk."

Inspector Bloodsoe shivered and then straightened. "I *will* discover what happened to your grooms, my lady."

"Please, be my guest," Julia said. "However, if you intend to do so by following me about, be prepared to not only be disappointed but humiliated."

"Humiliated?"

"Yes, because I will discover the truth before you." Julia infused her words with the utmost of confidence.

"Julia has the right of it, you know?" Garth smiled. "Would you care to lay a monkey on us discovering the culprit before you, Inspector Bloodsoe?"

"Never. As a representative of the Crown, it would not behoove me to enter into a gambling venture with not only a citizen but a suspect, at that."

"What?" Garth exclaimed. "Why am I a suspect?"

"It is clear that you are in collaboration with Miss Wrexton here. Your actions against me for her sake make it obvious that you are held within her power."

"Good God," Garth rolled his eyes.

"Within my power?" Julia gasped. "Far from it."

"In that case I am a suspect, too." Aunt Clare marched directly up to Inspector Bloodsoe.

"*Achoo!* Madame, please step back." Investigator Bloodsoe ordered.

"But I am in collaboration with Julia as well if it means that I care for her and believe in her innocence."

"You are not a man," Inspector Bloodsoe said baldly.

"This is very true." Aunt Clare looked at the inspector in a worried manner, as if indeed he was shorted on his wits. "And I never have been. Why do you note it so particularly?"

"Madame." Inspector Bloodsoe returned her look. "This case involves Lady Julia's grooms. They are men."

"Oh." Aunt Clare said, slightly dejected.

"In that case"—Ruppleton stepped forward—"permit me to introduce myself as a suspect as well as Master Garth."

"Who are you?" Inspector Bloodsoe frowned.

"I am Miss Julia's butler," Ruppleton said proudly.

"The butler?" Inspector Bloodsoe's tone showed what he thought of Ruppleton's standing as suspect.

"Indeed, sir," Ruppleton said solemnly. "The butler is notorious for culpability in many devious plots, is he not?"

"I have never found it to be so," Inspector Bloodsoe said, his tone withering.

"I see." Ruppleton was clearly deflated.

Julia realized that two very dear-hearted people were quite hurt that they were not considered worthy enough to be considered suspects by the insufferable Inspector Bloodsoe. "Personally, Inspector, I would put them on a list as suspects myself. Your first qualification was that one must be under my power. Cannot you see that both care about me very much? Surely that means they are in collaboration with me?"

This appeared to enrage the inspector. It was a formidable thing to view what appeared to be an undertaker in an apoplectic fit. "My lady, I have suffered enough of your jests and insults."

"And we yours, Inspector." Garth stepped forward.

"And as for you, my lord," Inspector Bloodsoe said, "I have not apprehended you for attacking a minion of the Crown, but if you attempt to lay so much as a finger on me again, I shall."

"You are in a miff merely because Julia has challenged you," Garth said softly. "And since you are now offering me a challenge, I shall return it. I will not lift a finger against you unless you dare to accost her as you did tonight. Or you make the mistake of harassing her in any way, shape, or form."

"That sufficiently covers it, Master Garth," Ruppleton said in an approving tone.

Julia warmed. Secretly, she thought the same.

"My lord, if I prove her guilty, I will apprehend her."

"We will discuss that if that day ever transpires," Garth said, his eyes alight. "Until then, Bloodsoe . . ."

"I understand, my lord." Inspector Bloodsoe nodded. His face had turned brilliant red, and he ended with an odd choking sound. Julia's eyes widened in question, but he said no more. He simply bowed, and turning, he disappeared into the shadows.

"Gracious," Julia murmured. "We certainly set up his back."

"Do not tax yourself, dearest." Aunt Clare stepped close and patted her arm. "I am sure he will regain his temper and come around again."

Garth snorted. "He will without a doubt. He has not had a moment to interrogate Julia."

"True." Aunt Clare nodded. She beamed. "My,

wasn't this an exciting night? However, I believe that I will have Ruppleton take me home now that I know Garth is here to protect you. I am so very sorry if we interrupted when we ought not have."

"No, no." Julia hugged her aunt with true warmth. "Thank you for attempting to come to my aid. Now do go home. I shall be there directly."

"Yes, dear." Aunt Clare peeked at Garth. "I thought you quite dashing tonight, Garth, dear."

"Do go on with you, sweetheart!" Garth winked at her. "I'll be puffing off my own consequence for the next month if you continue in that vein."

"Then we must go." Giggling, Aunt Clare turned and wandered down the path.

"Good night, Lady Julia and Master Garth." Ruppleton offered a quick bow before chasing after Aunt Clare.

With their leaving, it fell silent, so very different from the clamor and trauma of minutes before. Julia breathed in a deep breath. "Gracious, what an evening." She walked over and sat upon the stone bench.

"Yes." Garth joined her upon the bench.

For a moment they sat in the silence, the silver of the moon bathing them. Julia slowly turned to look into Garth's eyes, wishing to know what he felt. It was there in his eyes, what she herself was feeling.

They laughed in unison.

"Oh, dear me." Julia clasped hold of his arm in her merriment. "What a famous investigator I make."

"True. One day on the case and you've already held a country squire and wife at pistol point."

"And embroiled you with an officer of the Crown." Julia's heart caught a moment. "Do you think you will be able to survive it all?"

"Certainly. You have me within your power, you

know?" Garth smiled widely. "Women who wield fire-arms always impress me."

"Indeed?"

"I like them far better than men with pistols."

"Those jealous lovers." Julia looked sympathetic. "They do cause trouble, do they not?"

"They never seem to understand," Garth agreed with a good-natured grin. He stood and strolled to the forsaken champagne bottle that lay on the path. "Amazing. It is still intact." He picked up the bottle, mischief in his eyes. "We really must do something about this, I believe."

"Indeed, yes. A stabilizing drought would be help-ful."

"Purely medicinal." Smiling like the most wicked of doctors, Garth popped the cork. He walked toward her but then halted. His face lit in satisfaction. "Ha, ha! There are the glasses."

"Where?" Julia looked about. She immediately spied the silver tray upon a silver cart to her back left. It was amazing that she had not noticed it before. Her eyes then shuttered wide. No, what was truly amazing was the array of delicacies upon the cart. There were choco-lates, trifles, and fresh fruits. Two crystal champagne glasses and one long-stemmed red rose topped off the spread. The Billingsgates had indeed planned a roman-tic interlude.

"Heaven!" Julia swallowed hard. "How Byronic. We did destroy a celebration, didn't we?"

"I didn't know old Archibald had it in him." Garth strolled over and picked up the red rose. He ap-proached Julia and bowed. "Our duty is clear, ma-dame."

"What? Must we go and attempt to make Archibald and Phyllis return?"

"No." Garth's eyes glinted in the moonlight. "They

are most likely all the way to Little Dippington by now. No, it is our onus to do justice to it."

Julia hesitated. Then she took the rose, smelling its sweet scent. "I suppose you are right."

"Of course I am." Garth poured the champagne into the glasses.

"Otherwise it will all go to waste."

"Which would be a crime." Garth gave her one of the glasses. The other he raised up. "Here is to . . ."

"Archibald and Phyllis?" Julia laughed.

"No." Garth's smile was gentle as he sat down beside her. "I was going o say, To you, Julia Wrexton, a partner I believe I shall enjoy working with very much. We *are* in this together, my dear Jules."

"Thank you." Julia sipped her champagne quickly to hide her sudden flush of pleasure.

They talked over the day then, laughing and teasing. Time passed, and still they sat drinking the champagne, eating the chocolates and fruits. They talked over the day yet again. An outsider would have become heartily bored, for only the two of them could enjoy reliving the day so minutely or understand those shared moments.

And with that they created new shared moments. Julia would now remember the tilt of Garth's head as he laughed. The moonlight as it shimmered in his hair. The tingle of the champagne as she drank of it. The stars dancing in its depth as she looked in the crystal glass. The aura of the night.

It was romance. Despite anything Garth or Julia did, or did not do, the aura was romance. And that moment arrived, as it was destined to. Garth halted abruptly in the middle of a sentence. Julia had been laughing, but she froze instantly. Her heart waited in anticipation.

He would kiss her. She knew it. It was in his eyes and his face. Julia smiled slightly. The moment was perfect and would be perfect. Tonight, unlike any other night, she not only wanted his kiss but could freely admit to herself of that wanting. Exactly what had changed, she did not know. It might be poor Archibald and Phyllis's champagne mingled with the brilliant moonlight. Or it might be the rekindling of a trust she had thought lost forever.

Julia lowered her gaze before she stared wantonly into Garth's eyes. She suddenly knew the answer. It was not a rekindling of old trust, for that would be a revival of her trust in the boy Garth. It was, rather, a birth of trust, trust in the man Garth. Julia looked up then, swaying toward him without thought.

Something akin to fear entered Garth eyes. He stood and cleared his throat. "Hmm, yes."

Confusion washed over Julia. She shook her head slightly to clear it. She had misread the moment entirely. Garth had not meant to kiss her. It had been the champagne and moonlight only for her. Desperate for a distraction, she glanced at the tray as she rose with dignity. "What should we do with this?"

"I would imagine we should leave it." His tone was odd. Then he smiled wryly. "I may be wrong. Archibald might return for it, after all. The glasses are crystal and the tray silver."

Julia's laugh was self-conscious. "Something tells me you were right the first time. He will not return."

"Your instincts as sleuth tell you this?"

"Heavens, no." Julia grimaced. "I believe I will declare myself off duty in that respect. I have made so many mistakes tonight, it is clear I am severely lacking in that department. And you were right. This was clearly a dreadful hoax tonight."

Garth frowned. "That or our party was frightened off from the commotion we created."

"Perhaps." Julia said it without much belief.

"Come, let us go." Garth held his hand out to Julia. Startled, she looked at him wide-eyed. His smile was purely self-deprecatory. "I know that to kiss you would be out of bounds, but I'll be hanged if I will walk through the dark paths with a beautiful lady and not at least hold her hand. It would destroy my reputation completely."

"Tsk. Tsk. We could not have that happen," Julia said, choking on a laugh.

All the brilliance of the night returned. She held out her hand, and that awaited thrill coursed through her as he intertwined their fingers. Garth *had* wanted to kiss her. She had not been wrong. The entire evening found its purpose. It did not matter that they had been victims of a hoax and were still no closer to discovering the truth.

"I am glad you see it my way." Garth chuckled as they turned to walk hand in hand down the dark path. He appeared quite pleased with himself.

"Indeed," Julia's lips curled in a small smile. She would keep the secret to herself that she would have seen it his way if he had kissed her as well. Pretending to frown in deep concentration, she said, "I do wonder what happened and where my grooms are."

Garth growled. "Tonight I do not care. To perdition with them."

"But you must care." Julia feigned an innocence. "You are a suspect as well."

"I do not care about that, either." Garth grinned without fear or remorse.

"I do hope they are alive and safe," Julia persisted. "*All* of them."

"Would you stop talking about your bloody grooms. Let us just enjoy the evening."

Julia smiled as they continued strolling through the dark, hand in hand. She was already enjoying the eve-

ning. She should feel terribly guilty. seven men, men
who had been her prospective bridegrooms, were missing, and the Lord only knew what fate they might have
suffered, but walking hand in hand with Garth obliter-
ated those fears for the moment. Tomorrow she must
face them again, but not tonight.

"I will raise you," The marquess of Hambledon said
coolly, shoving his chips across the polished table. A
glass of excellent Bordeaux rested beside him.

Lord Mancroft puffed slowly upon his cigar. He
leaned back in a comfortable winged-back chair to consider his hand. The chair was of an unusually bright
red color, as were the other accents in the large room
about them. With wisps of pink gauze, large cushions
of figured satin, and massive, brocaded ottomans
strewn about, the exotic motif was the finest seen in
any bordello. "Very well, I· call."

The marquess flipped over his cards. Lord Mancroft
slapped his own hand down hard upon the table.
"B'gads, Danford, you have the devil's own luck."

"I agree." Lord Beresford nodded from where he
stood, his arms crossed upon Lord Mancroft's chair
back. "That is why I refuse to play one more game with
him. He will not gain one more vowel of mine, I assure
you."

"You said that last night." Lord Redmond grinned
as he took up the deck for the next game.

"And tonight," Lord Viscount Dunn said. "But only
after you went down to him, by how much?"

"I would rather not say." Lord Beresford grimaced.
He tossed back a bumper of brandy and drew up a
vacant chair. "But you can count me in for this one."

The men laughed.

"In that case, I'll not sit this one out, either," Matthew Severs, the earl of Raleigh, drew up his chair, setting his goblet of port upon the table. "Monteith, are you going to join us?"

"No," The earl of Kelsey sat far away from the card table. A candelabrum sat on the curio table beside him. A stack of racing magazines and Latin volumes of various literatures surrounded that. He was clearly enjoying his cigar and a book, which looked large and antiquated. "Though I thank you."

A knocking sounded at the room's door.

"Here they come, men. Watch the drinks now." Matthew Severs grinned. The seven men promptly stood, holding their drinks aloft.

A moment passed. A noise, similar to that of a large bolt being released, sounded. The door swung open. A plague of twelve cats darted into the room. They chased and sprang at the different men, clearly greeting their particular favorites. The men smiled and bowed as a lady entered after the felines.

"Good evening, Aunt Clare!"

Nine

"Hello, dear boys," Aunt Clare greeted effusively as she entered. "Do, do sit."

Since the twelve cats had already jumped upon the chairs or swirled around their particular gentleman, it took cautious moments of brushing cats off and sitting while still holding their glasses high.

Lucas Montieth, the earl of Kelsey, who had already been sitting and now had two cats vying to taste his wine, objected. "Aunt Clare, how can all your cats be lushes?"

"They never were before this, Lucas, I promise you." Aunt Clare sighed. "Only since the advent of you gentlemen into the house have they become so. I fear it was that one singular evening when I . . . I partook of a glass of wine with you gentlemen and I permitted them to do so as well. I only meant for it to be a celebration when Julia and Garth promised each other to work together to find the culprit. And he swore she would learn to trust him. And they both vowed to save each other. It was very effecting." She sighed. "I knew then that all our efforts had been worth it. That there was indeed hope and we needed only to keep them together until . . ." Aunt Clare stared off in a blissful reverie for a moment. "Still," Aunt Clare said with due consideration, "my kitties have but one vice, which they just took up. That is still better than we humans can manage, I believe."

The seven men nodded. Not a one was brave enough to declare that her darlings, especially Percy, harbored a few other vices than drink.

"What happened tonight?" Matthew asked in an obvious bid to change the conversation. "Did the evening go as planned?"

"No. It was a debacle, I fear." Aunt Clare sniffed, and tears welled in her blue eyes. "Quite disappointing."

Murmurs of sympathy permeated the room. Purrs rumbled softly beneath them.

"Tell us what happened, Aunt Clare?" Lucas suggested, his voice gentle.

"I simply do not know where to begin. I believe our mistake was setting out the champagne and repast far too early." Aunt Clare sighed. The sound of the bolt being shot back on the door interrupted her. The door opened, and Ruppleton and Wilson entered.

"Your nightcaps, my lords." Ruppleton carried a tray laden with various bottles and decanters. The men cheered and moved toward him.

"And a midnight tidbit of duck à l'orange." Wilson grinned as he rolled a large cart with silver covers before him.

"Wilson"—Charles leaned forward in eagerness— "will you join us for cards tonight?"

"I will gladly do so once I see the kitchen cleaned, my lord."

"You are making him an extremely rich chef, Danford." Matthew laughed.

"He is the only man I have never beat," Charles admitted without a flinch. "It is a rare pleasure."

"Yes, but that must wait." Lucas waved his hand, his

gaze firm. "Ruppleton, what happened tonight? Aunt Clare said you set the repast out too early?"

"I fear we did, my Lord." Ruppleton nodded as the men claimed their various liquors and wine. "Two chance passersby decided to partake of the food and champagne before Lady Julia and Master Garth arrived."

"Their names were Archibald and Phyllis Billingsgate." Aunt Clare nodded. "Percy met them first. He was very naughty. When he saw Phyllis take up Julia's and Garth's champagne, he objected and sprang upon her."

"She screamed at Percy's sudden appearance, I am sad to say." Ruppleton's face was long.

"And would not stop." Aunt Clare's blue eyes were wide. "Even when Percy withdrew. It is not as if he pressed his company upon her after that."

"Percy retreated?" Matthew's eyes gleamed with laughter. "That I never thought to see."

"The lady possessed quite a range to her voice, my lord," Ruppleton murmured.

"Percy realized his misbehavior and returned directly to me," Aunt Clare said proudly. A spate of coughing fell upon the men. "Then Julia *and* Garth arrived, which pleased me no end. I was very afraid that Garth would not follow Julia as he should, but he did."

"That was good." Lucas said in a cautious tone. "Then what happened?"

Aunt Clare shook her head. "Phyllis fainted dead away when Julia drew a pistol upon Archibald."

"What?" Lucas exclaimed.

"S'death," Matthew muttered.

"Julia, the dear girl, was under the impression that Archibald was attacking Phyllis when he was in truth attempting to calm her."

"My God, Julia carries a pistol?" Lord Harry Redmond gulped.

"Only upon this occasion, Harry, dear, as far as I know." Aunt Clare smiled. "She explained that."

"However." Ruppleton frowned. "We must take into consideration Miss Julia's presence of mind and her courage when making our future plans."

"Oh, my, yes." Aunt Clare blinked. "You have a very important point there. Perhaps we should forgo the notion of hiring a man to threaten her in order for Garth to save her."

"Yes, Miss Clare. We would not want Miss Julia to actually kill anyone," Ruppleton said. "Even in assumed self-defense. I myself am satisfied with Master Garth's bold actions of tonight, which transpired without our contrivance."

"Bold action?" Harry inquired. "What did Stanwood do?"

"It was quite surprising. That nasty inspector Bloodsoe had been following Julia all along," Aunt Clare reported.

"When Miss Julia drew the pistol," Ruppleton said, "he nabbed her."

"Then Garth nabbed him." Aunt Clare beamed with pride. "He was quite fierce, and so charming. He knocked that nasty Inspector Bloodsoe straight to the ground."

"I believe he would have given Inspector Bloodsoe a proper drubbing," Ruppleton informed the awestruck men. "But Miss Clare made her presence known."

"I am sorry, Ruppleton, but I felt forced to do so. It would have been delightful to watch, no doubt, but Garth was going to 'drub' Inspector Bloodsoe without knowing who he was. I did not think that fair or right."

"Yes, Miss Clare." Ruppleton sighed. "One should

not drub an officer of the Crown without compunction, I imagine."

"Gadzooks." Viscount Herrington Dunn groaned. "Could anything go more awry?"

"Oh, yes, indeed it did," Aunt Clare nodded. "Archibald and Phyllis disturbed me before I could place *the letter.*"

"A shame." Matthew pursed his lips. "What had you finally decided to write?"

"I promised Julia and Garth great reward if they would enjoy the repast and wait three hours." Aunt Clare confessed. "I had planned for a minstrel to play for them at eleven and hoped that the wonderful romance of the gardens would prompt Garth to propose."

"You would have needed more than that." Matthew laughed. Then he coughed. "I mean more champagne, to be sure. You only left one bottle?"

"We did have a plan if Master Garth did not propose," Ruppleton said quickly.

"Good, good." Lord Reginald Beresford pushed away Shakespeare, who had been taking advantage of their distraction to stealthily nose his way into the earl's glass of port. "It is important to always have two or three plans in reserve."

"We were going to have a mysterious messenger arrive at one o'clock bearing a message of where they were to go next. We even worked up a riddle for them."

"Not good." Lucas frowned in contemplation. "Employing a riddle with those two would only cause them to brangle over it."

"Not to mention that Julia might have shot the messenger," Matthew murmured.

"Matthew," Aunt Clare reproved.

"Accidentally, of course." Matthew presented an innocent face.

"It would be better to keep the notes simple and straightforward." Lucas's gaze was narrowed upon Matthew in warning.

"Yes, I suppose so. O-only it is quite, quite lowering." Aunt Clare gulped and dashed at her tears. "I feel as if I have failed you sweet boys tonight. You all have been so kind and patient since I have abducted you. Quite wonderful, in fact. Especially since I am taking darling Julia away from all of you. But I assure you, Julia belongs to Garth, and Garth belongs to Julia. They have loved each other from childhood, but they simply have lost sight of that."

"It happens," Matthew sympathized.

"I could not have permitted her to marry any of you." The cats deserted their gentlemen and went to the distraught Aunt Clare. "She would have been miserable."

"And we would have been miserable," Matthew vowed. Then he jumped. "As you explained, Aunt Clare, a person can only be happy with their own true love."

"It is hard to withstand." Lucas sighed with gusty fervor. "For me . . . I never did offer for her hand, but you helped me to see that it would have been a grave error if I had done so."

"Such dears." Aunt Clare sighed. "You all will have your own true loves, I promise you."

"Do not lose hope, Aunt Clare," Reginald said with a bracing vigor. "Sooner or later Stanwood will make a slip and he will be in the parson's mousetrap. I mean . . . he will realize his love for Julia and propose."

"That's the ticket!" Harry Redmond nodded. "Just keep throwing them together in compromising positions. They will tumble to it in the end."

"And perhaps . . ." Lucas murmured in consideration. "Make the notes you send more demanding and threatening. Make it sound like both simply must attend. That must be stressed most heartily. In fact, do not leave anything to debate. Tell them their lives may very well depend upon it."

Aunt Clare gasped. "I could not!"

Lucas smiled rather evilly. "No, of course not. The notes must come from a different persona. Someone mysterious."

"I do not understand."

"I do," Ruppleton said, his voice eager. He looked to Aunt Clare. "We must consider."

"Oh, yes." Aunt Clare stood and smoothed out her skirts. "Gracious, we have our work cut out for us, to be sure. I should not have permitted myself to fall into the doldrums. If you dear boys can be patient, so can I." She brightened all the more. "And it is not as if tonight were a total failure. Even without coercion, Garth *did* show his manliness."

"So did Julia." A sotto voce remark was made. Which groom it came from was not defined.

"Well. Ruppleton, Wilson, and I will leave you gentlemen." Aunt Clare took a deep breath. "We have plans to make."

The men all rose directly.

"If you have any difficulties with making plans, do come to us." Matthew bowed most courteously. "We can supply you with anything you might need. What are the most romantic places, away from crowds, mind you. I would imagine between the seven of us we have enough experience to snag them."

"You dear, sweet boys." Aunt Clare sighed. "You will not regret your good-heartedness. I will do all that I can to make certain of it. But indeed, we cannot stay for a coze. We have *plans* to make."

Ruppleton bowed to the room at large. "We shall do better, my lords. See if we do not."

The grooms fell silent until after Aunt Clare, Ruppleton, and Wilson and all the cats had departed. Giles Mancroft took it upon himself to trod over to the large door and place his ear to it after the clang of the bolt sounded. "They are gone."

"I win, then." Charles said. "I told you their plans would come to naught."

"I thought Julia and Garth might have at least kissed," Herrington grumbled. "I thought the one thing you could lay a monkey on would be for Stanwood to kiss a female in the dark paths. He has lost his touch."

"A good sign." Matthew grinned. "A man going soft is sure to become a tenant for life."

"Too bad he does not need a fortune." Giles sighed.

"Ha, if he did, he would be locked up here with the rest of us," Reginald snorted.

"At least you had a valid reason for joining this soiree," Lucas said, his tone dry. "Me, I was abducted upon just the thought that I would propose to Julia Wrexton. I would never have done so, I assure you."

"You can boast that now." A bewildered look crossed Charles's face. "But that all changes when the lady proposes to you."

"She has a way with her." Reginald sighed. A challenge entered his eyes. "Since you are not engaged to her, Monteith, why not request Aunt Clare to release you. Or you might escape if you do not wish to hurt her feelings."

Lucas shrugged. "It makes no difference to me if I am in here or out there. Indeed, in here we have all the benefits of White's without the drawbacks. On the whole, we have better service, far better food, and not every dandy and buck choosing to interrupt one. If I do say so myself, Miss Wrexton chose a most excellent group of fellows with which to be incarcerated."

"You *are* a pip, Monteith," Charles said, his voice indignant.

"Besides, if I leave before you chaps, it will be me to receive the first barrage of questions. From what Wilson says, the world thinks me murdered. Worse, they would think it Aunt Clare when in truth it was my own clumsy fault that I went to stir the fire. I make no doubt I owe my life to her and Ruppleton. If they had not chosen to arrive at the very moment I had fallen in my drunken stupor, I would have passed out and bled to death."

"Gads," Reginald muttered. "You were fortunate in that. Me, I might as well hide out here myself. Vivian was already furious with me when she found I was to marry Julia. Since I ha—did not make it to her that night with a trinket or two, I never doubt I will be in her bad graces for some time to come. Not a charming prospect."

"Why should you be frightened of your mistress?" Lucas asked, frowning.

"Vivian has the ear of royalty." Reginald sighed glumly. "She had the bed of royalty for a short time, you see, and she made the most of it. If she cries enough to old—well, to those in higher places, I might very well find myself on a ship in His Majesty's service or something equally unconvivial." He quaffed his wine. "Never, gentlemen, be unwise enough to go and search for a squealing, wounded cat in the shrubbery outside your light o' loves house when you should be attending her instead."

"Not after knowing Aunt Clare, to be sure." Herrington shook his head. "I would never have gone after a cat. I am growing to respect the creatures, but I am still not partial to them. They snabbled me because I went after the poor dog in the alley that Percy was savaging. I thought I was saving the poor cur. Then I thought I was helping a faint little old lady retrieve her cat. And I ended up here." He sighed wistfully. "I wonder if Gadstone has sold that jacket I ordered."

"Faith, Herrington, but you are a man-milliner," Harry jeered. "What does it matter if you missed an appointment with your tailor? I have been considered to have thrown my own race. I had a bundle riding upon it." He lifted his glass in a salute. "Never stop in the middle of a race to assist a poor little old lady with her cat upon the roadside. I ended up here, while my tiger MacGregor took off with my curricle to Ireland."

Matthew shook his head. "That was confoundedly shabby of him."

"Aunt Clare got to him, and you know how that goes," Harry continued. "He was going after his long lost love he had left behind. Poor chap, he will likely find her with ten brats at her skirts and a brawny husband by her side."

"True. But that is Aunt Clare for you. She can make you see stars and moons all for love, can she not?" Matthew shook his head. The men stared at him. He lifted a brow. "Well, do you care to tell me otherwise? The lady has a way of talking to you, and then, before you know it, you have told her all those odd little secrets you would not even tell your own self."

"I only did that when in my cups," Charles said stiffly. "I was the easiest mark, I believe. They had only to pay off the hack driver that Stanwood commissioned and bring me here instead of my own house. I was so jug-bitten, I never knew where I was until a day later." Embarrassment darted across his features. "Only I am afraid I talked in my sleep. Aunt Clare knew I regretted proposing to Julia even before I knew it."

"You are wrong, you know. I was the easier mark by far." Giles shook his head. "To think I fell for Wilson's own niece dressed as a fancy piece. I confess, they had her looking as fine as five pence. She didn't look like the normal straw damsel, I promise you. She sparkled with diamonds and pearls. But still, to be fooled and drugged by the niece of your betrothed's chef is quite lowering. Come to find, they actually snitched some of Julia's clothes for it. But what man notices that?"

"Faith, I must count myself fortunate." Matthew smiled ruefully. "They only stole me from aboard my ship. Well, they tried. There we were dockside, awaiting the tide. Ruppleton fell overboard in the process, and I dove in after him. *Then* they stole me. At least I had already given my captain his orders to sail. I hope his voyage will prove fruitful, now that marriage to Julia is out of the question."

"Under the hatches that much, are you?" Herrington asked with sympathy.

"Up the river tick without a prayer. I guess remaining here for the nonce is not such a bad notion." He cleared his throat. "Aunt Clare is a queer one, to be sure. But you cannot help but be fond of her. She attempts to be accommodating at every turn." A sad, melancholy look descended upon his face. "Even if she is but a dotty old spinster, it is refreshing to know there is still someone who believes completely in love and goodness. I do not want to be the one to disappoint her."

"True, True. Though she would not know it, she saved us." Herrington shivered. "Jupiter, after what Ruppleton and Wilson have told us about Miss Wrexton and her crazed, mercurial temper, I feel that I ought to kiss Aunt Clare. Who would have guessed that Julia

Wrexton could be such a . . . dreadful witch. She has always appeared the perfect lady, if rather cool and distant. But, blast it! That was her allure for me. She was so perfect. Then to hear . . ." He choked. "To hear of her fiendish temper. It shakes a man's faith, it does."

"She bamboozled us, is what she did," Harry said. "But then she is a sly one. Look at Aunt Clare; she thinks her niece an angel."

"S'faith. It is because she sees the best in everyone." Matthew shook his head.

"Aunt Clare could be gulled by anyone. Poor Ruppleton and Wilson—it must be the devil's own time to know and live with the truth." Reginald said.

"They are such faithful and loyal servants." Harry nodded, his lower lip pursed out. "They shield the dear lady well."

" 'Deed. They do." Giles shivered. "Forsooth, I am glad they did not hide their teeth with us, however. If they had not taken me aside and told me the whole sad story, I would still be in the dark." He snorted. "And they were afraid I might blow the gaff to Aunt Clare after that. I do not know about you gentlemen, but that is something I would never do."

"Egads no!" Herrington exclaimed. "We must have honor even if Lady Julia does not. Imagine, she has succeeded in pulling the wool over the eyes of the entire *tôn.*"

Reginald worried his lip. "It makes one almost feel like a cad for letting Stanwood in for it."

"Better him than us," Charles said firmly.

"That's a kind fellow." Matthew laughed.

"I am sorry." Charles pokered up. "But if there is one man who might be able to handle a termagant, it is Stanwood. There is not a woman he cannot handle, I have been told. And the two did grow up together. I make no doubt he is like the rest of Lady Julia's family. Her insanity is a natural behavior to him."

"Here now, Ruppleton and Wilson never said Julia was insane," Harry objected. Doubt crossed his face. "Did they?"

"They didn't say that exactly, but from the hints they've dropped, it is as plain as a pikestaff." Charles's voice finally showed strain. Indeed, it quivered. "I am sorry for Stanwood, but I am glad I have escaped such folly."

"You are not out of the woods—or should I say Aunt Clare's grooms club—yet." Lucas said. "You are not shot of Julia Wrexton until Stanwood marries her."

"Confound it," Harry exclaimed before Charles could retort. "There is no need to keep reminding us of it. We all know it. Why else are we all hiding out here? And the devil of it is, Aunt Clare had to set her sights on a man that is nobody's fool. Stanwood is too clever by half about women. He might be about the game for an age before being trapped."

"Then why not merely draw straws," Lucas suggested. "If one of you will return and live up to your pledge and marry Julia Wrexton, the rest of use would be free."

"Sacrifice one for the good of all?" Matthew shook his head. "No. I will wait for Stanwood's comeuppance. And I will suggest all that I can to effect that blessed occasion, and I advise every man amongst us do the same."

"Here, here!" It was an agreement in unison. Indeed, a song of men going into battle could not have been more rousing.

"Besides, as you said, Monteith, this place is not too intolerable." Matthew grimaced. "I do not care for the red decor, but there you have it."

"Yes, when one is abducted and held hostage"—Lucas smiled—"one cannot have everything."

"Gammon." Matthew grinned. "Aunt Clare would do anything she could for us, but she *will* persist in thinking that men have the fantasy of living in what looks like a bordello. She thinks it exotic and exciting, don't you know?"

Garth snapped his eyes opened and exhaled slowly. The light of dawn was just slipping into his room. Lord, what fantastic dreams he had had. Dreams that had pushed him to a fever point. They had been about Julia. He should feel appalled, or at least ashamed. Lost between sleep and wakefulness, he realized he did not. The dreams, as passionate as they were, had felt completely right, frighteningly right. He closed his eyes and let those feelings overcome him. It still felt right.

A small tap sounded at his door. "Garth?"

"Julia?" Garth opened his eyes slowly. Ah, that was it! He was still dreaming, after all.

"May I come in?" Julia's voice came from behind the bedroom door. It was no longer in his fantasy. "I need to talk to you."

"What?" Garth sat up, the coverlet falling from him. He glanced down at his naked chest and then glared at the door. "No, do not enter."

"I have something I must show you," Julia whispered. He saw the door handle turning.

"Stop. Please wait a moment . . . or else I will have something to show *you*," he muttered. Blast Julia's impatience. He sprang out of bed and dove for his smoking jacket.

"Now may I came in?" Julia called, her tone exasperated.

Garth had the jacket only halfway on when he saw the door swing open. He dove back to the bed and pulled the covers over him. He gritted his teeth and jerked at the jacket beneath the covers as Julia entered. "Oh, by all means, I enjoy rude awakenings. . . ." Garth froze. His jaw dropped.

"Look what I found slipped beneath my door." Julia rushed toward him, holding out a missive. "It was there before I awoke. Can you imagine?"

"No and yes." Julia wore the most exotic sapphire dressing gown. Of glowing satin, it was cut in an Oriental design that fit her unfettered body closely. No, he could not imagine Julia wearing such seductive night attire. But now that he saw it on her—yes, he could imagine. He could imagine some terribly lusty things, things to do with those looped buttons that ran from her throat to her waist.

"Read it. It is from a Monsieur X."

"Who the hell is Monsieur X?" Garth growled. It was a gut reaction. Some man was slipping billet-doux under Julia's door. No doubt, because *he* knew Julia wore such night attire. It was the outside of enough!

"Garth?" Julia pedaled backward. Only then did Garth notice the paleness of her face, the fright in her eyes, and that her hand shook.

"Give it to me," Garth said none too graciously. Julia's unusual, vulnerable look was heartrending. Mixed with the sapphire robe, it would be any man's undoing. Garth forced his temperature down and his gaze to the paper.

I know what happened to your grooms. Meet me at Grillon's, the Rose suite, at noon. Lord Stanwood must accompany you and no one else. If you value your life.
                                             Monsieur X

"Good lord," Garth muttered. "A room at Grillon's."

"What do you think?" Julia crossed her arms and turned to pace back and forth at the foot of his bed.

"I do not want to think." Garth closed his eyes swiftly. He could not concentrate while watching Julia's full, lithe figure striding and turning, her satin skirts swishing. "I have a headache."

"Do you. I am sorry." Julia came around the left side of the bed and sat down upon it. "I should not tax you with this, then. But Garth, I am frightened."

"So am I," Garth muttered. Julia was actually on his bed, as in his dream. However, what had felt right in his dreams now merely felt threatening, very threatening. His dream Julia might respond correctly, but he was not such a great looby as to think he could attempt anything with his real Julia. He would no doubt get floored if he tried.

"You are afraid, too?" Julia's eyes widened.

"What? No, no, I did not mean that." Garth stifled his groan. Lord, had he honestly confessed he was frightened. Wake up, old man, wake up. He drew in a deep breath. "Julia, we may discuss this later . . ."

"We cannot."

"After we have dressed . . ."

"The family must not know of this."

"Totally dressed." Garth persisted.

"We must protect them."

"And we have had tea, very strong tea. An entire potful I think."

"Garth!" Julia pounded a frustrated fist on her thigh, he noticed. "You are not listening. We must discuss this now. That is why I came here. We must not let anyone know about this. Especially Aunt Clare. You saw how frightened she was yesterday. And we certainly do not wish to have her trying to help us again as she did last night. It is too dangerous."

Garth groaned. "You are right. But you are not supposed to be in my bedroom."

"What a time for you to worry about propriety." Julia's voice was musing and absent-minded. She worried her full lower lip in a delicious manner. "Monsieur X. Who could he be? And how was he able to sneak into the house?"

"Julia," Garth said testily, "why did you not dress before you came here?"

"I could not wait to talk to you. Garth, there is no doubt about it. Monsieur X is threatening us. Why? No doubt he wrote the first letter. Yet now he is brave enough to give us his name. Though it cannot be his real—"

"You could have dressed first," Garth persisted. He finally gave into the burning question in his mind. It was better than considering the other things burning in him. "Do you always dress like that for sleep?"

"Hmm?" Julia's eyes all but crossed in concentration. She blinked and shrugged. "Of course. Indeed, this was a creation of my own."

Garth choked. "Y-your own?"

"Yes. Why?" He suddenly gained Julia's full attention. "Do you not like it?"

"That is an improper question."

"Improper?" Astonishment washed Julia's features. Her eyes narrowed. "It is not improper. Madame Celestine was very impressed with my design. She even asked if she could be permitted to make it up for her other clientele. All of them of *bon tôn.* Indeed, she thought the duchess of Watermark would care for one of similar design. And the duchess is such a stickler."

"Oh, Lord." Garth wished he had not asked. She not only wore that kind of attire to bed; she had the ability to dream such things up in her head. "I cannot believe that you . . . you design such clothing."

Julia stiffened. The flush to her cheek, the fire in her eyes, the slant to her bosom, were not helping Garth one wit. "Why? I told you I needed no advice upon fashion. My taste is considered excellent. I am not only an arbitrator of fashion but a leader of it."

"But of nightclothes?" Garth asked in desperation and exasperation.

"Why . . ." Julia's eyes widened; unfortunately it was in comprehension and far too clear of understanding. "I s-see. You . . . oh, no! You . . . you were thinking I was so . . . so unoriginal as to wear a cotton sack, as Betina did." She broke into merry laughter, her eyes sparkling in delight. "Garth, I am not a debutante. I am a woman grown. I wear the things I enjoy, and since it is in private, society cannot pass censure. But that you—you of all people—*would* . . ." She leaned back against the large headboard. She fanned her face with her hands. "Oh, my, that is amusing."

"It is not," Garth said lowly. "And would you keep your voice down? You said you wanted this to be a secret. If anyone discovered you—"

A rap at the door interrupted.

"My lord?" Benton, his valet, called. "Are you all right?"

Julia merely gurgled. The door began to open, and Julia scrabbled and squirmed to bury herself beneath the covers.

Garth rolled his eyes. For an intelligent woman, Julia could do some amazingly silly things.

Benton entered. Garth bit back a curse. If he had his old valet from France with him, none of this would matter. Benton, however, was newly hired when Garth had arrived in London. He neither knew nor trusted the valet as of yet. "Yes, Benton, what is it?"

"Are you all right, my lord?" Benton asked, his face suspicious and curious.

"Indeed I am." Garth pretended to stretch. "A fine morning, don't you think?"

"I-I thought . . ."

"What?"

"I thought I heard voices in here," Benton said, frowning.

"Voices?" Garth looked directly at Benton. The valet was definitely not up to snuff. "There were no voices."

Benton's eyes roved to the huge lump beside Garth. His face turned prim and pinched. "I see, my lord."

"I am sorry your hearing is going, old man."

Benton moved closer, his gaze fixed. "Shall I help you dress, my lord?"

Faith, but the valet was a rat terrier. "No. In fact, I believe I will sleep in this morning. You may leave now."

Benton remained still. Garth was forced to applaud Julia. The lump remained just as still.

"Benton?"

Benton started. His face showed severe disappointment. "Yes, my lord."

Benton turned and walked slowly to the door. He then spun quickly to look at the bed. Julia remained a motionless lump. Benton sighed and departed.

"You may come out now," Garth said.

The covers erupted. Julia sat up, her hair tangled, her eyes shooting sparks. She looked at the door and pulled a face. "What a little sneak. I'd sack him. Why, I could have been one of your bits of muslin, and he could have interrupted us making wild, passionate love."

Garth swallowed with difficulty. "Get out of this bed immediately."

Julia looked confused and hurt. "Why are you so angry?"

"I am not angry," Garth gritted. "I just sound angry."

"No, indeed. You are angry. Quite."

"Very well, I am angry." He could so easily reach over and kiss Julia. She had no notion how he wished she were his fancy piece and that he could make wild, passionate love to her. Yet she was Julia. Garth could not treat her like his fancy piece. Worse, the truly deep-seated fear was what would happen if he did kiss her and make love to her? In his dream it had felt perfectly right. What if in reality it was perfectly right? It would not and could not then be a passing fancy. No, it would have to be for much, much longer. The thought was dangerous. "Just leave."

"No." Julia crossed her arms. "I will not leave until you tell me why you are angry. I tried to hide as well as I could. If you were angry about that—"

"It was bird-witted."

"That is because I am not experienced in hiding from servants and fathers and husbands as you are. Nor am I trained on what you should do to escape." Her posture actually eased, and Julia settled back against the headboard. "I never realized how unprepared I am for all this cloak-and-dagger stuff until now. Perhaps you'd best teach me what I should do in instances like this past one. I clearly bungled it. I well-nigh suffocated myself under those covers."

Garth groaned. She had actually wiggled back. She was settling in for a comfy coze. Or fight. With Julia, it would not matter. She clearly did not wish to leave. It was the outside of enough! A woman should not be permitted a comfortable coze in a man's bed in the morning, not until after both were tired and satiated from . . . Garth groaned. He was going insane. "I am not *teaching* you anything. Now leave."

"Garth, I need your direction." Julia frowned. "I think it very small of you that you will not share your experience and knowledge with me."

Small! That was the problem. Frustration goaded Garth. Julia was acting as obtuse as a stone. No, rather as a granite boulder that wasn't budging. Desperate measures must be taken. "Very well. You wish me to teach you how to hide and escape, correct?"

"Yes." Julia nodded in earnest anticipation.

Garth rolled from the bed and stood. "Let us bypass the 'hiding' lesson, since the problem is that you are already hiding in my bed." Insight struck Garth and with it astonishment. "Because you *are* frightened."

"I am *not* . . ." Julia flared, her eyes snapping. Then she flushed. Her expression turned wry. "Not very much, that is."

Garth drew in his breath. The problem was greater than he thought. He must be cruel to be kind. "Then permit me to teach you how to escape."

"Yes," Julia appeared relieved. "Tell me."

"No," Garth nodded. "This is to be an . . . an actual . . . practice run. What should you do, Julia, when a man takes his smoking jacket off?"

"I don't know?" Julia quipped. "You *are* wearing something else under—"

"No. Only me."

Julia sat up, her face astonished. "You cannot be serious."

"I am."

"But . . ." Julia appeared mesmerized as Garth reached to untie his jacket.

"And then joins you in the bed you refuse to leave." He changed ploys and purposely pulled at the smoking lapels to expose his chest. He hoped he didn't expose anything else.

"Garth! No!" Julia slapped her hands over her eyes and rolled toward the edge of the bed. She was visible one moment, and the next moment, after a thump, she had vanished.

"Julia!" Garth bolted to the bed in consternation.

"I am all right!" Julia appeared. Indeed, she materialized in one swift spring. Her expression was once again the normal, composed "I am the Citadel" look. Her gaze, however, lowered to half-mast when she peeked at Garth. She then jumped, and her face blanched. She covered her eyes with her hand once more. "I-I am leaving! Now! I promise you."

"Oh, Lord." Garth flushed deeply. He had forgotten that his robe was unloosened and that his movement had rearranged it. His state very drafty, in truth. "Julia, I did not intend . . ."

"No. I understand . . ." Julia, one hand on her eyes and one hand held out and searching, actually traversed the room before Garth could overcome his embarrassment and emotions. She succeeded in breaking all records in leaving a room blindfolded (or handfolded to be precise). That is, until she found the doorknob and opened the door with too much force. It cracked Julia in the face.

"Julia! Are you all right?" All things were forgotten. Garth's embarrassment, his state of half-dress, everything. He strode across the room and enveloped Julia in his arms. He saw a huge red welt on Julia's hand. If she had not had it covering her eyes, the door would have hit her nose or head. He gulped. "Julia?"

"Yes." Julia lowered her hand and with it the telling bruise. She looked up at him. Embarrassment, fright, and all the other emotions Garth experienced chased across her face, an instant story. "I am all right."

"Thank God!" Those emotions driving him, Garth kissed her, and quite ruthlessly at that. He did not think he was being small about it. Indeed, he was being very big about it. He pulled back gasping. He was comforted to hear echoing gasps from Julia. They were both behaving like fish out of water. Which was far closer to the truth than Garth cared to consider. He grimaced. "Now, get the bloody hell out of here."

"Yes, that is a good idea." Julia spun and bolted out the door.

Garth slammed it shut. Everything—blood, thought, and emotion—boiled within him.

"Oh, God!" Julia's voice sounded from outside.

"What is it?" Garth jerked the door open.

He saw Julia's alarmed face. "Close the door!"

"Yes." Garth slammed it shut, but not before he saw Julia take in a swift but full look. Gads, he must appear the most immodest man alive. He counted to ten and then asked, "Julia, are you still there?"

"Yes?"

"What happened?"

"Benton just saw me." Julia's voice came through the wood.

"What?" Jealousy claimed Garth. "He should not have seen you dressed like that. The undeserving worm. He had no right to see you dressed like that."

"And I suppose I should not have seen *you* dressed as you were, either." Julia's deep laughter drifted through the door.

It was music to Garth's ears. He had just been the most barbaric and the most inept with a woman he had ever been in his life. He was not sure which bothered him the most, but he thought it might be the inept choice. He was generally a man of experience and style. The past embarrassing scene showed neither quality. Yet Julia's laughter was so full of acknowledgment, full of accepting humor, that everything was all right. He vowed he could kiss her for it.

"Julia!" Garth opened the door.

She had vanished. Garth closed the door, telling himself firmly that it was a good thing she had left. He turned back to the bed. Suddenly, he heard Julia's laughter again. He envisioned her there, wiggling down into the covers.

Blast his lower passions. He had been positively asinine. It would have been nice to just have a coze with Julia in bed. It would have been nice to plot and plan. It would have been nice for him to have comforted her, spiritually, that is. Instead, he had forced her to flee the room. He had let his fear ruin it all.

Garth ignored the thought that it had not been just his desires that had forced him to drive Julia from his bed and room. He ignored the fact that all his fears might be justifiable. He refused to accept the fact that now his new dream would be of making love to Julia in her terribly seductive nightgown and then having a comfortable coze with her afterward.

Ten

Personal Journal of Inspector Bloodsoe, Officer of the Crown
Pertaining to The Case of the Missing Grooms:

I have followed the suspects for the past two weeks. I have come to the conclusion that Lord Stanwood is not actively involved within the plot. Rather, he must be the Black Widow's next victim. At this very moment, she lures him into her deadly web.

She and Lord Stanwood are continuously together. Their behavior signifies that they are engaged within an affair. They slip off to the most secretive of places. I have seen them go to a suite at Grillon's Hotel, where they indulged in a private luncheon. The room was reserved in the blatantly false name of Monsieur X. Of particular note, I wonder that she had not employed that of Madame X.

The two have also driven to an inn at the outskirts of town without any form of chaperonage. The particular inn, of a Gothic sort, has been noted among the tôn for its illicit atmosphere and its availability for rendezvous. What I find truly ironic is the fact that the inn has also been a favorite of Lord Beresford's for his own assignations. He was, it appears, a rather amorous man amongst particular ladies of the theatre. This was, however, prior to his engagement to Miss Wrexton and his subsequent disappearance. This I had from the innkeeper, who was quite surprised when questioned to discover that Monsieur X was actually Miss Julia Wrexton, who had also been affianced to Lord Beresford. The benighted man could only declare that he thought Miss Wrexton far too lovely a lady to have been bespoken to either.

As I was unable to view Miss Wrexton and Lord Stanwood closely for fear of being discovered and possibly wounded from it, which would slow me in my duty, I have determined to follow other clues as well. To this end, I have also investigated the Wrexton servants. I, in truth, would have done this regardless, though I would not have expected them to swear to their mistress's crimes. She is not a common or stupid killer.

The interviews, as a whole, were what I expected. Almost the entire staff vowed their loyalty and respect for Miss Wrexton. They did, however, comment upon the eccentricities of the household. It appears the elder Miss Wrexton's cats require every kind of victuals, meals fit for a king, mind you. None, however, claimed mistreatment or had seen open atrocities. With two exceptions, that is.

First, the gardener. He is most obviously of Italian decent. Note: I did not request his origin, which might have been an oversight. Yet his strong accent and behavior proved his origin so strongly that to ask him might have insulted him. He is a rather excitable man. When asked his opinion of Miss Wrexton and Lord Stanwood, his reactions were vehement. He declared that both were murderers. When I persisted in my questions, the man would but point to two particular areas of the garden and refuse any more information of which they murdered. I then requested him to explain it more clearly. I am sorry to say he fell into his father's language and made little sense. Therefore, as a conscientious inspector, I must reserve *my judgment until I can determine his full meaning. I have procured an Italian book of translation for that purpose. Also a shovel.*

Second is Lord Stanwood's valet, who gave an important report to this investigation. He left my lord's service (his choice of words and not mine) approximately two weeks ago. From his testimony, he made my above assumption a fact. He vows that one morning he heard voices, male and female, projecting forth from Lord Stanwood's room. After gaining permission from Lord Stanwood himself, he entered. He asked Lord Stanwood of the voices. Lord Stanwood vowed no one was there. The valet swore there was a lump in the blankets the exact size of a woman beside Lord Stanwood in bed. He was particular to note that not only was the lump the size of a woman but the bumps and curves (his choice of words and not mine) were that of a woman as well.

Lord Stanwood summarily dismissed him from the room. The valet, when questioned, admitted the lump did not move, nor did he see beneath the covers. However, he left Lord Stanwood's rooms but resolutely remained without in the hall. Within minutes he viewed, with his own eyes, Miss Wrexton leaving Lord Stanwood's chambers. If there could be doubt, the valet was quite definitive of Miss Wrexton's attire, which was not meant for a proper morning call (his choice of words and not mine).

This, unfortunately, is where I begin to fear for the validity of his testimony. He proceeded to describe Miss Wrexton and her night rail, a shimmering, sapphire, erotic garb (his choice of words and not mine) to such a passionate degree that I fear he, too, has fallen to the siren's spell.

Indeed, I admit that conscious of his danger, I warned him that Lord Stanwood's sacking of him most likely saved his life. Better to be sacked than fall under the power of a murderess. It surprised me to hear directly from the valet that Lord Stanwood had not sacked him. I admit I had assumed that part. The valet's devious behavior in the circumstances is generally not what a promiscuous but socially conscious peer would tolerate. Indeed, in all honesty, I would have to say if I had been in Lord Stanwood's position, I would have sacked the man.

The valet swears that he went to the butler, Ruppleton, with the matter. He reported that the butler, clearly aggrieved and worried for him and his untenable position, advised him to keep such matters quiet, for it never helped to go against a powerful employer if one wished for references. He then promised the valet to find a far better position, one that would not compromise his integrity.

I know, without a fact, that the butler, Ruppleton, is loyal to his mistress and family. Yet I cannot help but be impressed with his efforts for the valet. Rather like Solomon with the baby, he made choices that protected both his mistress and the servant. The valet now works for old Lord Venetian, who is of such an age as to be completely free of romantic endeavor, even to his equally aged wife.

I have secured these two testimonies in regard to the case. Due to all my discoveries, I have become torn in my duty and the direction I should take. It is clear that the Black Widow at one point or another will strike Lord Stanwood. At the nonce, he should be safe until he unwisely proposes to her. With this belief, I have turned a portion of my investigation over to the disappearance of the other grooms in hopes of finding clues there. The trail, unfortunately, is cold. The collective disappearance of her grooms not being reported until now. My regret is that I am quite positive she will not return to the *scene of her crimes. She appears too involved with her newest victim.*

I believe the lady to be quite clever, as are often those of a psychotic nature, for what other motive would a woman have to acquire fiancés and then do away with them? It is common for a woman to murder the man once she is married to him and can obtain his wealth. That she does so before wedding them, however, is not common. She is, to revise a common saying, killing the golden goose before it can lay the golden egg.

All her grooms are of fine stature and good families. One cannot assume she became engaged to a poor choice, only to aspire after another that appeared better. She then would simply need to terminate the first. Engagement, that is. Murder is an extreme defense against gaining the name of "jilt." Yet this would not weigh with a psychotic and would then make sense.

Of a personal commentary. I feel sorry for Lord Stanwood. I will strive to do all I can to save him from her.

Pertaining to the Case of the duchess's Stolen Necklace: I fear I have no new information, being too involved with the Case of the Missing Grooms. Likewise my other cases. Nothing is more important than solving this case. I feel it most deeply. A tragedy of great proportion may be prevented.

"What the devil is the fiend's game?" Garth's gaze scoured the intimate gazebo as if it were a battleground instead of the most romantic and intriguing of settings.

"I do not know." Julia swallowed her champagne. "B-but perhaps he will show tonight."

"I hope to God he does," Garth growled. "He is leading us upon a wild-goose chase, if I have ever seen one. I am tired of billets popping up in every corner and cryptic notes to no purpose."

"At least he has offered us excellent dinners. Monsieur X has stellar taste in that regard."

"Considering the hours we have wasted and the places to which he has made us travel, it is the least he can do for us." Garth's tone was surly.

"Indeed." Julia tried to ignore the painful twinge in her heart. Wild horses couldn't have drawn it out of her, but the simple truth was that in a strange way she had begun to look forward to the chase of Monsieur X.

If they succeeded in finding him, she might not feel that way, but to date they had not. Yet the places they had visited due to his missives were, without a doubt, alluring. Garth and she had visited a suite at Grillon's Hotel. The finest dinner had been laid out with a note instructing them to eat and he would join them but he had very important business to attend to on the nonce.

Once Julia's nerves had settled, she and Garth had enjoyed capons basted in a walnut sauce, trout Meunière, and the most scrumptious array of pastries. She had actually enjoyed the afternoon. That is, other than the awareness of their purpose and the tension of knowing the next room housed a huge canopy bed draped in Indian silk.

Julia flushed. It had been the same when they had been told to travel to that quaint inn on the outskirts of London. With its stone walls and sloping roofs and what almost looked like castle battlements, it was a storybook setting. Monsieur never appeared, but the innkeeper, who had apparently been paid beforehand, had been so eager to please. Indeed, they had remained and indulged in a most excellent spread of pork roast with cider, shepherd's pie, and vegetable tartlets, topped with cold ale for Garth and sweet wine for Julia.

Only when the innkeeper had interrupted them three hours later with a wink, inquiring if they wished a room for the night, did Garth and Julia realize the passing of time. Julia worried her lower lip. They had decamped so swiftly that not until they were well on the road had she lost that nervousness around Garth. Or, for that matter, a terrible tension that had nothing to do with proper, ladylike thoughts.

Now, here they were at another charming place. Indeed, Julia was beginning to be in awe of Monsieur X. She had never known that there were so many unique places so very close to London yet. This charming inn presented private dining in a quaint gazebo set upon a quainter millpond. The pond was lit with strings of fairy lanterns about it. The gazebo itself was intimate, with great, exotic plants circling them. Those, too, were interlaced with fairy lanterns. "I wonder how Monsieur X knows about these fantastical places."

"I do not. I am beginning to believe Monsieur X to be—" Garth halted.

"What?" Julia asked.

"Nothing. It is of no significance," Garth said, his voice tight. "The only thing I have to say is . . ."

A rustling in the plants occurred. Garth paused. Julia's own heart jumped. She stared in astonishment as a small, wizened lady appeared. Her face was seamed and ancient, yet the clothes she wore were of brilliant colors and in good repair. She stepped forward with great dignity. "Would ye care to have your fortune read?"

Julia relaxed and smiled. Gypsy fortune-tellers were not unusual, after all. No doubt she was part of the entertainment in the establishment. "No, thank you."

The crone's eyes narrowed. She held her hand out toward Garth. "Perhaps you would like yer lady's fortune read?"

"She is not my lady." Garth laughed. "And if she does not wish to peer at her fortune, she might have a perfectly good reason not to do so."

The Gypsy woman cracked a smile. "You are a fine-looking gentleman. And kind. You do not believe that old Myrah can read your fortunes?"

"No. I am sure that you read them here almost every night." Garth smiled and offered her a wink.

She cackled. "No, I but pass by here tonight. I shall read your lady's fortune for you without the need of coin."

"Thank you," Julia said. "But . . ."

"You are frightened?" Myrah asked.

"Perhaps," Julia admitted honestly. "Things have been rather unpredictable of late."

Myrah reached over and took Julia's hand in hers. Unless Julia wished to fight for its possession, she would have to permit Myrah to read her palm. The slightest shock ran through her as the old woman placed a finger to her palm and smoothed the lines of it.

Myrah remained silent a moment. "Your life is in great turmoil. Trouble. There is a strong absence. You are seeking."

"Yes," Julia admitted. "I am."

"You do not know what you seek."

Julia blinked. "No, I fear I do."

"But it is very close." The Gypsy woman continued, clearly not hearing her.

"Truly?"

"*He* is very close."

"Monsieur X!" Julia gasped in excitement. Now the woman made sense. Her eagerness overrode her discretion. "Do you speak of Monsieur X?"

"What?" Myrah peered up. She cast her gaze to Garth and then back to Julia. She chuckled. "I do not know who this Monsieur X is, but he is not who you seek. He is not who you need." She dropped Julia's hand and turned her gaze upon Garth. "Your palm, my lord."

"Yes, my lady." Garth offered his palm with good humor.

She took his palm and ran her hand over it but once. She then released it. "I am glad you did not pay old Myrah. Now old Myrah can tell you what she sees. Not what you wish to hear."

"In that case, permit me to pay you so that you may refrain from sending me into the doldrums."

"Too late, my lord." Myrah turned and included Julia in her sharp gaze. "You should know the truth by now without old Myrah to tell you."

"There is danger?" Julia asked, a chill coursing through her.

Myrah smiled. "There is danger."

Julia fought the tingle of fear. "Tonight?"

"Yes, tonight. Tomorrow. The next day and the one after the next. Always there is danger within the heart. You must be brave." Myrah pointed at Garth. "*He* must be brave. Your fortunes are entwined and must not be separated."

"True." Julia lifted her brow in wonderment. "We might very well be forced to share the one if things are not set aright."

"I do not mean money!" Myrah frowned darkly and waved her hand. "That is not your fortune. Your two destinies, all that you are, are twined together. You have tried to break the bond. You fear. But someone watches you, watches you closely. That love is strong for you, my lady, very strong." She looked at Garth, her aged eyes solemn. "As your love must be strong, my lord. Do not forsake your lady or the cost shall be high."

Garth started, an unreadable expression passing through his eyes.

Myrah nodded. "I told you, you would not wish to hear."

Julia, confused for a moment, finally understood. "Gracious no! You do not mean . . . he and I . . . we . . ."

Myrah lifted her head sharply. She looked past them, her dark eyes narrowed. "I go now. Someone listens. And someone comes."

She turned and departed.

"Did you hear her?" Julia found she whispered.

"Of course I did." Garth lifted a brow. "She is a most imaginative gypsy."

Julia flushed. "She said someone comes. It could be Monsieur X. Finally, he intends to show himself."

"Excellent." Garth picked up his glass of champagne and drank deep from it. "I have some caps to pull with him, to be sure."

Julia leaned forward. "But she said there would be danger."

"Indeed she did." Garth's tone was dry. "At least she did not say we were going upon a long journey. That I could not have abided."

The leaves about them rustled again.

"Softly." Garth reached over and placed a hand upon Julia's. She gripped it in spite of herself.

"My lord and lady . . ." The proprietor stepped through the fronds.

Julia sighed in exasperation. She thought she heard Garth curse beneath his breath. "Yes?"

The proprietor bowed. "Has the dinner been to your liking?"

"Yes. Thank you. It was delicious."

"For dessert we have prepared honeyed apple and saffron doucet. Will that be acceptable?"

"Indeed yes!" Julia leaned forward eagerly. She adored apple doucet.

Garth chuckled. "You have made my lady very happy. That is a particular favorite of hers."

"Excellent. Excellent." The proprietor's eyes twinkled. "We can but hope that you will become a happy man soon as well. If you will follow me, then."

Garth lifted a brow. "I beg your pardon?"

The proprietor smiled. "Your chambers are prepared."

"Chambers!" Garth's brows snapped down. "What chambers? No! Do not answer that."

Julia swallowed a groan. Not again. "Indeed no."

The proprietor looked confused. "But I was ordered to serve the dessert within the chambers. Also, the musicians are there. They will play for you."

"No, by God!" Garth exclaimed. "No chambers."

"Indeed." Julia looked down. "We-we do not need dessert that much."

"But the musicians?"

"We will forgo the entertainment." Garth said sternly.

Julia offered a wavering smile. "The gypsy was sufficient entertainment."

"Gypsy?" The proprietor frowned. "What gypsy?"

"The one who was just here. She is a very imaginative fortune-teller."

The proprietor stared. "I did not hire a fortune-teller."

"You didn't?" Julia frowned.

"No, my lady, I did not." The proprietor frowned. Then he brightened. "But I do have dessert and musicians and the most glorious chamber awaiting you."

"You may serve the dessert to us here." Garth's words were clipped. "That is all."

"Very well." The proprietor sighed. "If that is your desire."

He departed through the leaves.

Julia flushed with pleasure. "Thank you, Garth. For . . . for the dessert, that is."

"Indeed. It would be unfair to deprive you of dessert merely because Monsieur X is a satyr."

"Garth!"

Garth sighed. "Julia, I cannot continue like this. Can you?"

"What do you mean?" A chill passed through Julia. Was Garth going to quit the search?

"Have you not noticed that every place he has demanded we visit has been romantic? Seductive? Confound it. There is always an infernal bed in the offing for us."

"Oh, that." Julia swallowed hard. What did he think she was? A stone? "Yes, I have noticed."

"Always it is *if you value your life.* He doesn't seem to give a hang for our sanity." Garth's expression turned fierce. "You must forgive me, Julia, but I cannot tolerate this anymore. There must be an end to it."

"I understand." A numbness invaded Julia. Garth was going to withdraw.

Garth reached across the table and clasped her hand. "That Gypsy had the right of it. It is time for us to be brave. It is time we become engaged."

"What?" Julia gasped. He wasn't withdrawing. He was— Julia shook her head to clear it. "Are you asking me to marry you?"

Garth stared at her mutely. Julia's breath caught. It was shocking, but if he were, she was not sure what she would answer. Strange. The word no did not enter her mind—or her heart. Whereas she had accepted proposals from six men, proposals she had actively sought, and with every one of them the word no had screamed out within her.

Garth did not move, but it was there in his eyes. He would ask her again.

Then it was not there. It disappeared within a moment. Determined intelligence schooled his face. "N-no. I am saying we should become engaged. Didn't you hear what Myrah said?"

"I thought I did." Julia said slowly. "What part are you talking about?" Since it wasn't that they were destined to be together . . .

"She said that someone watches you, watches you closely. That must be Monsieur X. And she said that he loves you dearly."

"Ah, yes. Indeed, that is what she said." Julia nodded and forced a smile, all the while castigating herself as a ninnyhammer. Garth made sense now. She had been insane the moment before. No doubt it was all due to Monsieur X's choice of settings. Garth was right, that is what had caused her to slip into fantasy.

"Monsieur X is attempting to set us up in some manner." Garth's grip tightened. "The villain is testing one of us, either you or me. I do not know which it is or why, but it is time we turn the tables and draw him out."

"By becoming engaged?" Julia pulled her hands from Garth and, standing, moved quickly to the picket railing. She stared out in determination across the millpond. Garth had proposed to her to lure Monsieur X out; instead, he had nearly lured her out into a frightfully feminine display.

"Julia?" Garth stood and strode to her. He glanced about and lowered his head to whisper. "If Monsieur X did something to your grooms, he only did it after they became engaged to you."

"Yes. Yes. I understand. You intend to be the bait."

"Softly. Remember what Myrah said."

"Interesting. The things I remember she said and the things you remember she said are very different." Julia bit her lip. "What did you hear her say?"

"She said someone listens. It must be Monsieur X."

"Oh, yes." At the moment Julia didn't give a rap about Monsieur X. Her heart was aching. She had almost said yes to a fake proposal from Garth. Gritting her teeth, she looked up. "What should we do now? He's heard all of this then . . ."

She halted as she saw into the depth of Garth's eyes. Desire was banked within them. He lowered his head, nuzzling her ear. "Accept my proposal loudly now and . . . pretend that you mean it."

"Very well." Julia steeled herself. She would not act the silly goose again. *Pretend, Julia. Don't let it be real.* Clearing her throat, she stepped back from Garth and spoke very loudly. "Yes, Garth. I will be honored to marry you."

"As I am, my love." Garth spoke his line just as loudly. He stepped forward and placed hesitant arms about her. His expression was odd as he lowered his voice. "Now we kiss."

"Y-yes." Julia quivered. It was hopeless. His arms felt marvelous about her.

Garth, in a stilted movement, lowered his head and brushed her lips with his.

Julia let out a sigh. "There."

"Yes." Garth lowered his head again, only this time swiftly. Then his lips captured hers most savagely. Yet the emotion behind it was real and strong, and nothing fake about it. Julia groaned, and her passions flared in eager response. Only Garth's touch and breath and heat mattered. They were hers, and she melded into him, offering her touch and breath and heat in return.

"Stop, Black Widow!"

Julia didn't have a moment to think. Garth tore his lips from hers. A body came rushing at them. She struggled from Garth's arms at the same moment he released her. He spun, putting her behind him. Only

behind him happened to be against the picket railing.
She crashed into it and then through it.

She screamed as she plummeted into the pond. Julia,
her heart pounding in fear, forced her head above
water, frightened for Garth. It must be Monsieur X.
"Garth!"

"Julia!" Garth bellowed as he clearly struggled with
another man.

"Oh, my God." Julia, treading water, almost went
down in surprise. The man struggling with Garth was
none other than Bloodsoe.

"You mustn't marry her!" He gripped Garth. "She
will murder you!"

"What?" Garth shook his head. "Release me!"

"I am here to save you! You must listen!"

"Julia!" Garth cried out. "Are you all right?"

"Yes."

"You are in danger. She's a murderess!"

"Release me!"

"She's a fiend!"

"Cease!" Garth attempted to shove Bloodsoe from
him. Only Bloodsoe clung like a limpet. Both men went
flying into the water. Julia squeezed her eyes shut at
the splash.

"Help me! Help me!" Bloodsoe's voice called out.
"I cannot swim! I cannot swim!"

"Oh, no!" Julia snapped her eyes open.

Fear shot through her. Bloodsoe looked to be frantically crawling over Garth, all but driving him down
beneath the water. Julia had heard of it before. Pan-
icked men could kill strong swimmers in such situ-
ations. Praying, she struck out toward them. Only she
couldn't make progress in her skirts. She refused to let
that fear drain her. Suddenly, she couldn't see either
man. "Garth! Garth. Please answer me!"

The water roiled from where Garth and Bloodsoe had gone down. Garth's head appeared. "Julia!"

"Thank God!" Julia's chest hurt painfully from the sudden relief. "Are you all right?"

"By God I am. But I had to knock Bloodsoe out."

"Good!" Julia called. "He deserved it!"

"My lord! My lady!" An alarmed voice called from the gazebo. The proprietor stood at the broken fencing, his face distressed. "Are you all right?"

"Yes." Garth called. "Never mind us. We decided on a moonlight swim."

"Now you will want your chambers, yes?"

Julia began laughing. "No! But I want my apple doucet!"

Eleven

"Are you ready?" Julia wrapped her blanket around her firmly as she stood before the town house entry door. The millpond water had done severe damage to her dress as well as arranging its lines in the most immodest fashion. She licked her lips from the last bit of apple doucet, which she had polished off in the carriage. The proprietor had been so kind as to send several servings with her.

"As ever I will be." Garth grinned at her. He had wrapped his blanket about him like a Roman toga. He also had one arm of Bloodsoe's looped across his shoulder. Meeker possessed Bloodsoe's other arm. The unconscious inspector sagged limply between them.

"*Snarf* . . . what?" Bloodsoe's head bobbed up. "What?"

"Ah, he speaks." Garth observed. "I didn't hit him as hard as I hoped."

Bloodsoe flung his head back. When he took in Garth, horror filled his eyes. "You tried to kill me!"

"No, you clunch, I didn't." Garth shook his head. "You were about to drown us both. Sorry if I took exception to that."

Bloodsoe's head listed, and his eyes rolled about. "Where are we?"

"We've brought you to my house." Julia said.

"Oh, God!" Bloodsoe moaned. "You do want to kill me."

"Why, what shabby gratitude," Julia said as she opened the door to the town house wide. "I think we are being most courteous to you considering you are a weasely eavesdropper who managed to send us all into the brink."

"Not to mention your name-calling. It's rather offensive, old man," Garth murmured as he and Meeker stumbled through the portal.

"Here we are. Home, safe and sound." Julia followed them in and closed the door. A puddle of water pooled about them on the marble floor.

"Gad's hounds," Bendford Wrexton cried out from the library door. Apparently he had been either just entering it or just leaving it. Either way, it was unfortunate. "Just what in bloody hell happened now?"

"Oh, dear. Not so safe."

"Good evening, Lord Wrexton." Garth's tone was nonchalant. "You may leave us, Meeker."

"Thank you, my lord." Meeker's voice was laden with gratitude. He abandoned his side of Bloodsoe, bowed hastily, and vanished from the foyer within seconds.

"Bendford, what is the matter?" Aunt Clare's voice called. She, too, emerged from the library, Percy at her skirts. Her eyes widened as she took in the sodden trio. "Gracious!"

"What was it this time?" Lord Wrexton asked in a tired voice. Clearly he was attempting to hold his temper, a rare and sad trial for him. "And what are you doing consorting with the enemy?"

"He is not the enemy." Garth said mildly. "He tried to save me, don't you know?"

"Save you? Lord Wrexton lifted his brow high.

"Yes." Garth chuckled. "From Julia, no less."

"Murderess." Bloodsoe muttered.

"What did he say?" Lord Wrexton roared.

"He's rather confused from the dunking he received." Julia smiled as winningly as she could.

"Dunking?" Lord Wrexton's face turned ominous. "What dunking?"

"We had a slight accident." Garth said. "Bloodsoe was a jot too enthusiastic in his crusader role."

"Murderer," Bloodsoe said more firmly, and pushed away from Garth. He wavered, weaved about, but regained his stance.

"Bloodsoe did this?" Wrexton's look was disbelieving. "Not Julia?"

"Indeed." Julia frowned. "I was completely innocent of any wrongdoing this time."

"Seductress!" Bloodsoe said.

"Be quiet." Julia hissed.

"What?" Lord Wrexton frowned.

"He sneezed." Julia flushed. "None of this was my fault, Father."

"Truly, sir." Garth said. "It was an accident."

"*Achoo!*" Bloodsoe said. "They tried to kill me."

"If that was their purpose, I would approve most heartily. But no, I know Julia did not do anything so right-thinking."

"Bendford, for shame." Aunt Clare clucked. "You will have poor Mr. Bloodsoe thinking we wish him ill."

"Well, we do, confound it. The ferret is always sneaking about, trying to condemn Julia for some absurd reason or another."

"I caught them." Bloodsoe lifted his head. "I saw the Black Widow seducing Lord—"

"Aunt Clare," Julia interrupted quickly. "Do you think we might have some dry clothes for Inspector Bloodsoe? I fear he will contract a fever if he is not attended."

"But I stopped them!" Bloodsoe, at that moment, did appear feverish.

"Yes, he stopped us from finishing our dinner." Julia said firmly. "That is all."

"How could you have gotten a dunking if you were only eating dinner. Where the devil were you?"

"We were at a charming inn that has dining right out over a millpond."

"What!" Lord Wrexton actually goggled. "Millpond? Gads . . . Garth, my boy. You didn't . . . you weren't at . . . well, you weren't, were you?"

"Yes, sir. Forgive me."

"Gads! What the devil were you two doing there?"

"Do tell me more, dear." Aunt Clare skittered up. "Was it romantic, then?"

"It was quite romantic," Julia admitted.

"Romantic!" Lord Wrexton looked appalled. "The millpond isn't meant for romance, Clare. It's meant for . . ."

"Seduction!" Bloodsoe stated. Then he sneezed.

"Er, yes." Lord Wrexton pinned a thunderous glare upon Julia. "What were you two about?"

Julia sighed. "We had gone there in hopes of finding a clue as to who . . . who took my suitors, Father."

"Untrue," Bloodsoe objected. "She lured Lord Stanwood there. And she has caught him this time. They are engaged. Now he will die."

"What?" Lord Wrexton gurgled.

"What?" Aunt Clare's voice was breathless. "Did . . . did . . ."

Julia swallowed. She glanced at Garth. His gaze was full of wry amusement. She shrugged. "Er . . . yes. Garth proposed."

"I don't believe it!" Bendford said.

"And did you accept?" Aunt Clare clasped her hands together. "Please say you did."

"Yes, Aunt Clare." Guilt filled Julia at her deception, but she was committed. She winced. That surely was not the correct term. "I did."

"Finally." Aunt Clare's eyes shone with pride and love. "Oh, how wonderful for you. What made you two realize your true love at last?"

"True love? At the millpond?" Bendford shook his head. "That is not what happens, Clare, at the millpond."

"What made us . . . ?" Julia thought hard. She then laughed. "Why, in truth, a gypsy fortune-teller made us realize it. She told us we belonged together."

"What!" Lord Wrexton appeared dumbfounded.

"A Gypsy fortune-teller? Now why didn't I think of that?" Aunt Clare breathed.

"She h-hired the gypsy!" Bloodsoe said. "I know she did."

"I did not!" Julia exclaimed in astonishment.

"Yes, you did, Monsieur X!" Bloodsoe said it with great melodrama.

"What the devil is he blathering about now?" Wrexton growled.

"Gracious," Aunt Clare exclaimed. Everyone looked at her. She blinked. "Excuse me. I must go tell Ruppleton the good news. I must tell Ruppleton and Wilson!" Aunt Clare lifted her skirts and turned. She actually trumpeted, "Ruppleton! Oh, Ruppleton!"

"They will not be married," Bloodsoe avowed.

"What?" Aunt Clare froze halfway across the foyer.

"I will stop her. She is the Black Widow. Her other grooms' disappearances must be accounted for first. And I have proof of her dastardly involvement."

"Stow it, Bloodsoe. Bedamn, I need a drink." Lord Wrexton turned to the library door. "Everybody come in here now!"

"Could we not go and change clothes first?" Julia attempted.

"Now, Julia!"

His roar caused everyone to file into the library. Julia glanced to Garth. His eyes were filled with mirth. It lifted her spirits directly.

"Come, my love." Walking over, he clasped her hand and blatantly drew her to the settee and sat, pulling her down beside him. He looked at Lord Wrexton, who had pounded over to the bar. "I am surprised, sir, that you are not happy about us wedding. It seems to me it would settle matters quite tidily."

"I am happy! If I could believe it, that is." Lord Wrexton grabbed up the brandy decanter. "You two have been at each other's throat all these years . . ."

"They were at more than that, my lord," Inspector Bloodsoe whispered as he dropped into one of the chairs.

"What happened to change that?" Lord Wrexton's gaze was definitely suspicious as he poured himself a bumper. "And do not try to gull me with some twaddle about Gypsies telling you so. Destiny for true lovers is just so much tripe."

"Bendford, dear, it is not tripe," Aunt Clare reproached as she drifted in and alighted upon a chair. "Indeed, I have told you that Julia and Garth have been in love since they were children. Did you forget?"

"They cannot marry," Bloodsoe persisted. "I demand to know what happened to her other fiancés. The Crown will not overlook it."

"Truly?" Aunt Clare leaned forward in concern. "That could hinder their wedding, you say?"

"Without a doubt, madame."

"Miss Clare?" Ruppleton entered the library at the moment. "I heard you call."

Aunt Clare sprung up. "Ruppleton. It has happened. Julia and Garth are going to be married."

Ruppleton's face broke into a broad grin. "Congratulations."

"Inspector Bloodsoe says that they cannot marry until the Crown knows what happened to Julia's other suitors. So if you will excuse me." Aunt Clare all but dashed past him. "If you could please serve drinks to everyone. They are frightfully wet."

"Certainly." Ruppleton answered to empty air, since Aunt Clare had cleared the library that swiftly. He moved toward the cabinet where Lord Wrexton had already supplied his own needs, a dazed, pleased expression upon his face. "This is certainly time for celebration."

"It is not!" Bloodsoe said. "I won't let them marry."

"Pah." Lord Wrexton drank his brandy swiftly.

"I have evidence." Bloodsoe's voice oozed portent. "Your gardener will testify, I will have you know."

"My gardener?" Lord Wrexton shook his head. "Confound it, man, your dunking has affected your brains."

"Our gardener?" Julia herself could only stare.

"Yes." Bloodsoe lifted his chin and cleared his throat. "He will testify that you are a murderer."

"What?" Garth exclaimed.

"Of course, he declares that you are a murderer as well, my lord." Bloodsoe looked stern. "Which I had not considered before but will in the future, I assure you."

"Oh, Lord!" Julia bit back a giggle. Garth frowned at her in inquiry, while a slow, steady rumble came from Lord Wrexton. She looked at Bloodsoe. "Just what were you doing digging in the gardens? I believe it was four nights ago."

Bloodsoe appeared shocked. "How did you know?"

"I am the wicked Black Widow."

"See, my lord!" Bloodsoe's voice was triumphant.

Lord Wrexton shook his head. "What the devil were you digging in our gardens for, you great looby?"

"He was looking for the bodies, Father." Julia said. "And actually, Bloodsoe, I know it because Antonio quit our employment that morning. He threw poor Aunt Clare into quite a dither from what I heard. He swore that Garth and I had been destroying his garden again and he could no longer work for such blood-thirsty murderers."

"He did?" Garth's face lit with amusement.

Ruppleton nodded. "That he did."

Bloodsoe paled. "I see."

"He has returned to Italy, where there is respect for the living."

"He has?"

"Ha! Hoisted on your own petard, Bloodsoe. You drove your own witness off by digging up his flowers. That makes you a murderer as well."

"You should not be so glib, my lord." Bloodsoe persisted. "I vow that you will be next to disappear if you do not listen to me."

"Damn, but I've had enough." Wrexton slammed his drink down. "I'll not have you talking such fustian to me in my own library. You will not stop Julia and Garth from marrying, do you hear?"

"I hear, my Lord. But I will stop them. I will bring in the Crown if I need must."

That caused a roar and bombast from Lord Wrexton, to be sure.

Julia chuckled slightly and snuggled closer to Garth as the two men proceeded to engage in verbal battle. "Faith, it is better than watching the great Siddons, is it not?"

Lord Wrexton took the lead with a tirade, his voice

rolling and lowering, modulated to reach the farthest reaches of the House of Lords. Bloodsoe fought in the quiet manner. Determinedly, he would slip in one statement to every five of Lord Wrexton's. Indeed, in such a determined manner that he could not have been considered vanquished. He hung in there like one of the royal physician's leeches.

Julia leaned into Garth. "Perhaps we should take pity on them and tell the truth."

"No." Garth frowned. "Don't you dare tell them we are pretending. This has turned out far better than expected. Let Bloodsoe broadcast it."

Julia sighed, guilt pinching at her. "But what about later . . . with Aunt Clare? She will be so disappointed."

"No. We cannot tell them the truth and hope to fool the world, or Monsieur X."

"My lord." Ruppleton's voice breathed.

Garth looked up. "Yes, Ruppleton?"

He was holding a tray with drinks. He bent and offered Garth not a drink but the entire tray. In fact, he shoved it into Garth's hands. "Do forgive me, but I must attend to . . . the champagne. We must have champagne as well."

"Of course, Ruppleton." Garth said politely, though his eyes showed his surprise. Ruppleton was gone before even that.

"You bloodsucking parasite," Lord Wrexton shouted at Bloodsoe. "Now you listen to me, and listen to me good!"

"Do hurry!" Aunt Clare waved at the seven men who made their exodus from their red-and-gold prison. Twelve cats escorted them.

"I think we should consider this more closely," Lucas

said, the very last to leave the room. "It is too smoky by half. The fortune-teller is all wrong."

"You only say that because you lost the bet," Danford said. "I told you tonight would be the night."

"I thought the Millpond Inn should do the trick. Matthew said. "It is one of the few investments of mine that prospers still."

"Indeed." Lucas's tone was dry. "But we still have not considered all the angles."

"No, you must appear." Aunt Clare's sweet face was firmly set. "That dreadful Bloodsoe man says that he will stop Julia and Garth's marriage because her other grooms are missing. If I present you now, he cannot persist in the investigation, can he?"

"True." Giles nodded. "You cannot say someone is missing if they are standing before you."

"Yes," Harry agreed as they chased down the second flight of stairs. "It is best we take Bloodsoe by surprise and set the blighter right upon the instant. We cannot have him throwing a spanner into Julia's marriage. Not after all this work."

"Gadzooks, no. I will see to that. Mother will listen to me . . . and the Crown will listen to her."

"I still believe you might wish to consider Julia's and Garth's reactions." Lucas brought up the rear.

"Why? Now that they have recognized their love, they will be grateful to us, I am sure." Aunt Clare's face glowed. "And quite relieved to know that you are all safe and well. Julia does fret so over any little mystery to which she does not have the answer."

"They will need to be completely in love for them not to feel duped," Lucas persisted.

"Monteith has a point there." Matthew frowned. "Both are proud. We dare not set their backs up or they will both go off in opposite directions just to spite us. Their pride will demand it."

"I am sure you are wrong. Garth and Julia are not at all like that. Besides, Julia declared it was a fortune-teller who had made them realize their love for each other." Aunt Clare beamed as she led them forth into the foyer. "They cannot blame us for contrivance, then, can they?"

"No, only some poor Gypsy who needed coin for a bottle of wine." Lucas's tone was ironic as the men came to a hushed, huddled stop. "Thank God for that."

Shouts and roars came from the library door. The men automatically formed a defensive group. The cats surrounded them in a second ring.

"Forsooth," Reginald muttered. He looked back the way they came. "Perhaps Monteith is right. This does not sound like the proper time for telling secrets."

Herrington's grin was weak. "Almost makes you homesick for upstairs, what?"

"Gracious!" Aunt Clare clasped her hands together. "Bendford is rather loud, is he not?" She then held her hands out. "Now, before we go into the library, I wish to tell you dear gentlemen again . . ."

The library door opened, and Ruppleton slipped out. He slammed the door shut and turned. Upon seeing the men, his face crumpled, and he waved frantic hands at them. "Go. Go. It's all a bubble!"

"What?" Aunt Clare gasped.

"Master Garth and Julia are merely pretending to be engaged." Ruppleton did not even attempt to lower his voice. Lord Wrexton's shouts from the library made it quite unnecessary. "They want to draw out Monsieur X."

"Egad!" Harry muttered. "We've been had."

Lucas chuckled. "Imagine, they have gotten seven for the price of one."

From behind the door, Lord Wrexton's voice rose to

even greater heights. "Now, get out of my house you Friday-faced, bandy-legged mawworm! And don't drip on my carpets as you go!"

"S'death." Matthew cried as the library door swung open. "Take cover!"

The men scattered. The cats, caught beneath legs and boots, howled and leapt. Herrington tripped over Shakespeare and slid halfway across the marble floor. He did not try to rise, but crawled straightaway into the salon. Reginald crashed shoulders with Giles as they both strove to escape through the parlor doorway.

Discovery of the grooms appeared imminent. Ruppleton whirled and dove toward the library door. He slipped on a remaining puddle of water. He scrabbled, flapped his arms for balance, twirled, and rammed directly into Bloodsoe, who was coming out. They were both propelled backward, an effective stopper to the library door.

Both men down for the count, the other grooms successfully dispersed. Matthew dragged Lucas into the sewing room. Harry bolted into the music room. Charles played the odds and ranged himself in the corner up against the large grandfather clock.

The sound of opening doors and closing doors was negligible. Lord Wrexton's new roars and Ruppleton's groans were joined by Bloodsoe's vociferous sneezes. The cats had chased after Aunt Clare, who had rushed to assist both butler and inspector.

"Dear me," Aunt Clare exclaimed. "What a frightful error. But do rise, gentlemen. Everything is all right now, I do assure you."

"Thank you, Miss Clare." Ruppleton rose slowly and staggered to the center of the foyer. He appeared dazed. A large knot reddened his brow.

"Cats! *Snarf!*" Bloodsoe scrambled up with far more

vigor. He actually leapt two feet in the air in an effort to escape the feline mass.

"Why the devil are all the cats down here, Clare?" Lord Wrexton strode from the library, peering about belligerently.

"Why?" Aunt Clare blinked. "I-I thought they should be present for—for Julia and Garth's announcement?"

"H-how very sweet of you, Auntie." Julia appeared with Garth by her side. She was forced to tug her blanket up as Peaches and Cream vied to climb it the fastest. "Perhaps we should get them some milk in celebration?"

"Oh, no. Champagne will do," Aunt Clare murmured absently. She had not realized before exactly how underdressed Julia truly was. It was quite proper for Garth to see her this way, but the other poor boys must be eating their hearts out now. "Julia, dearest, I do believe you should go to your room and . . . and change into something more suitable. You—you are not at all dressed for company."

"So now you notice her bedraggled, shameful state?" Lord Wrexton threw up his hands. "Clare, you are a wonder."

"Thank you, Bendford." Clare smiled, quite pleased. After all, her boys were safely hidden for the moment. "Garth, dear, why do you not go as well. You will catch a cold like that."

"Ha!" Lord Wrexton refused to give the floor. "It is Bloodsoe who's going to catch cold at it. And he's one that can go bloody well change. I don't like him in my house."

Bloodsoe stiffened. "My lord. I do not care to be here, either. If I could escape, I assure you, I would."

"Be my guest. Everyone remain where you are so that Bloodsoe suffers no setbacks on his way to the door." Lord Wrexton said it most spitefully. "And do not bother to return, Bloodsoe." He suddenly barked a grand laugh. "You will not receive a wedding invitation, I assure you."

Bloodsoe sneezed, appearing miserable. "I have warned you, and my conscience is clear. There will be no wedding between Lady Julia and Lord Stanwood until my investigation is complete and I know the whereabouts of and what happened to the other grooms."

Yes." Lord Wrexton waved a hand. "Now be off, you slippery cod."

"My lord." Bloodsoe sniffed and meandered rather drunkenly toward the outer door. "Treating me with disrespect will not change matters. I am not easily diverted from a case."

"Yes, yes, Inspector Bloodsoe, I am sure." Aunt Clare took Bloodsoe by one arm, and Ruppleton took him by the other to steer him. "Perhaps a mustard plaster would be beneficial when you arrive home."

"I am the best there is, I will have you know. I cannot be hoodwinked! Not Inspector Bloodsoe! *Achoo!*"

"Good-bye, Bloodsoe," Lord Wrexton chortled. "Give me a call when you find those chaps. I don't doubt, the way you go about matters, that Julia and Garth will have grandchildren by then!"

"Bendford!" Aunt Clare murmured sternly. "That was unkind. Why do you not go and enjoy a brandy . . . in the library, of course."

"Very well." Lord Wrexton turned but clearly could not resist one last taunt. "I vow the man could not see what lies directly in front of his long nose."

The grandfather clock began to chime the hour that very moment. Bloodsoe stared up at the clock. Aunt Clare expelled a most exasperated breath. To the side could be seen Charles Danford's boot just barely showing. "Do be quiet Bendford, dear. We all have our blind sides. Even you, dearest."

Twelve

"We have put the announcement in both the *Morning Post* and the *London Gazette.*" Julia studied her list as they entered the carriage and sat. "What should we do next?"

"What? It is not on your list?" Garth teased.

"No," Julia frowned. "We wish to make this look proper. What would we do next if we were newly engaged?"

"I know what I would do next." Garth's tone was wry. "Though I do not think you best put it on your list."

"What is it?" Julia dove into her reticule, looking for something with which to take note of Garth's additions.

Garth grinned wickedly. "I would take the opportunity of this enclosed carriage to properly maul you."

"I see." Julia dropped her reticule. She hid her face and smile as she picked it up again. Gracious, would that not be positively enjoyable? She could not bring herself to castigate Garth upon his lascivious behavior. In truth, she was having too much trouble turning her own thoughts from it. "No, I can see how that should *not* be scratched upon the list."

Garth laughed and peered out the window. Julia fell silent, scratching off items on her list. What would they really talk about right now if they were going to be married? Julia started doodling. Would they talk about the honeymoon? Would they discuss the exact date? She scratched on the small slip of paper all the more. Would they debate where they would live? Julia pursed her lips. She then gasped.

"What?" Garth asked.

"Nothing. Nothing at all." Julia stared in consternation at what she had unconsciously scribbled.

"No, it is something." Garth leaned over. "What did you write?"

"I was merely wondering what we would be talking about if we were truly engaged."

"And what did you write?" Garth asked.

Julia handed the paper to him.

"Children?" Garth's eyes started wide, and then his gaze became closed. He handed the list back to her.

"Well?" Julia asked, discovering an uncharted hollow within her heart.

"Well what?" Garth clearly strove for a nonchalant look.

"Do you want children?" Julia asked. "I mean, have you ever thought of having them?"

A solemn and rather wistful look crossed his face. "Have you?"

"I do not know," Julia said, embarrassed. She bit her lip. "No. That is not true. When I was young, I always planned to have children, lots of them."

"I think I did, too." Garth smiled.

"I wanted my children to have plenty of brothers and sisters." Julia laughed. "Amusing, isn't it?"

"No." Garth's gaze was soft, his hazel eyes a warm moss green. "In truth, I felt the same way. I wanted the large, boisterous family that we never had."

Julia nodded. She did not need to question his choice of words. "But now you do not think that anymore?"

"No." Garth looked away. He grimaced. "One must

be married for that. At least it is the recommended manner, I've been told."

"Yes," Julia nodded. This time she looked away. When did she exactly lose that vision? She imagined it was at her coming out, when she discovered the world and men. Men who never captured her interest or her heart. Men who seemed to wish to hedge her about and ask her to be what she could not be. It became more than just being led in a dance. It became more like being pushed from one direction to another, at someone else's will. That was when the thought of children became one of confinement and control rather than her childhood dream of never being lonely and always having family, love, and laughter.

"That is the rub," Garth said quietly. "When I grew up, I believe I started trying to imagine what kind of father and husband I could possibly be? I do not remember mine whatsoever, of course, or my mother. And your father has been most excellent and as much of a parent as could be . . ."

"And Aunt Clare the perfect role for a mother and wife?" Julia asked in gentle amusement.

"But—" Garth halted. "Very well, I will own it. I would not even know how to go about it."

"Me, either," Julia admitted.

They stared at each other.

Julia looked down. How pathetic they appeared. Two orphans that knew when it came to families, real families, they would not have a clue as to how to deal with them or live within them.

"No children." Julia crossed through her scribbled question with resolution, ignoring that newly discovered hollow. She smiled brightly. "Well, then? What should we do next to foil Monsieur X?"

Garth, his face far too solemn, studied Julia. She felt a dreadful flush rise to her cheeks. He laughed abruptly. "I know." He called for Meeker to pull the carriage to the side. He was opening the door and had alighted before Julia could question him further. "Come."

"Where?" Intrigued, Julia gave him her hand and permitted him to assist her down.

"You must have a ring." Garth grinned like a schoolboy. "The most ostentatious ring imaginable."

Julia's mood lifted directly. Her favorite jewelry store was just down the street. "Rundell and Bridge, oh, yes, indeed."

They entered the select confines of the most famous and respected jeweler to the *tôn*. Julia, eyes sparkling, strolled down one counter. Garth wandered down the other.

A clerk appeared. Julia smiled. "Good morning, Albert."

"Miss Wrexton!" Albert's face paled. His normally obsequious demeanor showed strain. "H-how do you do?"

"Very well." Julia lifted a cool brow. She should have known that even an assistant to the jeweler to the *tôn* would have heard the gossip. She forced a bright smile. "Very, thank you. Indeed, I am going along famously, to be truthful."

"That is because she has made me the happiest of men, Albert." Garth strode over to stand beside her.

"Sh-she has?" Albert swallowed.

"Yes. I am Stanwood," Garth said jovially. "And I am Julia's latest fiancé, and last, I might add."

"I hope so . . . I mean, that is good to hear, my lord." Albert stammered.

"Yes, extremely good." Garth smiled down at Julia. "We would like to look at the most ostentatious . . ."

"And odiously expensive . . ." Julia added.

Garth nodded. ". . . Engagement rings you might have."

"Certainly." Greed and distress warred across Albert's face. Greed won. He bowed. "Permit me to prepare a display for you."

He disappeared into a side door and returned shortly. He cleared his throat. "If you would follow me."

He led them into a private room where he had rings displayed upon black velvet. Julia needed but one glance at the array. At the top of the grouping was one with a tremendous green sapphire cut in a round brilliant. Two swirls of diamonds, one a row of champagne diamonds and one of white wrapped around half of the sapphire and then swooped up and over a small segment of the huge sapphire.

It was absurd, but the sparkling water-green of the sapphire made Julia think of Garth's eyes. She wanted that ring. As she lifted her finger to point, Garth spoke. "That is the one without question."

Julia froze. She glared at him.

Garth raised his brow. "You do not agree?"

"I do," Julia admitted with a frown. "But you told him which one I wanted before I had a moment to tell you. You could have been wrong, you know?"

"A thousand pardons, my love." Garth's lips twitched. "Perhaps we should ask to see a few more than these. You are right; we should spend an hour at it at least. I shall pretend I do not know your taste or style whatsoever. That *was* frightfully brash of me."

"Beast." Julia sputtered on her laughter. "That is the perfect ring, and you know it."

"Excellent," Garth said, his eyes warm. He reached into his jacket. "I will write a draft on my bank for it immediately, Albert."

"My lord." Albert appeared shocked. "You have not inquired of the price."

"Once again, it appears I have spoken out of turn. These engagement rituals are confounding." Garth sighed. "What is the price?"

Garth didn't flinch when Albert confessed the outrageous price. Julia did. "Wait!

Garth looked up. "Yes?"

Julia gazed at the ring longingly. She wanted the ring regardless of the cost. She glanced at Albert. "Could we please be alone for a moment."

Albert stiffened. "I beg your pardon?"

Julia's brows lifted. She was not accustomed to being questioned. "I wish to speak to Lord Stanwood in private."

Albert flushed and looked down. "Er, yes. Of course."

"Do not fear, Albert." Garth rose and escorted the hesitant Albert to the door and opened it. "I promise I won't pop off."

"My lord!" Albert exclaimed.

"With the ring," Garth said solemnly. "Neither will the Lady Julia dispose of me while we are unattended."

"My lord. I had I no such thoughts. I—" Albert halted. Gurgling, he ducked his head and stepped out.

Garth closed the door on him and turned with a smile. "Now. What is your objection?"

"I have no objection, to the ring, that is." Julia licked her lips and then blurted. "Only, permit me to pay for it."

"Now *I* beg your pardon." Garth frowned darkly. "I will stand the ready for the ring, and there will be no debate. It would look odd for you to pay for your own engagement ring. Very odd. Monsieur X would sniff out a rouse, no doubt. And after Albert's behavior, you cannot delude yourself into believing he would not gossip. The *tôn* would hear, I am sure."

"But it is far too expensive for you. I wish to purchase it."

"No."

"Yes." Julia glared at him. "It is my responsibility. We are only doing this because of my situation."

"I will pay for it."

"No." Julia smiled as winningly as she could. "You are not looking at this correctly. If I buy it, it is actually Father who is paying for it. And you must own he deserves to pay for it. He is the perpetuator of this all, do not forget."

The slightest smile touched Garth's lips. "For which I am grateful to him."

"What?"

"That is, if we both escape this with our lives intact." Garth said wryly. His eyes darkened. "I am glad to . . . to know you again, Julia."

Julia flushed. "Thank you."

"I fear, however, I have a confession I must make."

"What?" Julia stiffened. Confessions mixed with Garth could prove lethal.

"Now remember"—Garth took her hand in his gently—"I promised Albert you would not murder me. Please, do not make a liar out of me."

"I will try not to." Julia could not hide her nervousness. "Now tell me."

Garth sighed. "I can easily pay for this ring, Julia."

"What?" Julia blinked. She did not know what she expected. This seemed innocuous enough. "That is all?"

"Yes, that is it, pretty much." Garth smiled with the nervousness Julia had experienced moments before. "Only, I can easily stand the blunt for this ring and more. My fortune outstrips your father's by two times or more, if I am not mistaken." He appeared shame-faced. "You see, I enjoy gambling. Gambling upon the exchange."

"You are gammoning m—" Julia froze. His eyes were too honest. She shivered as if doused with a bucket of cold water. "Oh, my God. You mean it, do you not?"

"Yes, Julia. I do."

"Oh, no," Julia moaned. "All this time I have been accusing you of coveting my fortune! Here I have been practically accusing you of being one step from the Cent-per-cents. In fact, *you* led me to believe that! Why? Why did you do that?"

Garth studied her for a moment. He sighed, and a self-deprecatory smile touched his lips. "It hurt me that you would think me so low a character as to chase after your money. You classed me with the fortune hunters, and I decided you could have a taste of your own medi-cine. Also, I would never have vaunted it before your father. Making money upon the exchange is ignoble for a nobleman. Only the cits should have the pleasure. Besides, you know your father, the only proper interest in life is politics."

"All this time," Julia murmured, "I was thinking that you—"

"I know, and I apologize. I should not have acted so. After all, it did make sense why you thought me a fortune hunter. I did arrive on the doorstep at your father's beckoning. Also, I *am* a rake, and I care for nobody."

"You are not!" Julia flushed from her vehemence. Swallowing hard, she shook her head. "I do not believe that anymore, Garth."

"I never expected to hear you say that." Garth's voice was soft. He grinned. "Blast, but I *am* buying you that ring. Give me no argument. Just to hear you say what you just did is worth every carat of it."

Julia laughed. "I do apologize for all the dreadful things I have called you. It is just that you . . . you are a frightful tease."

"I know I am, and I paid the price." Garth turned grave. "I destroyed your trust in me, Julia. I regret that."

"I was no better." Julia forced a laugh. "I can be rather shrewish when I wish to be. And I can jump to conclusions . . . even when they are not warranted. But for all that, I-I do trust you, Garth."

"And for what it is worth, I never truly thought all those things I twitted you about."

"Gammon." Julia retorted with spirit. "You did so."

"Very well, I might have." Garth grimaced. "It was my defense."

"Defense?"

"I felt that you had grown not to need me. Or care for me. The only way to disguise that pain from myself was to tease you as if it did not matter."

"I do not care what great fortune you have," Julia avowed. "I will pay for this ring, and gladly. I am going to keep it forever in memory of hearing you say that."

"Vixen," Garth said warmly. "But I intended for you to have the ring afterward. Did you think I would take it back? What would I do with it? No! Do not answer that."

Julia knew she was cornered. She threw up her hands. "Very well. You win. But only because if we tarry any longer, Albert will be sure that I have done away with you."

"Excellent!" Garth walked to the door and opened it. "Albert, we are finished."

It was a quick and simple matter to make provision for the ring. Garth pocketed the box, and they left the private room in a complacent mood. Then Julia froze.

The marquess of Hambledon's younger sister stood at the counter.

Upon seeing Julia, she gasped. Her eyes grew furious, and she cast a scathing look at Albert. "What is she doing here?"

"You can tell her all about it, Albert." Garth winked at the man and took Julia's arm to draw her to the door. Rattled, Julia permitted him to lead her in a daze. Just before they escaped through the door, Garth turned back and said in a stage whisper. "Now don't forget to tell her the size. How ostentatious! Or the cost. How . . . ? Well, I will leave that to you, old man. Don't fail me."

Garth dragged the stunned Julia out into the fresh air then, slamming the ornate door loudly behind. In a delayed reaction, Julia choked, gurgled, and then laughed. "I do hope he can do us justice."

"That's the Julia I know." Garth smiled his approval and drew her a few steps away from the door. He reached into his vest pocket and pulled out the box.

"Garth, you are not going to—do it upon the open street?" Julia peered around quickly.

"Why not? We have nothing to hide." Garth's grin was positively wicked. He lifted the ring high. Julia vowed that blinding rays shot from it in the morning sun. "For Monsieur X to see. For all the world to see, and . . ." Garth cast a quick glance to the jewelry store. "And for the rude little chit and poor Albert."

Julia looked to see both of them with their noses pressed to the glass. Laughing, she waved to them with the style of a queen. She turned a sparkling glance back to Garth. "Do. Do proceed, my lord."

Garth's eyes darkened. "Will you accept my ring as a proposal to confound them all and wear it in memory of this day."

"I do." Julia blushed. Her voice was husky and choked. "I mean, yes, I will."

Garth rather gravely placed it upon her finger, his hands warm upon her. "No matter what danger there is. We will beat it, Julia; we will beat it all."

Julia looked at the glittering, ostentatious, audacious stone upon her hand. She smiled up at Garth. "Thank you."

"Of course the only danger at this moment is that of Albert and the widgeon fainting dead away." Garth tucked her hand into the corner of his arm, and they strolled down the street. "Imagine how we shall put everyone's noses out of joint as we proceed with our whirlwind engagement."

"I am dizzy already."

"Madame, I warn you now, the world will know us as a couple most flagrantly in love."

Julia could not hide her smile. "I believe that would be acceptable."

"Do you?" Warmth and pleasure sparked in Garth's gaze.

Julia laughed. "Indeed, I shall hold you to your threat."

Garth seemed to lose step a moment, and then he recovered. He gazed about. "Hmm. Now what else should we buy? If we were going to be married?"

"I do not know." Julia could not care where they went or what they did. The day had already been made perfect. "What do you think?"

"I think I know the answer now."

"What answer?"

"If I-we were truly going to be married, yes. I would want children. four of them. How is that for a list?"

"No," Julia shook her head. "Five children."

"Why?"

"I do not know." Julia blinked. "I believe because that is what I wanted when I was five myself."

"Five is not an unreasonable number." Garth observed. "Your father would be ecstatic."

Julia laughed. Yes, the day was perfect. She ignored how the hollow in her heart had disappeared in that singular moment.

Pertaining to the Case of the Missing Grooms.
An update, respectfully submitted by Inspector Bloodsoe,
Officer of the Crown:

At last, I have progress within this case. Strong progress. I cannot credit how I overlooked the first true clue in this most perplexing case. I believe it was due to my overpowering fear for Lord Stanwood that clouded my vision. It distracted me from the true direction I should take.

However, since my near drowning, things have become clearer. First, Lord Stanwood can very well take care of himself. Second, and what has brought me to the wealth of new clues I have found, was when I wondered, as Lord Wrexton did, why Lady Julia had chosen the Millpond for her illicit assignation. It clearly was not a common establishment for a lady of the tôn to select. Therefore, I decided it behooved me to discover more about the establishment.

Following the trail of ownership, it was found to belong to the earl of Raleigh. It took much research, since it is uncommon for such a noble name to be involved with such an enterprise. I also discovered that the earl is involved in many other merchant endeavors. His family history is not savory. Indeed—No, it would not be fitting for me to write of it. Especially since I fear the poor earl has met a sad fate.

The fact is that Lady Julia's dining at the Millpond can no longer be considered a macabre irony, as I be-

lieved in my previous report. (Reference one visit by Lord Stanwood and Lady Julia Wrexton to the very same inn frequented by Lord Beresford in company with his paramours.) She is possessed of and using these men's possessions and or their cachet they themselves once possessed.

She truly is a Black Widow of the worst kind. She has destroyed them and taken what she has wished from them. Her motive becomes clear. The fact that she uses their possessions without compunction speaks of her groom's demise.

I did not expect her to return to the same mode of crime. After this breakthrough, I am pleased she has not. For now I have returned to them and found that she was not always neat in her machinations. Indeed, the evidence residing within my drawer condemns her. She is very much linked with her grooms' disappearances. It is my duty now to discover where she has buried the bodies. I cannot close this case without . . .

"Bloodsoe, I want a word with you!"

Bloodsoe's head jerked up. His hand slid to cover the journal's page. His superior, Chief Pattington, stood before his desk. "Yes, sir?"

"Is that the Black Widow case you are working on?" Chief Pattington craned his neck to try and read the page from upside down.

"You mean the missing-grooms case? Forgive me, this is my personal journal, sir." Bloodsoe closed it and promptly put it into his top drawer. "However, I am preparing an official report, sir."

"Official or unofficial, I need whatever you have." Pattington flung himself in the chair in front of Bloodsoe's desk and scraped it back across the barren floor. He kicked out his legs and propped his feet upon the desk. "Those bloody lords are coming down heavy on me."

"I am sorry to hear that, sir." Bloodsoe frowned. "I assure you, sir, I have almost cracked the case. The evidence I possess against Lady Julia Wrexton is damning, very damning. We shall have the Black Widow trapped soon. I have discovered—"

"I will take whatever you have right now." Pattington thunked his chair to the ground.

Bloodsoe froze. He blinked. "Sir, I have not completed the investigation. I have her motive now. I also have strong evidence, both in testimony as well as articles of evidence, that links Lady Julia to her grooms' disappearances. I need, however, to discover the bodies. Without the bodies . . ."

"We do not have time, I tell you."

"Not even for one body?" Bloodsoe asked cautiously.

"No, not even one." Pattington leaned forward, planting his elbows firmly upon Bloodsoe's desk. Pattington was as interesting a personality study as was the Black Widow, Lady Julia Wrexton. He was uncouth and hailed from the lower orders. Yet he had inexorably risen through the ranks, clearly because the *tôn* and those of higher rank were never permitted to see that side. The man actually wore two different personalities as if they were but different jackets. The one thing that made him tolerable was that he did it openly and without apology. "I am telling you, Bloodsoe, we have to nab Lady Julia Wrexton damn soon. Else we *will* have another body on our hands."

"You mean Lord Stanwood's, I presume?" Bloodsoe felt the sting of defeat.

"Precisely." Pattington nodded sternly.

Bloodsoe waited. Pattington for once did not say what Bloodsoe expected of him. It was amazing that the chief was proving to be delicate about the issue.

Bloodsoe finally drew in his breath and decided to say it for him. "However, if Stanwood is killed by Lady Julia, we will be there for it. We can catch her . . . er, red-handed, as it were."

"What?" Pattington's elbows nearly fell off the desk. "Good God, but you are coldhearted, man."

"Sir?"

Pattington sat back into the chair. "I had not considered that issue, not a bit. No, if we do not haul Lady Julia into custody soon, Lord Stanwood is going to get himself murdered, whether in a duel or in cold blood. God only knows why, but he and she are determined to court disaster. They are going out in society now. She is vaunting a ring the size of a cannonball. It amazes me that the two are still invited to the best houses, but there are those who support her father." He pursed his lips. "They must be the few who ain't trooping into my office and bedeviling me with demands for her neck in a noose. To make it worse, the two actually appear May mad. The thought that it might truly be a love match is driving the *tôn* rabid."

"I see."

"If that isn't enough, gossip has it that the earl of Raleigh's little brother has arrived in town and is looking to call Stanwood out. The young pup is green from the country and doesn't know of Stanwood's reputation."

"Ah, yes." Bloodsoe frowned. "And what is that reputation, sir?"

"The man has never lost a duel, Bloodsoe."

"I did not know that, sir."

"Well, thank God most of the *tôn* does. That is what has kept Stanwood's and Lady Julia's enemies from open attack. For the nonce, that is." Pattington waved his hand. "But now we have this young fire-eater from the country stepping in where wiser men won't. And with matters the way they are, I can't depend upon Stanwood not to lose his temper and have pistols at dawn with the halfling. Either way, I'll have another bloody mess on my hands."

"Indeed, sir."

"I want Lady Julia, and I want her now. In fact, I would have liked her clapped up yesterday to tell the truth. The marquess of Hambledon's mother alone is enough to make any evidence you possess stick like plaster. They are turning the screws tight, Bloodsoe. If we fail, we will be out on our ear. We won't even be able to join the watch. But if we succeed, it will be a feather in the Crown's cap." He grinned and stood. "Or a feather in the Crown's crown, ha! I like that. Don't you like that Bloodsoe?"

"Yes, sir." Bloodsoe refrained from sighing. "But . . ."

"Also a promotion for me." Pattington's face grew stern. "So nab me Lady Julia."

"Sir, I must say, in all good conscience, I do not have enough evidence."

"You are far too particular, Bloodsoe. That has always been your problem. Just give me what you have and we will make it enough evidence."

"Sir, that is not possible."

Pattington stared at Bloodsoe. He shook his head and then stepped across the small office and closed the door. He walked back, his voice low. "You do not understand the political unrest caused by this case, Bloodsoe."

"No, sir. I do not."

"The parties in question are all very strong toffs in politics. If Lord Wrexton weren't so bloody strong himself, we could have settled this case long ago. Lady Julia would have had her swing on the gibbet. But he is a strong old ox when it comes to politics, and no one likes to tangle with him. That is not to say they are not doing so, because they are. What should be a private case between these families is lifting the petticoats of the Crown. These blue bloods are bringing their fight right into the House of Lords."

"I see." Bloodsoe felt the oddest, strangest twinge. "But sir, what if Lady Julia is innocent?"

"What if she is?" Pattington stared at Bloodsoe steadily.

"What if . . . if it *were* someone else?"

Pattington shrugged. "You have not found someone else, have you?"

"No, sir."

"There you have it. Do not bother over it so. You are the best man we have. That is why I put you on the case."

Bloodsoe cleared his throat. He was feeling distinctly uncomfortable. That odd twinge persisted. He felt an ill feeling in his gut. It was as close to a "hunch" as he had ever felt. Bloodsoe did not believe in hunches as a whole. Worse, it was the worse time to finally experience one. "Sir, as the best man for the case, I must inform you that we are not prepared to apprehend Lady Julia as yet. We must have a body. Or . . . or something more in that line."

"Then get it, Bloodsoe." Pattington turned and walked to the door. "I'll try and get you another week on this. But I make no promises."

"Sir?"

"Yes?"

"Do you think Lady Julia did it?"

"How the devil would I know?" Pattington shrugged his shoulder as if a fly had lighted on it. "She may have. The entire family is eccentric. Gads, but Wrexton's sister, the cat lady, used to keep the *tôn* raising their brows when she was young."

"Aunt Clare? Why?"

"She turned down her fair amount of suitors in her time."

"She did?"

"I know what you are thinking." Pattington grinned. "She was skitter-witted and daft even back then, but her family had power and money. The very two things that are guaranteed to make a peer drop to his knees and offer his hand and heart. But she vowed she would only marry for love, and she's done just that. Touched in the upper works." He shook his head. "It looks to me like Wrexton's daughter is following in the same path, as an eccentric, that is. Seems, though, she had got herself enough fiancés, unlike her aunt. But did she truly expand the energy to kill them all?" He lifted his hands up. "That is your department."

Bloodsoe studied his chief in astonishment. "How do you know so much about the Wrextons?"

"Not just the Wrexton's, Bloodsoe, but everyone in the *tôn*. That is my department. You can't move up the ranks without knowing your ranks." Pattington pointed a finger at him. "Now get me Lady Julia."

Thirteen

Julia laughed and twirled in Garth's arms to a waltz beneath glittering chandeliers. On a night like tonight, she wanted to pretend that everything was right in her world. She truly was Garth's fiancé, and they were happily engaged, looking toward an exciting future of love and happily-ever-after.

No one in the ballroom glared at them or harbored ill will. Meaning that Lady Danford and all of Charles Danford's cousins did not watch like birds of prey from the distance. Nor were there any relatives or friends of Lord Redmond or Viscount Dunn present. Indeed, there never had been a Charles Danford, Lord Redmond, or Viscount Dunn. There never had been a Monsieur X, either. There had never been anyone but Garth.

Garth smiled down at Julia, a warm and mischievous smile. Then is when Julia's heart whispered its secret. It was true. In her heart of heart, there never had been anyone but Garth. Julia stumbled in shock.

"Are you all right?" Garth frowned.

"Yes. Yes, I am." Julia nodded. Why had she not known it before? What would she have done if she *had* known it? her heart whispered back to her. Julia shook her head. She was not certain, but surely she would have done something different.

Garth studied her intently. "I know what we need."

"You do?" Julia raised a brow.

"I do." Her other brow shot up as Garth spun her out of the dancing throng and, with one more twirl, brought her to the veranda doors. She laughed as he opened them and drew her out to the stone veranda that terraced in three tiers to a fantastic garden beneath.

"Garth?" Julia's tone teased, yet she drew in a relieved breath. "Whatever are you thinking? People will talk."

"Never say so?" Garth's eyes glinted as he took her into his arms. "Let us at least make them change the subject of gossip."

"How?" Julia asked with wry humor.

"Like this." Garth lowered his head and kissed her. His kiss was gentle. To Julia, for that weary moment, it was life itself.

"I fear I lied." Garth slid his lips to below her ear, brushing that tender spot.

"You lied?" Julia's fears were drowned in pleasure.

"I said I knew what we needed." He held her closer, and he kissed the very curve and corner of her mouth. "In truth, this is what *I* needed."

"No." Julia shook her head, her lips grazing across his. "You were correct the first time."

Garth chuckled and kissed her sweetly once more. Julia stood in a dazed glow. At that moment, it seemed enough to hold their kiss and each other into eternity itself. Indeed, it seemed more than enough.

"But how will this change the gossip?" Julia finally drew back. She remained burrowed within the haven of Garth's arms.

"Hmm?" Garth rested his cheek upon her head, rubbing it against her hair. "Let us see. The gossip is now that you are an innocent woman and I am a treacherous seducer. A premier rake who took you in, you poor little lamb." Julia sputtered in her laughter and laid her head on his chest. The steady beat of his heart caused her own to gain faith. "No? Then, let us see—"

"I am not a murderess?" Julia asked lazily. "Just a woman in love?"

Garth tensed. His heart beat so fast against her ear, she felt a terrible intruder. Worse, she could not believe what she had just said. She had talked of love, whereas it had never been spoken before. She *was* a terrible intruder. She looked up in consternation. Garth's expression was withdrawn. Her heart failed her, and she castigated it. Why had it finally let her know the truth now? Why, at this frightfully late and complicated date, had it spoken? No, not spoken, rather, blurted it out?

"Julia? I—" Garth halted.

"No . . ." Julia shook her head, appalled. "I . . ."

"Aha! There you two are!"

Julia cringed. She looked to the corner of the veranda. Faith, fate was unkind. She forced a smile. "Inspector Bloodsoe, how very nice to see you. How long were you spying on us this time?"

"Damn and blast." Garth sighed and withdrew his arms from Julia. He turned to the inspector, his frown furious. Bloodsoe pedaled backward. "How did you get in here?"

"I told a servant I was here as added staff for the evening." Inspector Bloodsoe gazed at Julia, alarm enlivening his face. "I have not been here very long, madame. However, what you two have been engaged in transpired long enough for three couples to come out, see you, and return to the ballroom. I counted them. In fact, the gossip inside is what steered me to you."

"Famous!" Garth muttered.

Julia winced. "And what is the new story about me this fair eve?"

Inspector Bloodsoe stood without words for once in

his life. His pale complexion actually turned a shade darker. He approached slowly, a spark of intensity within his gaze. "Lady Julia, I have come here to ask you the question point-blank." He stepped back as Garth growled. "Very politely, I assure you. Please, Lord Stanwood, do not trounce me until I have spoken with Lady Julia. It is of grave importance. I . . . you, my lady have avoided my inquiries persistently. I regret that I-I was not firmer, that I permitted myself to be distracted, that—that I do not know the answers to this case still."

Julia experienced the worse premonition. Inspector Bloodsoe in such a diffident state was uncommon. She studied him closely. "What do you mean, Inspector Bloodsoe?"

"I fear there is no more time, my lady. This case is coming to a close, with or without your testimony. You will be apprehended."

"Bloodsoe, I have had more than enough!" Garth rumbled like a tiger rudely awakened from a nap. "I will no longer be patient."

"I do not mean any disrespect, my lord!" Inspector Bloodsoe raised his hands.

Julia grabbed Garth's clenched fist and arm. She threw her weight upon it to keep it in check. "Do proceed, Inspector Bloodsoe."

"I have enough evidence that connects you with the disappearance of your grooms."

"What?" Julia's knees almost gave out. "Tell me."

"Julia, any 'evidence' he has is pure gammon."

Julia could feel Garth's arm muscle bulge, his fingers flex. "Tell me what you have discovered, Inspector Bloodsoe."

"I will attempt to detail the information for you as it pertains to each groom individually."

"Good God!" Julia's knees did give out.

Garth snatched her up. "Damn you, Bloodsoe!"

"My lord, please refrain from attacking me until later." Bloodsoe stood stiff and tall. "My lady, in the case of Charles Danford, the marquess of Hambledon, I have a witness who will testify that your carriage was seen outside his house at the late, late hours. The servant in question swore it sported your family crest upon it. She had awakened because some dogs had set to howling. She went to investigate. She saw the carriage across the street."

"Impossible!"

"Next. I found a diamond-and-pearl ear bob in Lord Mancroft's room the night he supposedly disappeared with a straw damsel. It belongs to you, my lady. I know this because it was of such a unique and expensive quality that I took it to Rundell and Bridge. I asked if they had crafted it and to whom the ear bobs had been sold."

"Good gracious, I have not worn that pair of earrings in ages!"

Inspector Bloodsoe did not halt in his delivery. "In regard to Lord Beresford, I have nothing yet."

"Thank goodness." Julia was actually beginning to wonder if she did not have an evil twin who was wandering the earth.

"And I also have no strong information in regard to Lord Redmond. I do know there was a drunken tollgate man who swore a Scotsman known to be Lord Redmond's tiger raced by him in the curricle at the time he was posted to see Lord Redmond. He said the man was shouting something about love and that he was going home. I have sent a man to Scotland to locate the tiger and curricle."

"I see."

"Now in Viscount Herrington's case, he was to see his tailor but never appeared. But the tailor once again spoke of yelping dogs. Now that I have orated these happenings, I have just realized that there is a connection. All of them have dogs involved. Lady Julia, do you own dogs?"

"Of course not, as if I could with Aunt Clare's cats about. Percy is a positive devil with them. There was that Great Dane— No, you do not wish to hear about it, I am sure."

Bloodsoe shivered. "No, madame, I fear I would not have the stomach for it."

"Very well." Julia attempted a cool façade. "There is no connection there, I assure you. What else do you have?"

"Your lace handkerchief with the Wrexton coat of arms was lately discovered upon the boat from where Matthew Severs disappeared. The captain returned from his journey yesterday. As I had figured, the earl did not sail with him as first expected."

"Ridiculous. I never use a handkerchief!" Julia trembled. "I assure you, all of this evidence can prove only one thing."

"And what is that, my lady?" Inspector Bloodsoe asked.

Julia's very soul shivered. "Monsieur X is trying to frame me. We now know his motive, to be sure."

"Monsieur X? You cannot divert me. He is you, and you are he."

"I am not, I vow it. He—he is the one who . . ." Julia gasped and looked at Garth, wide-eyed. "There were howling dogs with the earl of Kelsey's disappearance. Monsieur X must own dogs."

"Kelsey?" Inspector Bloodsoe's nose quivered. "I know of his case. He is thought to have been murdered."

"I . . ." Julia paled and gripped Garth.

"It is none of your concern, Bloodsoe," Garth said.

"Now if you will leave us. You have distressed Lady Julia."

"My lord, I have given you all this information in order that you may believe what I tell you. Lady Julia does not have any time left. If she cares a straw for her family or you, she will cooperate with me."

"What would you like to know, Bloodsoe?" Julia asked wearily.

"I wish to know where you hid the bodies."

"Good God!" Garth roared. "You idiot!"

Garth made to spring at Bloodsoe, but Julia wrapped her arms about him tightly. "Run, Bloodsoe, run."

"You bloody well better, you addle-brained clod-poll!" Garth all but dragged Julia across the veranda toward Bloodsoe.

"My lord, Lady Julia must tell me." Bloodsoe retreated accordingly. He looked at her, his eyes desperate. "Where did you bury the bodies, my lady?"

"I did not bury them!" Julia was appalled.

"Never say you cast them out to sea?" Now Bloodsoe looked appalled himself. "My lady, we must have the bodies. Or at least one!"

"Eeks!" A female voice cried.

Julia, Garth, and Bloodsoe froze. As if one, they turned in the direction of the voice. A man and woman had stepped out onto the veranda. Julia flushed in mortification. They had been so involved, no one had recognized their presence.

"Pardon!" The man swung his frightened lady back toward the doors. "We did not hear a word. Nothing at all, I assure you."

The couple stumbled back into the ballroom. Julia groaned. The couple did not go much farther than that. Why should they? Half of the ballroom was peering at them through the long windows.

"Thank you, Inspector Bloodsoe, for offering them

something else to gossip about." Garth glared at Bloodsoe. "If you wish to come with me, I will show you a body."

Inspector Bloodsoe remained rooted to the stone floor. "No, my lord. Not if you mean it to be mine."

"Smarter than I thought." Garth grinned wolfishly.

"No, Garth, you cannot do anything to him." Julia sighed. "We must hear him out."

"I know, but let us at least leave our audience for the nonce. If we are going to discuss bodies, let us do so in the garden." Garth took Julia's hand and drew her down the steps. She noted that Bloodsoe followed, albeit cautiously. "Hopefully it will prove more private. Though why in blazes you had to choose a ball for this discussion, Bloodsoe, is beyond me."

"I am trying to tell you, my lord." Bloodsoe called out as Garth increased the pace. "There is very little time left."

"What the devil do you mean by that?" Garth cast a dark look back at him. "No, wait. We are not far enough away."

Garth led them deeper into the garden. He finally came to a stand, his gaze narrowed upon Bloodsoe as he came in a slow last. "This should be sufficient. Now what do you mean, there is little time?"

"Indeed." Julia looked at him wryly. "If you wish me to find all these bodies, I must have time. You cannot expect me to just dig them up directly."

"Stanwood!" A voice cried out. Julia did not recognize it. "Where are you, Stanwood?"

"Good God, what now?" Garth shook his head in exasperation. He raised his voice. "I am here. What do you want?"

"I demand satisfaction from you." The voice sounded closer.

"This is what I meant!" Bloodsoe frowned grimly. "My lord, I advise you not to answer."

"Who the devil are you?" Garth called. "And why do you want satisfaction?"

A young lad with flaxen hair and a frightfully outdated jacket appeared through the shrubs. His step was cocky, his expression eager. "Ah, there you are, you bastard."

"If I am not mistaken"—Bloodsoe lowered his voice—"that is Andrew Severs. The earl of Raleigh's young brother."

"I see." Julia nodded, her eyes widening.

"I am Andrew Severs!" the lad announced, gray eyes sparking as he stepped before them. "Matthew Severs's brother."

"Excellent work, Inspector." Julia nodded to Bloodsoe. "I must revise my opinion of you, it appears."

Bloodsoe actually flushed. "No, no. I was given the information beforehand."

Garth appeared mystified. "Matthew Severs?"

"Groom number six." Julia offered beneath a covering hand.

"Ah! Yes! Very well, Andrew Severs." Garth greeted the lad calmly. "Now that we know who you are, would you care to tell me why you wish to call me out?"

"You are Lady Julia Wrexton's fiancé, are you not?" Andrew turned to study Julia. He grinned then and offered a flourishing bow. "My lady, how do you do?"

"I am not quite sure." Julia said. "It depends on if you intend to destroy the rest of my evening by calling Garth out or not."

"Yes, I suppose that would cast a damper on it for you. A thousand apologies, my lady, but you must understand, in my brother's absence, I cannot, in honor, permit Lord Stanwood to steal you away from him."

Julia's eyes widened. Before she could speak, Bloodsoe stepped forward, his expression fairly eager. "Then you do not believe that something dire has happened to your brother?"

"Of course something dire has happened to Matthew." Andrew grimaced. "Lord Stanwood has pirated away his future bride. If that isn't dire, I do not know what is."

"You do not believe he is dead? Have you heard from him, sir?"

"No, I have not. I would not be here if I had. I am not such a clunch as to meddle in my brother's business if he can do it for himself." Andrew frowned. "But I know he is not dead. I would feel it if he were."

"I see." Bloodsoe's face fell.

Andrew grinned. "We have that kind of talent in our family. No, Matthew is not dead, and I will not permit Stanwood to steal his bride. We Severses are pirates ourselves; we take such behavior to heart. It is too insulting by half."

Bloodsoe stiffened. "You openly confess to piracy?"

"He is an officer of the Crown, sir." Julia felt pressed to say.

"That must be why he looks half-dead." Andrew cocked his head to the side to study Bloodsoe.

"I beg your pardon." Bloodsoe murmured.

"No need to do so." Andrew nodded. "To be honest, I knew who you were before I came out here."

"You felt it?" Garth asked dryly.

"No, no. The ballroom is abuzz with it, don't you know? Who but an officer of the law would demand a lady to tell him where she buried the bodies, and that while at a grand ball. Bad *tôn*, what? And now that I see the chap, no humor, either. And he uses words like confess." Andrew looked scornfully at Bloodsoe. "I will not confess to anything, Mr. Inspector. Other than wanting to duel with Lord Stanwood, that is."

"Young cawker." Garth shook his head, laughing. "You know very well I will not go out with you."

"Why not?" Andrew drew himself up to his full height.

"Because you are half my age." Garth snorted. "I'd look a regular cake, wouldn't I? It is clearly against the code of honor, and I do not understand why you even thought you could draw me out."

"Blast and damn." Andrew's look of dismay was comical. "I was afraid you would say that."

"Right, there you go, then." Garth grinned. "Toddle back to the ball, why don't you? Take Bloodsoe with you."

"Confound it, Stanwood!" Andrew frowned. "It just is not fair or right. You do not *need* to marry Lady Julia. You are a regular nabob from what I've heard. Full of juice. While we are under the hatches. We need Lady Julia in the family. You don't." He bowed to Julia. "My lady, won't you please reconsider? My brother Matthew is the jolliest of men, a regular Trojan, I promise. He isn't a rake or cad or anything difficult to wed." Andrew gazed at her with the utmost sincerity. "We really could use you and your fortune in our family."

"You confess that?" Bloodsoe's mouth dropped open.

Andrew frowned at him and shook his head. "There you go again with that confessing thing. Why shouldn't I confess it? It would be a shame for Lady Julia to waste her fortune on Stanwood here when we need it so much more."

"Do not press it, Severs." Garth cast him a threatening look. "My ring is on Julia's finger, and you best grow accustomed to it, I warn you."

"Why? You said you will not go out with me."

"True. But I might serve you some of the home brew if you persist."

"Please do, my lord." Bloodsoe encouraged.

"What?" Julia stared at him in astonishment, as did the men.

He did not flinch. "At least Lord Stanwood loves you, my lady. This Severs apparently was a fortune hunter and wished to marry you for nothing but your money."

"He is firmly seated with the lower orders, isn't he?" Andrew appeared intrigued. Then he grinned. "I am beginning to like you, old chap. Our family has burnt entire villages to steal the woman they loved." Andrew turned a speculative gaze upon Garth.

"Do not look at me." Garth laughed. "I have no village for you."

"I didn't think I could be so lucky." Andrew began to strip out of his jacket. "Fisticuffs will have to do, I suppose."

"My lady," Bloodsoe said lowly to Julia. "This is exactly what I meant by there is little time. If you do not show me the bodies in order that I may apprehend you, Lord Stanwood will sooner or later be killed because of it."

Andrew lunged at Garth. Garth stepped aside, and he tumbled past.

"Not by this lad, of course." Bloodsoe said. "But you yourself realize that Lord Stanwood cannot fight every man who insults you. Six grooms are missing, all of them possessing extensive families. Brothers, cousins . . ."

"Please." Julia bit her lip. Garth had just taken one blow from Andrew, who crowed in delight. Garth then popped back a shying left.

"Hmm." Bloodsoe's brows shot up. "Is Lord Stanwood er . . . throwing the fight?"

"Yes." Julia sighed. She shivered. "Don't you think if I could find those dratted grooms, I would. Every single last one of them. But I did not do anything with them. I do not lie. It must be Monsieur X who did. But who he is and why he is doing all this, we have not yet discovered. Garth and I have tried to draw him out, but so far we have not succeeded."

"My lady, I would like to believe you." Bloodsoe frowned, his face surprised. "I find that astonishing, but I do. It must be because I experienced—" He halted.

Andrew was making a flying leap at Garth. Julia purposely turned her attention to Bloodsoe. "Experienced what?"

Bloodsoe looked sad. "A hunch, my lady."

"A hunch?"

"Yes." Bloodsoe's gaze was mournful. "However, I do not believe in hunches. And the evidence against you—"

Julia spun on him. "I do not give a rap about the evidence against me. I had nothing to do with my grooms' disappearance." She stepped up to him and stared him in the eye. "Here is a confession for you. You appeared surprised to discover that Severs wanted to marry me for my fortune. I knew that. I did not love him, either. Nor did I love any other of those men. Yet I did not hate them."

"Then why . . . ?"

Julia flushed. "My father gave me an ultimatum. He said I must marry within six months or else he would give my fortune to . . . to someone else. So I set out to get married as swiftly as possible. That is why there were six. When one appeared to fail me, I went and found another one."

"Madame, why did you never tell me this?" Bloodsoe's face worked, clearly his mind working even faster. "It . . . it sheds a different light upon matters."

"We have not exactly enjoyed the best of moments

for honest discussion." Garth tripped Andrew. Andrew cursed. "It was a private family matter. I certainly did not wish it to be known."

"Who is to receive your fortune if you do not marry?"

Julia turned her attention to the two fighting men. "Garth."

"My God. Do you . . . ?"

She shook her head. "I do not believe it. In the beginning I did accuse him of being involved. Only to the extent that I thought he had talked my grooms into jilting me, or something like that. Now I know he wouldn't have even done that much." Julia looked at Bloodsoe rather helplessly. "You may care to think . . ."

Bloodsoe shook his head. He actually looked frightened. "I do not. My-my hunch was . . . was right, I fear."

"I do not know if I should be happy for that or not."

"I-I am sorry, my lady."

Julia nodded. "So am I. You do not know how sorry I am."

"You love him, do you not?"

Julia laughed wryly. "I do. I never knew it before, but I do. Do not take your 'hunch' to heart. I might very well prove to be the Black Widow, after all. I will kill the only man I love."

"I do wish it had been you. If you had come up with one body, we could save Lord Stanwood."

"Hmm." Julia narrowed her gaze upon Andrew Severs, who Garth now held off with a large hand. The lad's fists were windsailing harmlessly.

"My lady," Bloodsoe said. "It cannot be just anybody."

"You are right." Julia bit back tears. "What am I to do? We . . . all our pretending has done nothing."

"Pretending?"

Julia sighed. "Garth and I are only pretending to be engaged to try and draw Monsieur X out so that we can catch him. But we have had no luck."

A sudden shot rang out. It whizzed past Julia.

"Until now, it seems." Bloodsoe jumped forward, toppling her to the ground.

"Julia!" Garth roared and dashed over. Another shot whistled past him. He dove on top of Julia and Bloodsoe.

Andrew, deserted and the only one left standing, peered about. "Blast! What is going on! Who the devil is shooting? Stanwood, I am not finished with you yet." He strode over to the three on the ground. The third bullet ruffled his hair. "B'gads! Now I am." Andrew dropped to the ground, the latest addition to the group. Everyone groaned. "Sorry, didn't know I would get so chummy with you so fast. Can anyone tell me exactly who they are trying to kill?"

Bloodsoe's voice drifted up. "Your guess would be as good as ours, sir. I have had only one hunch and wish for no more."

"*Oikes*. That ain't good." Andrew muttered. "I am totally in the dark here."

The unison of responses made him groan.

"Julia and Garth." Lord Wrexton strode into the breakfast room. "I wish to have a word with both of you in the library when you are finished here."

Garth raised a brow. "Certainly, sir."

Lord Wrexton cast a nervous glance at his sister. "It is a private matter, Clare. You need not join us."

Aunt Clare's face showed hurt. "Yes, Bendford."

"That is good." Lord Wrexton murmured beneath his breath as he turned and left the breakfast room.

"Gracious." Aunt Clare stared after him, her blue

eyes crossing with concern. "I wonder what Bendford can be thinking?"

"You think *you* do?" Garth cast a worried look to Julia. Anger swept through him. She was heavy-eyed and pale this morning. After what transpired last night, it was not surprising. Garth clenched his jaw. If he ever found Monsieur X, he would rend the man limb from limb for what he had done to her. "Well, Julia? Should we beard the lion in his den now? Or would you like to turn truant and run?"

"One cannot escape Father." Julia sighed. Without a glimmer of a smile, she rose. "We best see what he wants."

"Julia, dear." Aunt Clare's blue eyes mirrored Garth's own fears. "Are you all right, my child?"

"I am fine." Julia smiled, but it did not reach her eyes. In truth, they were bleak. "Do not be concerned. I-I am merely tired, that is all."

Garth stood abruptly. He smiled as gently as he could. "We must go now, Aunt Clare."

"Yes, dear," Aunt Clare reached for the teapot. "Do see what Bendford wants. I'll just remain here and finish my tea."

Garth bowed and followed Julia from the room. He lengthened his stride to catch up with her. "Julia?"

"Yes?"

"*Are* you all right?" Garth fought the urge to take her into his arms and soothe her worries away. That or kiss her until she slapped him. Julia was always so pluck to the backbone that her low spirit frightened him. Faith, he would take the battling, shrewish Julia over this dazed, withdrawn one any day.

"I said that I am fine." Julia looked away. "I did not sleep well, that is all."

"Which is readily understandable." Garth settled for

clasping her hand. "We will find Monsieur X, Julia. We will. Do not lose faith."

"No, of course not." Julia tugged her hand from his. Garth frowned but remained silent as they entered the library.

"What did you wish to say, Father?" Julia walked over and sat in a chair.

Garth was left to find one a distance away. "Yes, sir. What is it?"

"Ah, yes, there you two are." Lord Wrexton immediately sprung from his chair and, walking to the door, closed it firmly. He turned and drew in a breath. "I have been thinking."

"Oh, Lord." Julia murmured. "Please, no."

Garth stifled his laugh as Lord Wrexton's breath wheezed from him. "Just what do you mean, by that, young lady?"

"Nothing, Father." Julia refused to meet his gaze, either.

"Very well." Lord Wrexton squared his shoulders. "I heard about last night. Of course, everyone has heard about last night. The gossip mill has everyone taking stray shots at you from the tweeny to Prinny himself. Bloodsoe must have been a bloody idiot as well. They say he was so addlepated as to ask you where the bodies were. Gads, but Mildred Danford should be proud of herself."

"She didn't look that happy last night," Garth said dryly. "Indeed, she looked as if she would like to chew glass."

"Good! Good! It will go worse for her if my suspicions prove true."

Garth raised a brow. "What suspicions?"

"I'll lay odds that your marksman last night was one of Danford's relatives. If I find the evidence I expect to, she is going to be terribly sorry." He halted. His manner changed, and he waved a hand. "Well, that is neither here nor there. We have more important matters to attend."

"Like what?" Garth asked, since Julia only watched her father with suspicious eyes.

"I have been thinking." Lord Wrexton cast Julia a warning glare. She did not respond. "Good. It is clear that matters are growing out of hand. And even if I prove it was one of Danford's relatives shooting at you, it will not really stop all this madness."

"True." Garth nodded cautiously.

"And it must stop." Lord Wrexton's voice rang with portent.

Julia finally showed a flicker of interest. "How would you suggest we stop it, Father?"

Lord Wrexton rubbed his hands together. "You and Garth marry immediately."

"What!" Garth exploded in astonishment. That he hadn't seen it coming showed just how overtaxed he was. He glanced to Julia to see her reaction.

Her face was calm, her gaze actually cold. She apparently was not shocked. "Why, pray tell, should Garth and I marry now when it appears everyone wishes to kill him because of it?"

"Think about it, girl. They are hedging their bets right now. They all want to claim you a murderess, but at the same time, if you are innocent and you can marry into their family, they want that instead. Take that choice away from them. Marry Garth out of hand and it'll put paid to their hopes, I promise you." Lord Wrexton grinned in delight. "Damn, but this time it will be you making it to Gretna Green. It will do my heart good."

"No! We are not going to do it." Garth said it sharply, his gaze steady upon Julia. The blood had drained from her face. He knew how she felt. Everything rebelled at the notion. Damn, but she did not deserve any more scandal or indignity. "Gretna Green is out of the question."

Lord Wrexton frowned. He turned a questing gaze to Julia. "Well, Julia. What do you have to say?"

Julia looked to Garth. Then her gaze skittered away. He could not read what she thought. "You heard Garth. We will not marry. We will not go to Gretna Green."

"Why not, confound it?" Lord Wrexton's face darkened. "It only makes sense. You two slip out on the sly, tie the knot right and tight, and come back with flags flying high. No one can argue with you then, my girl. And no other man can think to vie for your hand because Garth will have it. If any of those other fickle, jack-pudding fiancés crop up, it will be too late for them, by God."

"My, but you have thought this all out carefully." Julia said tersely.

"Yes, I have." Lord Wrexton nodded, clearly missing Julia's tone. "What does a fancy social wedding matter, I ask you, if you don't have your groom. I am sick and tired of this. Besides, it is Garth this time. We do not want *him* disappearing on us."

"It certainly works out for you, does it not?" Julia narrowed her gaze. "Are you sure you are not Monsieur X?"

"What?" Bewilderment crossed his face. "There's that infernal name again. Garth, what the devil is she talking about?"

Garth smiled slightly. "Nothing, sir. She is only thinking that your suggestion hints of self-interest here."

"Damn right it does." Lord Wrexton frowned without repentance. "I am this close to getting Julia married to you. This close to getting the grandchildren I have dreamed of all these years. And I do not want to lose that. I do not want to see you shot. Now tell me if that is self-interest?"

"I am sorry, sir." Garth drew in his breath. "But . . . no. Julia and I will not go to Gretna Green just to . . . to escape this danger."

"Then I will get you a special license. Does it really matter? You are going to be married, anyway. Why must you delay at such a cost?"

Garth bit back his words. He could not say that Julia and he were not really going to marry. He could not say that if they did, this would be the worst way to begin the marriage.

Desperation crossed Lord Wrexton's face. "I will pay you."

"What!" Julia snapped to furious, glaring attention at that.

"Both of you." Lord Wrexton's face turned cagey. "I will give you both separate settlements of funds, iron-clad. If you are afraid of being financially reigned in with Garth, Julia, you need have no concern. You may have your financial freedom."

"That is not what I was worried about! I will not permit you to . . . to try and bully us into this." Julia flushed deeply. "No, Father, this all has happened because of you trying to sell me off in the beginning. Now you cannot try and pay me off. No! I refuse."

"Garth." Lord Wrexton looked to him with entreaty. "Be reasonable! You are a man. You can think more clearly."

"Ha!" Julia snorted. Her brown eyes glittered. "What does it matter how clearly you both think if I will have none of it. And I swear, I will not!"

Garth stiffened. He had been patient and bending, yet she still classed him with her father. Hadn't anything they had been through mattered to her? Garth's voice came out sharp. "You heard her, sir. There is not a chance of it. And I am sided staunchly with Julia. Neither logic nor money would sway me."

Lord Wrexton, his face darkening, looked sternly to Julia. "Say what you want. Accuse me of self-interest. Say that it is all my fault. But what are you going to do to save you and Garth from this situation, Mistress Mule? For once, do your duty as you should, for God's sake. Marry Garth, and marry him posthaste. It is the only way out of this imbroglio with both your lives intact, and you know it."

"No, it is not, Father." Julia lowered her gaze. She visibly shivered, and then she lifted deadened eyes to Lord Wrexton. "Do not worry. I shall do my duty. Now please leave us, Father. Garth and I must discuss other matters."

"What?" Lord Wrexton stared. Suspicion entered his eyes. "What other matters would there be, since you have turned down my offer?"

"I said, please leave us."

Julia's tone was so very cold, with a hint of threat, that even Lord Wrexton cleared his throat. "Very well. I will leave you to discuss the issue. Remember, if you change your mind, I can have you two safely shackled within a day. *And* I will pay you anything you wish as well."

Lord Wrexton strode from the room and slammed the doors. Then his voice rumbled from without. "Damn, Clare. Is that you? You were eavesdropping, b'gads! Now come away from here. Julia and Garth are discussing private matters."

Garth would have laughed if the situation weren't so tenuous and so infernally difficult. He watched Julia closely. "I am sorry, Julia. Your father is . . ."

". . . My father." Julia smiled bitterly. "He is right, however; we cannot ignore this. Something must be done."

"What do you suggest?"

Julia dragged in her breath. "I want you to leave England tonight. You must return to France."

"What?" Garth stared at her, unable to believe what she had just said or the cool manner in which she delivered it. "Why?"

"Father is right, drat his conniving soul." Julia would not meet his gaze. "We meant to net Monsieur X with our pretense. Yet ever since we became engaged, he has remained silent as a grave. It is everyone else who has gone up in arms. Literally. You are in danger. If we do not marry, you must leave."

Garth froze, unable to speak. Minutes seemed to pass. He could not utter a word. Julia would neither look at him nor break the silence.

God, his heart performed a somersault. It shouted with excitement. Marriage! You could marry Julia. You would have her kisses, her passion, and those morning cozes in bed. And four, no five, children to raise and love. A family. No loneliness. Julia! Julia! Julia!

Garth's heart exalted at the notion. Then Garth's mind objected. No, Julia had already bit her father's head off at the proposition. He could not expect to fare better. Faith, she had told him to leave for France without a flinch. He may realize that marriage to her was what he wanted desperately and that leaving her now was the last thing he desired, but he could not expect it of her.

Worse, fear rose from the pit of his soul, that dark place far from both his heart and head. *Do not be a fool, Garth,* a voice whispered. *You could never be a decent husband. You could never be a good father. What would you know of it, anyway? Are you trying to reform at this late date? Do not make a cake out of yourself.*

"You would not care to get married, would you,

Julia?" Garth offered her a wry smile. "Faith, can you imagine what kind of parents we would be?"

Julia drew back as if struck. Garth knew himself for a coward. He had painted her with his brush of fear and hurt her. He could not draw back, it seemed. His evil genius goaded him. Julia must say it first, if she could, she must commit in some fashion. "Well, do you want to marry me?"

Julia gazed at him steadily. Her eyes showed him a greater courage than he possessed. They showed him a wealth of love. "No. Not if you do not want to marry me."

As far as words went, it was no profuse cry of love. She was not a desperate lady fainting at his feet. She was Julia, his Julia. She would meet him halfway. But, by God, it was clear in her direct gaze. He must meet her the other half. He would have to speak. He could not hide if he were to be her mate. Garth froze.

"Very well. You must leave for France." Julia said softly. She rose and smoothed out her skirts. "You will be safe if they know you have bolted. That you have . . . forfeited my hand."

Garth bit back his roar of pain and anger. Damn and blast, he could not propose marriage, but he did not want to give her up, either.

"No, I will not desert you." He ignored her look, the one that said that he had just done exactly that. "I will not do it, Julia."

"I do not think you have a choice in the matter." Julia's tone was level. "I am deserting you. Monsieur X will no longer lead me about with a ring in my nose, and neither will you. From now on, he can request and threaten all he wants, but he will need do so in person, for I intend to ignore everything else." She turned her back to him. "The same goes for you. I will not pretend anymore." He voice caught. "Not at the expense of your life."

Garth rose slowly. "Do you really expect me to walk away? Do you expect me to leave you in this danger?"

Julia whirled on him. Her eyes glowed with a fierce anger. Or could it be a fierce pain? She attacked so swiftly, Garth could not determine which. "You do not understand, Garth. I am not giving you an option. Yes. I do expect you to walk away. I do not *need* you. Is that clear? I-I will be better off without you. Far better off."

Emotions ripped through Garth: anger, raw pain, longing, and forsaken love. He clenched his jaw and his fists. He had to. Else he would have shaken Julia. "Very well. If that is what you wish. I will leave."

"By t-tonight?" Julia persisted.

"Tonight." Garth gritted.

Julia looked down and tugged at the sleeves of her dress. "Excellent."

Garth nodded. "Fine."

"Yes, fine!"

The library door burst open. Aunt Clare stood in her fluttering gown of thin white muslin over a white sarcenet slip. Red silk roses bestrewed its bodice and hem. She looked like a valentine, except her blue eyes were stricken. Almost as stricken as Garth's heart felt. "No! My dear children, no!"

"Yes, Aunt Clare. I do not ever want to see Garth again." Julia, her head lowered, lifted her skirts and dashed from the room.

Aunt Clare cast Garth a pleading look. "Go after her, my dear. Go after her and do not let her go again."

"No, Aunt Clare." Garth said through the chilling numbness settling into his heart. "You heard her. I know you did. She does not need me. I will leave this evening."

"But . . . you . . ."

"I have much to do, Auntie. Please excuse me." Garth stalked from the library then. He could not look into Aunt Clare's tearing blue eyes again

"Oh, dear." He heard Aunt Clare's gentle voice. Then as he proceeded, he knew he had imagined it, for he swore he heard her say, "Blast Bendford, anyway! The—the royal clunch."

Fourteen

Julia cantered through the park, her maid correctly following behind. The trail of the jonquil net scarf tied around the crown of her patent hat of raw silk waved behind her in the morning breeze like a banner as a knight begins a joust. The skirts of her aubergine riding habit were tucked about her. She was prepared for some serious riding. Indeed, it had been too long.

Gratefully, there were very few people enjoying the fresh air. She did not care to see anyone. Not that she did these days. These days, people never stopped to chat with her. They might stop to gape at her—and point—and then chat with their fellows, but that was as far as it went.

Garth had left sometime last night. He had packed his bags, and after saying farewell to everyone—that is, everyone but her—he had left. She sniffed. Thank God, he had obliged her as she had requested of him. She knew if he had remained any longer, she might very well have broken down and made a complete ninny out of herself by begging him to marry her instead of going to France.

Julia's shoulders slumped in dejection. She straightened them angrily. She had done the right thing. Indeed, the only thing she could have done. Garth had been in mortal danger because of her. He had to leave England. She could not have married him, as her father had hoped, not when Garth would have only done so to keep her safe.

Before this, Julia had refused to marry because she could only imagine how intolerable it would be to be forced to curry to a man's whims and megrims. Now she realized that that would have been a cinch as long as they were Garth's whims and megrims. She knew him. She knew his oddities inside and out, and none were that impossible to her. No, those she could have accepted. Now she realized that she had merely been weaving an excuse from air dreams. The truth was that living with a man who did not love her would have been the truly intolerable situation. Especially when she herself was in love with that man so completely, so desperately.

Garth most definitely did not love her. Her mind wandered back to that morning in the library when he had first swept her off her feet. That was when he had showed her how he would propose to the woman he loved. Her heart cried out with pain. What a far cry that memory was from last evening's scene. She shivered, still remembering his negligent "Would you like to marry me?"

Faith, if there was love there, it was lukewarm at the very least. Julia smiled wryly. Such cruel lessons life administered. Before all of this, she had believed she would marry anyone rather than live in penury. Now she realized she would choose financial penury any day rather than emotional penury. Garth had tweaked her about her lack of passion time after time. Well, he had awakened her passion. Now the tigress was out of the cave and would not settle for a blasé mate. She wanted the fire, and if she could not have it, she wanted nothing.

In truth, in an odd, twisted way, she should be grateful to Monsieur X. It had been a long road covered in a rather short time that had changed her from the woman she had been to the woman she was now. She had discovered she wanted love and family. Faith, she had even discovered the one true love she desired. Despite the raw pain inside, she was glad for the journey and for who she had become because of it.

Now, Aunt Clare was a different matter. She appeared completely devastated by Garth's leaving, putting paid to their separation. Indeed, Julia had decided to ride in the park this morning, simply to escape the climate at home. Her aunt Clare was so unhappy that she had actually rounded on Lord Wrexton, declaring it was his fault.

He, too, had been forced to escape this morning. Apparently, he had awakened to all twelve cats sleeping upon him. He discovered his jacket quite singed. His breakfast, from what Julia had heard, was even blacker. Julia smiled. In a way, she thought he did deserve it. Yet she knew it was not his fault. It was not anyone's, in fact. Garth did not wish to marry her, and she would not sit about and cry over it. At least not in public or in broad daylight.

"My lady!" Bloodsoe's voice shouted.

Julia sighed. Was she forever to be haunted by the inspector? She turned to peer back. Her mood lifted immensely. Bloodsoe, hanging at a lopsided angle from his saddle, galloped toward her. Clearly, he was no skilled equestrian.

Julia stopped her own well-trained Delilah and waited. "Good morning, Inspector."

"Hello-o-o!" Bloodsoe greeted as his horse galloped past.

"Pull on the reins, Bloodsoe," Julia called. She frowned. She recognized his mount now. It was from her very own stables. The family knew Toby well. The horse was the slowest slug imaginable. Just how Bloodsoe had coaxed the horse into such a fantastic pace was beyond her.

"Ah! Yes!" Bloodsoe sawed on the reigns. Toby halted abruptly. Bloodsoe, apparently not expecting such swift obedience, toppled off.

"Gracious!" Julia slid from Delilah and ran to him. "Are you all right?"

"I fear I do not understand horses." Bloodsoe lay sprawled in a daze for a moment. "You cannot reason with them."

"Not exactly." Julia bit back her smile. "Do you know it is quite improper to gallop in the park?"

"And very painful at that." Bloodsoe rolled over and slowly rose. His face showed complete alarm. It was directed upon her, however, and not Toby, who had meandered away for a juicy sprig of grass. "My lady, my journal is missing."

Julia frowned. "Why are you riding Toby? Or any horse, for that matter?"

"Your aunt told me where you were and lent me this horse." Bloodsoe peered about narrowly. "You are not listening, my lady. My journal is gone from my drawer. My personal journal. As are all the articles of evidence and the testimonials. You must escape."

"What?" Julia blinked. "Why must I escape?"

"My personal journal is where I have written all the evidence against you. I refused to give it to Pattington when he asked. I informed him I needed more time before I could give him an official report. I think he has stolen the journal and intends to use it against you. He intends to apprehend you."

Julia shook her head slowly in confusion. "But how can he? You said you needed the bodies . . . ?"

"Yes. It was *I* who needed the bodies. Even just one would have been nice." Bloodsoe halted. Shaking himself, he flushed. "*Pattington* does not require one. He told me that he could make anything stick if he was pressed to do so. Or Lady Danford could. I believe she is at the forefront of this."

"Oh, Lord." Julia murmured. "Father swears it was one of her clan who shot at us. He said he was waiting for information against them. She . . . she is . . ."

"You must escape." Bloodsoe frowned. "Where is Lord Stanwood?"

Julia's chest constricted in pain. "He—he left for France. Last night."

"What?" Bloodsoe expression was of complete disbelief. "No. He would not leave you."

"He did." Julia offered a sad shrug. "I sent him away."

"No." Bloodsoe objected. "You did not."

"I did. I did not want him to be in danger."

"He left you? He truly left?"

"I told him I wanted him to go."

"But he must testify to the fact that Monsieur X exists. He should not have left for France."

Julia glared at Bloodsoe. "If you say that one more time, I swear I . . . I shall cry."

"My lady. I am sorry. Please, anything but that." Bloodsoe turned alabaster white. "Did anyone else other than you and my lord know about Monsieur X?"

"No. We did not want to involve the family. We kept it secret in case Monsieur X had sources within the house." She brightened. "Wait. You know about Monsieur X!"

"I would not make a good testimonial, my lady" Bloodsoe shook his head. "I did not write the most complimentary things about you within my journal. They will not believe me now. I had no time to enter my *hunch.*"

"I see." Julia flushed. "What are we to do?"

"You, my lady"—Bloodsoe gasped and pointed—

"are to gallop in the park. Indeed, I would suggest riding neck-or-nothing if you are proficient enough."

Julia turned and looked. A group of men raced at them. "Oh, Lord."

"They followed you. Or me." Bloodsoe moaned. "My lady, please escape."

"A famous idea, Bloodsoe." Julia ran to her mount and bolted onto it, heedless of the modesty of her skirts, thankful that Garth insisted she learn to mount a horse herself, unassisted, when she first started learning to ride. She was even more thankful he taught her to ride hell-bent for leather. She kicked Delilah into a gallop, leaving Bloodsoe and her maid behind. Now if she could only leave the law behind!

"Just what the devil are you rambling about, Clare?" Lord Wrexton frowned at his sister. "And do try and make sense this time around. I am in no mood for roundaboutations this morning. I just walked into the house, and you have not even let me past the first step. I warn you, I am sadly out of curl. And much of it is due to you."

"I am sorry, Bendford, though what I have done to make you unhappy—"

"Twelve cats, Clare! I slept with twelve cats. Do not tell me that was a mistake."

"No, admittedly it was not. The kitties felt it only right to do so." Clare wrung her hands. "But, Bendford, something has happened far more serious than that."

"I doubt it." Lord Wrexton rolled his eyes, his tone biting. "What? Did Alexander the Great cough up a hair ball? Or has Shakespeare refused the tuna in cream and tartar, now. Lord, what goes up those stairs to feed those creatures could feed an army, I vow. I am amazed they can even waddle."

"Bendford, dear," Aunt Clare said reproachfully. "You *are* in a black mood."

"Of course I am! I just told you that!" Lord Wrexton's tone was aggrieved. "I just lost the best son-in-law I could have ever had. Most importantly, Garth would have been perfect for Julia."

"Yes. I have told you that many times, Bendford." Clare discovered herself clenching her hands together rather than wringing them. "Bendford, that Inspector Bloodsoe was here."

"Blast and damn the man!" Lord Wrexton glowered at her. "What did he want this time?"

"He seemed terribly worried over a journal that he was missing. I think he believes Julia had taken it, for he kept saying he must see her, that there was no time. He sounded as if he thought the law would wish to apprehend her for it. Do you think that is possible?"

"Balderdash!" Lord Wrexton said. "That is sheer idiocy. Do not even concern yourself with that sneaksby. He's cracked in his upper works."

"Dear me." Care sighed. "And I lent him a horse."

"What!"

Clare bit her lip. "He said he must see Julia. That it was urgent and a matter of life and death. Oh, dear, if only Garth were here."

"Ha! I agree with that." Lord Wrexton snorted. "With my luck, now one of those other pudding-hearted grooms will show up to claim Julia's hand."

"No. They will not. But I do not understand. You liked them very well in the beginning."

"Yes, but I do not now. Not when I realize I could have had Garth for Julia. Those others seem like poor seconds."

"Bendford. How wonderful. I believe you are grow-

ing. I—" Clare halted. The front door behind Bendford opened. Her heart leapt as the best of visions appeared. "Garth, my dear boy."

"What?" Lord Wrexton's eyes lighted, and he spun.

"Hello, Aunt Clare." Garth, smiling wryly, stepped
in and closed the door.

"You have come back, thank God!" Clare ran to him,
her arms outstretched. "I am so glad."

"Let us hope Julia feels the same." Garth laughed
and hugged her.

"Garth, my son!" Lord Wrexton strolled over and
pounded him on the back several times. "So you have
returned. You realized I was right, heh? Well, no hard
feelings, son. It isn't easy to throw you heart over the
fence right off."

"No, sir. I am sorry" Garth's face darkened. "I did
not return to marry Julia. She made it perfectly clear
she did not wish to wed me."

"Did she?" Aunt Clare shook her head. "I thought
you had made it clear to *her.*"

"You should never listen to a woman, Garth," Lord
Wrexton shook his head. "It is you who have to make
the decision and then make sure they see that it is for
the best."

"Sir, we are talking about Julia." Garth challenged
him. "Have you really had such great success with that
approach in the past?"

"Hmm. I see what you mean." Lord Wrexton sighed.
"But . . . well, blast it. It might work better for you. We
will have to mull it over. Devise a plan."

"Just tell her you love her, Garth, dear." Aunt Clare
gripped his hand tightly. "That is what you need to do.
And . . . and propose with more . . . more fervency
than what I heard you put forth yesterday. Why not
propose like that time you were playing make-believe?"

"Clare, do not pester the lad." Lord Wrexton

frowned. "B'gads. You didn't listen to me yesterday, did you? You eavesdropped on the two, didn't you?"

"It is all right, sir." Garth laughed and ran his hand through his hair. "Aunt Clare has the right of it. I bungled it yesterday. I-I still do not know what to do. I only know that I should not have left. I deserted her simply because she told me to do so. If she were testing me, I failed."

"Do not be down in the mouth, lad." Lord Wrexton advised. "Just be firm with her and it will be all right."

Garth winked at Aunt Clare. "So I shall be. Where is she now?"

"Oh, my!" Clare's hand flew to her mouth. "I forgot . . . I mean, I was distracted. Garth, dear, that Inspector Bloodsoe was here this morning. He said it was of dire importance he find Julia."

"What?" Garth's face darkened. "I hope . . ."

A thunderous pounding at the door interrupted them.

"Blister it. What now?" Lord Wrexton stomped to the door and jerked it open. "Oh, it is you, is it? Go away."

"My Lord Wrexton, I must talk to you." Bloodsoe panted, hanging on to the doorpost.

"Bloodsoe!" Garth exclaimed. "Bloodsoe, what is the matter? Where is Lady Julia?"

"Lord Stanwood?" Bloodsoe stumbled past Lord Wrexton. "Thank God you are here. Lady Julia said you were in France."

"I was going there, but I changed my mind."

"They have apprehended her, my lord. They followed her to the park. She almost outraced them, but . . . but they caught her."

"Who did this?" Lord Wrexton bellowed.

"The authorities," Bloodsoe said. "They wish to try her for the abduction and murder of her grooms."

"Impossible!" Lord Wrexton roared.

"I thought so myself, my lord. There are no bodies. Not even one. A person must have bodies if one is going to hang someone for murder."

"The devil confound you. They cannot do that to my Julia." Lord Wrexton growled. "I will not let that happen. Why, it will be them who hang when I am done."

"Good gracious!" For the first time in her life, Clare saw twirling spots before her eyes. And a flickering darkness. She swayed.

Garth caught her quickly. "Are you all right, Auntie, dear?"

"My. It is rather like the fireworks at Vauxhall."

"Aunt Clare?" Garth asked.

Clare shook her head. She patted Garth's firm arm about her. "I am fine. Somewhat, at least."

"That's my girl." Garth grinned. "We need you to be strong."

Lord Wrexton glared at Bloodsoe. "If you are hoaxing us, you—"

"I am not. My superior, Chief Pattington, says that Lady Danford and the families of the other grooms demand it. He will do it without the bodies." Bloodsoe looked pleadingly at Garth. "Lord Stanwood, if you will come with me, please. You will be able to testify that there is another involved. You can testify to Monsieur X."

"Monsieur X?" Lord Wrexton frowned. "That bloody name again. Who the devil is Monsieur X?"

"Monsieur X?" Clare moaned. "You want Monsieur X?"

"Monsieur X must be the killer." Bloodsoe nodded solemnly. "If we can prove his existence and throw the blame on him, we might be able to save Lady Julia."

Garth's eyes darkened. "I will gladly come with you."

"No. A moment. Garth, dear, please, please, do forgive me. But you did tell me I should be strong." Clare drew in a deep, frightened breath. "I confess. I-I am Monsieur X."

"What?" Lord Wrexton thundered. "Do not go daft on us now, Clare. We do not have time for you to slip your leash with reality, b'gads."

"No. I truly am Monsieur X. I took Julia's grooms." Clare straightened her shoulders. "I know where the bodies are, Inspector Bloodsoe."

"No, Aunt Clare." Garth's arm about her tightened, almost painfully. His eyes were pained. "Do not do this. It is wonderful of you to try and protect Julia, but it will not serve. I promise you. If it comes down to such a drastic measure, I will take the blame before I permit either you or Julia to do so."

"Miss Clare." Bloodsoe bowed slightly. "I applaud your bravery. However, I do not believe the courts will believe you."

Clare flushed. "Why not?"

"Because you have difficulty hurting a bloody fly, Clare, let alone seven men, that is why," Lord Wrexton said quite ruthlessly. He frowned. "Now do cut line, Clare. We have no time for your heroics. We must go directly if we are to save Julia."

Clare stared at the three men, frustration and hurt welling within her. Even Garth, the dear lad, did not look as if he believed her. "M-may I-I please go with you?"

"No, Clare. We do not have time to bear-lead you about." Lord Wrexton's tone was pure impatience. "We must move fast if we are to take countermeasures."

"Please, Aunt Clare." Garth kissed her cheek. "You are the dearest aunt anyone could ever want, but you can best help Julia by remaining here instead."

Clare knew when the men had set their minds past changing. They did have trouble with considering matters if those matters were not as stable as a table. But then, who ever wished to be a table? She forced a smile. "Very well. I-I will remain here and . . . have my tea."

The rampant relief on the men's faces from her swift capitulation was anything but complimentary. Clare sighed. This was no time for wounded pride. She sent them off with a saintly wave. They left, planning and scheming very nicely.

"They do like to think they are chivalrous. It is quite difficult at times." Hastening over, she went to a tambour-top writing table and withdrew paper and ink. She did not hesitate overly much the note. Though one tear did blot it.

My faithful Ruppleton and Wilson,

The law has apprehended Julia. They wish to say that she is Monsieur X. They want to know where she has hidden the bodies. I must go and make my confession. It is all my fault.

Please do not follow. I do ask that you release the boys once you discover this letter. Give them my love and apologies. I-I never meant for things to go so very awry.

Monsieur X
(For the last time, I fear.)

P.S.: I have taken the kitties with me. I worry that Bendford will not accept care of them in my absence. Surely prisons require mousers? At least I pray I will only go to prison.

Fifteen

My God, how did this happen? Julia, hands tightly clasped before her, still dressed in her riding habit, gazed around at what was supposed to be a court. It was nothing more than a hangman's room. The judge, one Honorable Percival Threadwell, presided over the case. The prosecutor stood reading the charges against her. His delivery lacked the precision of Inspector Bloodsoe as he employed the absent man's evidence. What the prosecutor lacked in precision, however, he made up for in high dramatics and inflammatory language.

Each long-winded and convoluted accusation gained heavy gasps and cries from those who watched. Julia had required but one cursory glance at the audience as she had entered. She smiled bitterly. Her seven grooms might be missing, but not their families. Indeed, she doubted a single relative or friend of theirs was absent in that regard. Considering that she had been apprehended only a mere two hours ago, their full attendance reeked of political influence gone amock.

Julia lifted her chin, ignoring the chill that mercilessly played along her spine. While she and Garth had been off chasing the illusive Monsieur X, the wheels of injustice had been turning overtime, primed by some of the most powerful families in the kingdom.

She wondered if Monsieur X were pleased with himself at this moment.

As if to mock her very thoughts, the prosecutor boomed. "I read now from the official investigating report: *'This I had from the innkeeper who was quite surprised, needless to say, to discover that Monsieur X was actually Lady Julia Wrexton, who had also been fiancé to Lord Beresford.'*"

A scandalized murmur whirled about the room. Julia bit her lip. That must be the Beresford kith and kin.

"Untrue!" A voice shouted from the back of the court. "I was wrong! But I received a *hunch!* I know differently now."

Julia gasped and spun upon her bench to see the speaker, as did everyone else in the courtroom. Bloodsoe, deathly pale, stood within the entrance door. Her father and Garth flanked his sides.

"Garth!" The chill vanished from Julia's spine, replaced by a warm glow. Her heart sang out through her fear and gloom. Garth was here, not in France. He had not deserted her.

"What?" The Honorable Percival Threadwell peered at them. He possessed a thin, twitching face that was overpowered by his wig. He also had frightfully poor teeth. He seemed to cringe back into his seat of honor. "Who are you, sir? Wh-why do you interrupt these proceedings?"

"Your Honor, I am Inspector Bloodsoe." Bloodsoe stepped forward and offered a respectful nod. "I wrote the report now being read. I vow it was not meant to be official. Therefore, may I approach the bench? I wish to present new information to the court in regard to Monsieur X. Lady Julia is not he, and he is not she. It is he who is the murderer."

A frantic flutter occurred to the right side of the court. The Honorable Percival Threadwell's gaze turned with what appeared dread in his eyes to that particular spot. Julia, intrigued, followed his gaze.

Julia's fingernails bit into her palms in anger. Lady Danford, surrounded by her own familial court, sat there. The dreadful woman was actually dressed in the deepest black of mourning, as were her relatives. In her delicate, trembling hand, she held a black handkerchief. It was that telling flag she waved.

Threadwell of the poor teeth clicked them sharply, rather like a rabbit munching a bitter carrot. "I-I am sorry, sir. You may not approach the bench. The court does not recognize you. Pray sit down."

Lady Danford's handkerchief flapped again.

"Er . . . yes?" Threadwell attempted a ferocious glare. "Sit down immediately. Else you must leave the court."

Julia bit back an ironic smile. It must be difficult to be a judge owned by one particular peer, especially the rather taxing Mildred Danford.

Bloodsoe stood his ground. "But Your Honor . . ."

"Sit down, sir. Or I will have you taken from the court."

"Good gads, Threadwell," Lord Wrexton roared. "What in blazes are you doing? The man has a right to speak. It *is* his bloody report!"

Even from where she stood, Julia shook from the vibrations of her father's rumbling tones. Apparently, so did the Honorable Percival Threadwell, who had just been demoted to "Threadwell." He blanched. "Lord Wrexton!"

Lord Wrexton puffed out his chest, glaring. "Yes? I am here to denounce these proceedings."

"I with him." Garth stepped forward and bowed.

"And— Oh, Lord." Bloodsoe lifted his gaze a moment to the heavens. "So am I."

The black lace flag flew high. Threadwell flinched.

Looking down, he coughed. "Er, my lord, you must be seated. Else . . ."

"Else what!" Lord Wrexton challenged. His face showed his utter contempt. Julia bit her lip. She prayed her father would not overplay his role.

"Guards!" Threadwell cried, and waved his hands. "Confine these men."

"Oh, very well." Lord Wrexton trod over to an empty seat. He sat just as the guards reached him. He glared at them. "Do not dare to think it. Now be gone."

The guards, turning colors, turned to Bloodsoe and Garth. Bloodsoe scurried to find a chair at their advancement. Garth only saluted and strolled to lean against the back wall, since all other chairs were taken.

Lord Wrexton, even sitting down, did not lose the projection of his voice as he glared over to Lady Danford. "But I warn you, there are two sides to everything. And once you have heard the entire case against *my daughter*, I am sure you will realize that it should be sent to be considered by a jury of her peers."

"Yes, my lord," Threadwell squeaked. Lady Danford coughed into her handkerchief. "Er, I mean, silence. And if you interrupt once more, I will have the guards take you out in . . . in contempt of court."

"It's not the courts I have contempt for!" Lord Wrexton called out.

"Guards! Remain there!" The Honorable Percival Threadwell flushed. Clearly rattled and clearly the weaker personality, he looked, rather, to the prosecution. "Proceed, and swiftly, I beg of you."

The prosecutor cleared his throat and looked back to his page. "Er, 'Monsieur X was actually Lady Julia Wrexton . . .'"

"Pardon me. I am sorry to interrupt . . . !" A sweet voice interrupted, once again from the back of the room. "But *I* am Monsieur X."

"Oh, no!" Julia gasped as she spun. She blinked and blinked again. It seemed impossible, but she could not deny it. The twelve cats scampering down through the courtroom would not permit it. "Aunt Clare!"

"I am Monsieur X! Please, may I confess, Your Honor?" Aunt Clare traipsed directly up to the bench and the Honorable Percival Threadwell. Apparently he was too surprised to even gurgle. Mildred Danford's black lace handkerchief floated to the ground. The prosecution dropped his papers.

One bystander, and one alone, moved. Lord Wrexton stood. "Clare, for God's sake. Stop that nonsense and come back here!"

"I am sorry, Bendford, but I really must talk to the judge." Aunt Clare gazed up at the Honorable Percival Threadwell with solemn blue eyes. "Your Honor, my name is Clare Wrexton, and I am Monsieur X. I know where the bodies are. Julia does not, so could you please release her and take me instead?"

The entire courtroom went wild at that moment. Half was in response to the astonishing confession, and the other half was from the kitties' exploratory search through the crowd. Aunt Clare took that moment to turn and wave at Julia. "Hello, dearest. I am so sorry I caused this frightful imbroglio. I did mean it for the best, I assure you."

"Aunt Clare." Julia rose slowly, not even knowing she did so. "What . . . how . . . why?"

"I am going to explain that, dear." Aunt Clare smiled and turned back to Threadwell. "Inspector Bloodsoe said that you cannot hang Julia if I tell you where the bodies are. Is that true?"

The Honorable Threadwell blanched. His gaze skittered over to Lady Danford. Lady Danford was not waving her handkerchief. Alexander the Great had it, and was dragging it about, while the lady herself was swatting at Doubting Thomas, who had jumped into her lap. One quick smile crossed the Honorable Threadwell's lips. It disappeared immediately. He sat straighter in his chair and nodded to Clare. "That is true, madame. Just where are . . . the bodies?"

Aunt Clare drew in a deep breath. "They are presently residing on the third story of our town house. I put them there because I knew that no one else ever goes up there, except for me and my cats, that is."

"Oh, no." Julia moaned, a numbness overtaking her.

"That is, they have been there for the past fortnight." Aunt Clare frowned.

"God!" The Honorable Threadwell covered his mouth as if he might cast up his accounts. "Never say so."

"They might be gone by now. I wrote a letter to Ruppleton and Wilson to take care of them for me, since I was coming here to confess."

"Ruppleton and Wilson?" Threadwell asked.

"Yes." Aunt Clare nodded. "My butler and chef."

"Oh, God. How could I have missed that!" Bloodsoe's tormented voice was the one in the room. "The butler did do it, after all."

"And my chef." Aunt Clare nodded. She turned to glance at Bloodsoe, who had sprung up. "But you did not meet him, Inspector. He spent his time cooking them—"

"Oh, God, no!" Lady Danford screeched. The gasps and cries drowned Aunt Clare out.

Julia stood dazed in the bedlam. Aunt Clare's face was clear and innocent, her lips sweetly pursed. She frowned, shaking her head. "No! Let her finish! Let her finish."

"Yes." The Honorable Threadwell, green-hued beneath his wig, raised his hand. "Silence, please. W-we must hear the rest."

Aunt Clare turned back to him. Concern entered her eyes. "My dear Honor, are you feeling all right?"

"Madame," Threadwell gulped. "Wh-where would the bodies be now if Ruppleton and Wilson took care of them as you requested?"

"Why, wherever the spirit takes them, I would imagine."

"God." Threadwell wiped his face swiftly, knocking his wig awry. "How could you have done something so heinous, madame."

Aunt Clare flushed. "I am sorry, Your Honor! I did not mean to stir up such tempest. It is just that I could not permit Julia to marry one of those gentlemen when she loves Garth."

"Garth?" A look of confusion joined the horror on Threadwell's face.

"Lord Stanwood," the prosecutor hissed. "The one in the report."

"Yes, that is the one. He is back there against the wall. He did not go back to France, thank God." Aunt Clare beamed. "He and Julia have loved each other since they were children, you see. So I decided to make a push to assist them. I simply removed Julia's other suitors until she and Garth realized their love and destiny. I must say, all her grooms were perfect gentlemen about it."

"Oh, my poor Charles!" Lady Danford sobbed out. "Killed by an insane woman. Oh, my son!"

"She belongs in Bedlam!" A voice shouted.

"Nay! She belongs swinging from the gibbet!"

"No!" Julia found her courage and her mobility. She rushed to Aunt Clare's side. She was not the only one. Percy gave out the most barbaric howl and leapt over laps and heads to reach Aunt Clare. It was clearly a call to arms, for the twelve cats clawed over boots and skirts to race to her side.

"*Achoo* . . . that is it!" Bloodsoe yelled into the me-lee. "I got it! Monsieur X did not own dogs. She owns cats—dog-eating cats!"

"Aunt Clare could not have done what you think!" It was the only thing Julia could say. She didn't have the answers yet, but this was one thing she did know. "She is trying to save me. That is all. She is too kind to have—"

"Hang her!" Lady Danford screeched. "She mur-dered my son. Oh, my poor, poor Charles!"

"Yes, Mother?" Charles Danford's voice asked.

Lady Danford shrieked. The audience roared with fear and shock. Hands performed the sign of the cross or clasped in swift prayers.

Then the room fell deathly still as Charles Danford, marquess of Hambledon, strolled down the center of it. "My God. He's come back from the dead."

"No," Charles said, smiling. "Just from . . . er, Sur-rey!"

"Charles, my dear boy." Aunt Clare's face broke into a delighted smile. "What are you *doing* here?"

"We decided to drop in for the party, Aunt Clare," Matthew Severs, earl of Raleigh, advanced from the back as well.

Aunt Clare raised her hand to her brow. "My good-ness. You all came!"

Julia well-nigh fainted. Her six grooms advanced to-ward the bench. And a seventh man as well, the earl of Kelsey. She refrained, however, stiffening her knees and her back. She noted that many of the other ladies in the room could not. Indeed, they were falling from their seats like flies.

It was true. Somehow it *was* true. All of it. Aunt Clare *had* been Monsieur X. She *had* taken Julia's grooms. How, she did not wish to consider, and it didn't really matter. They were all there before her at this moment, alive and healthy. A peal of laughter escaped her. "Oh, Aunt Clare. How could you have?"

"I could not have without the assistance of Ruppleton and Wilson." Aunt Clare teared up, pride lighting her face. She waved to the two family retainers who stood in the back. Then she had the grace to flush. "I am sorry, dear. But as wonderful as these boys are—"

Julia choked. "You know them well now?"

"I do." Aunt Clare nodded as the Honorable Threadwell banged on the desk for silence. "They are dears, but I still could not let you marry them. You were meant for Garth."

"Er, yes." Julia glanced up. She could barely see Garth in the far back. Only by the posting of the guards could she determine his approximate location.

"I want order. I demand order." The Honorable Percival Threadwell's voice squeaked, and he stood up so swiftly, his wig slid completely off, displaying his balding plate. "Order in the court. Guards— Oh, never mind. Remain where you are." He banged again on his desk. Finally, the court silenced. He looked at Charles Danford in appeal. "My lord, I beg of you to explain to me what truly happened. This lady said that she had killed you."

"I did not!" Aunt Clare gasped. She looked at Julia in confusion. "Did I?"

Julia laughed. "You—we assumed when you spoke of bodies that that is what you meant."

"Oh?" Aunt Clare frowned. "I am sorry."

"My lord!" Threadwell exclaimed again. "Please, for pity's sake, tell us in your own words what this woman did to you."

"Did to me?" Charles lifted a brow. "Why, nothing. Nothing at all. I have the greatest respect for her."

"But she said she kept you on the third floor—"

Threadwell halted, as he received a stern glare from another Danford.

"Your Honor." Charles appeared at his most supercilious. "Do look at Aunt Clare. Does she look as if she could keep me anywhere against my will? Does she look as if she is a criminal? No, no, my absence was due to my deciding to go to . . . Surrey and inspect some new property I acquired in a game of chance."

"I went to Scotland to help my tiger find his true love," Lord Harry Redmond said with a glint to his eye. He winked at Aunt Clare, who giggled.

"And I was in Italy," said Matthew Severs. "On . . . on a different ship than I intended to sail on, granted. I did not, however, expect it to create such a brouhaha."

"I went with him!" Lord Herrington Dunn spoke quickly. Matthew frowned at him. He shrugged his shoulders, his face desperate.

Matthew turned to the Honorable Threadwell and smiled. "Yes. He is an enjoyable chap. I met him at his tailor's. He gave me great advice upon my jacket."

Lord Reginald Beresford cleared his throat. "As for me . . . I-I was called away to a friend's deathbed at a late hour. I was forced to leave directly." He glanced back to the crowd, his gaze upon an extremely elegant lady. "The friend passed away and . . . and left me his fortune. I-I shall gladly take care of—of my loved ones. I would not have—"

"Enough, already," Matthew murmured to Beresford.

"Oh, yes." Beresford paled. "That is all."

"I see." The Honorable Threadwell peered around. One lone man had not explained his past whereabouts. He squinted slightly, then he gasped. "My lord, Monteith, is—is that you?"

"Yes, it is." Lucas Monteith nodded.

"But how . . . why . . . ah . . . what happened to you?"

"Oh, I was on another boat. I met up with Severs and Dunn in Italy. We all had a jolly time, I assure you." He then frowned darkly. "However, we did feel quite irate when some small bird, actually two large birds, name of Ruppleton and Wilson, came to us and informed us that the lovely Lady Julia was being tried for some strange, ridiculous charges as to our personal whereabouts. Not having the honor of knowing Lady Julia well, I am here myself because I heard that the delightful Aunt Clare thought to create some famous tale to save her dear niece."

"Oh, Lucas, you are a sweet boy." Aunt Clare said, her eyes tearing. The reaction in the room to hear the earl of Kelsey termed as such was strong. "But I must tell the truth, I believe."

"No, Aunt Clare." Julia took up Aunt Clare's hand and squeezed it warmly. "You need only to be *honest*. You will not have to lie. You did do this for me, did you not? And for Garth? And you are proud of these gentlemen, are you not? They came here to speak from their hearts in your defense and mine. Such nobility cannot be overlooked."

Aunt Clare blinked and blinked. The men around them held their breath. She smiled. "Yes, dear. You are right. I will be honest this time. I like honesty far better than truth, anyway."

The men about her sighed a collective sigh of relief.

Charles Danford cast the judge a commanding glance as he bowed. "We do respectfully request, Your Honor, that this absurd trial be brought to a close."

The Right Honorable Percival Threadwell sucked through his teeth in obvious indecision. A high whining whistle accompanied it. He glanced toward Lady Danford. He blinked and was forced to stand. Then he nodded. She was passed out upon the floor in a dead faint. He fell back in his chair with a heartfelt sigh. "I myself see no case here." Bewilderment entered his gaze. "Since all bodies are accounted for and . . . and you gentlemen apparently er . . . were not harmed in any manner, I cannot rightly press charges against anyone." He glanced hastily over to the fallen Lady Danford once more.

"Once she faints, she generally remains so for a half hour." Charles Danford drew out his timepiece. "Time passes so quickly, does it not?"

Fear chased back to Threadwell's face, and he sprung back up. He banged on his desk. "This case is adjourned. Closed. Finished. I declare Lady Julia Wrexton exonerated from any charge brought against her by . . . ah, the Crown. Yes. Clear the court is my best advice."

"Wait!" A youthful voice objected from the crowd. Andrew Severs sprung up, his face dark. "I object!"

"Oh, Lord." Threadwell halted, his shoulders sagging. "What is it now?"

"I want to know who Lady Julia must marry!"

Threadwell shook his head with clear alarm. "No. That . . . that is not within my jurisdiction. In fact, nothing is after this. I quit."

"Sit down, Andrew!" Matthew ordered. "You heard His Honor. He has adjourned the court."

"But Lady Julia should marry you, blast it!" Andrew frowned. "She belongs in our family, b'gads!"

"No! She is to marry my Herrington!" Lady Dunn cried.

"Not so." Lady Beresford shouted. "It is my Reginald she must marry!"

"Nay! Giles has her hand!" Lady Mancroft shouted. She slapped at Lord Mancroft. "Tell them, Bertram."

"Oh, no, not again." Julia closed her eyes tightly.

The nightmare had returned. The courtroom erupted with shouts and cries. Faith, it sounded as if it were soon to be an auction for her hand. Julia wished she could sink through the floor.

"Order!" Sir Threadwell squeaked. "There must be order. This is the Crown's court. I want order if it is the last thing I have."

"There will be order," Andrew shouted, "when Lady Julia tells us which fellow she is going to wed."

"All right!" The Right Honorable Percy cried out, tearing at the few strands of hair remaining on his shining pate. "Lady Julia must tell the Crown now. Who are you going to marry?"

Julia stared at the judge.

"We will never get out of here alive elsewise." Threadwell's voice was hoarse. "For the love of God and your country, my lady, just choose one."

Julia's heart sank. He was right, after all. Swallowing hard, Julia turned to study each of her six grooms in turn. She overlooked the earl of Kelsey, who but shrugged at her. "I-I . . ."

"No, Julia!" Garth shouted from the back. "You are going to marry me!"

"Wh-what?" Sir Threadwell exclaimed. The room again roared with anger and objections. Garth ignored it all as he pushed away from the wall and strode toward the bench. The guards started after him. Threadwell waved his hand. "Leave him be. We have little time. This must be settled."

Julia's heart pounded so loudly she could neither hear anyone or look at anyone but Garth. She tilted her head up at a challenging angle. "I am?"

"Excuse me." Threadwell said. "But who are you?"

"I am Lord Stanwood." Garth looked down at Julia. "And I am Julia's last suitor. And her final suitor. I claim her as mine. She will marry me and no one else."

"I object!" Andrew Severs shouted. "Matthew, do something. Call the fellow out, for heaven's sake."

Garth spun and cast a stern, challenging look to the room at large. "My ring is on Lady Julia's hand, and I have her father's approval!"

"By God but he does!" Lord Wrexton jumped up. "He's the one I want!"

Garth bowed to Aunt Clare. "And her aunt's approval."

Clare clapped her hands together and sighed. "Indeed, my son."

He glared at the seven men about them. "And I call any man out who cares to debate my rights."

The men all stepped back in one obvious movement.

"Good. Good!" Threadwell nodded. "There you have it. Lady Julia is going to marry Lord er . . . Stanwood. Court adjourned."

"No!" The words burst from Julia. She was being swept aside by all, told what to do at that. It would not serve. Worse, her inner fears rose. Why had Garth proposed to her now? And what if she said yes? "I did not say he had my approval!"

"Oh, no!" Threadwell moaned. "Then who do you want?"

"Julia . . ." Garth's eyes darkened.

"Garth, dear," Aunt Clare stepped forward. She leaned up to whisper far too loudly. "Remember what I told you to do this morning? You must do it properly. Julia must hear you say it."

"Come on, Stanwood, you can talk her around." Lord Reginald encouraged. "You owe it to us. I mean, to Aunt Clare . . . I mean . . ."

"No." Garth shook his head. "I owe it to no one but Julia." He took her hand in his. His hazel eyes darkened to deep sea green. So like the ring that was upon her finger. His smile turned wry and nervous. "I declared myself to be her last and final suitor. In truth, I should have confessed that my claim was actually first, before all the others."

"Good tact." Danford nodded. Then he frowned. "I think."

Julia merely raised her brow in suspicion. Garth laughed, but then his gaze turned desperate. His eyes finally showed his heart. "I have loved Julia long before you gentlemen even met her."

"Garth!" Julia gasped in astonishment.

"I have loved her since we were children."

"He has." Clare sighed.

Grinning at her, his eyes melting her soul, Garth knelt upon one knee.

"Very good style," Severs murmured.

Julia, despite it all, giggled.

Garth eyes gleamed with answering humor. "Julia. My wild Julia. My beloved hussy."

"Gads. He's lost it." The exclamation came sotto voce from somewhere among the six men.

Garth's passionate gaze did not leave Julia's breathless one. "I need you. I need you to love me. I need to have your spirit and body beside me day and night. I will never own you, and I never wish to do so. Marry me."

"Now, dear!" Aunt Clare clasped her hands together. "Surely you can say yes?"

"Aunt Clare . . ." Julia paused. She broke into a brilliant smile. "You are so very right. I can say yes with all my heart."

The roar and applause from Julia's ex-suitors was deafening. Tears of joy slipping down her face, Julia flung herself at Garth. "I love you. I always have!"

Unfortunately, Garth was in a less balanced position. It did not stop him, however. He welcomed her into his arms, and they toppled most inelegantly to the courtroom floor. He delivered one sole kiss to her lips. Yet so passionate and loving was it that Julia knew that her world had become perfect. She had just said yes to what she had meant to be. She had said yes to her very life.

Garth drew back then and came to a sitting position. Flushing, Julia did the same. Laughing, he reached out and clasped her hand. He looked at the surrounding, gaping men, approving family, and disinterested cats.

He grinned. "Do go away now, won't you? You will have to find other fiancés than this one."

"Do not worry about them, Garth, dear." Aunt Clare cast her boys a warm look. "I shall do everything in my power to help them find their true loves. You just attend to dear Julia."

"That I shall, Auntie, dear. That I shall." His eyes agleam, Garth leaned over and kissed Julia soundly.

"Blast, I am going to have my grandchildren yet!" Lord Wrexton trumpeted.

Julia returned an equally mischievous look upon her love and destiny. "Indeed, Father. Five of them, in fact."

"Five!" Lord Wrexton's mouth fell open in awe. Then his face lit as if heaven had opened up to him. "Blast and damn. Let's clear this court! I have drinks and cigars to buy for everyone. I am going to have five grandchildren!"

"Faith," Garth said in a low voice for Julia alone. "I cannot wait for those wonderful cozes in bed with you."

"Indeed." Julia flushed. "Just cozes?"

Garth nodded slowly. "The way I have dreamed them, you will love them."

Julia shook her head ruefully and laughed. She never had a doubt in the world. Not one!

More Zebra Regency Romances